Praise for Ken Shufeldt
and *Genesis*

"*Genesis* leaves Left Behind in its hair-fraying, nerve-frying, blood-freezing apocalyptic dust!"
—William Martin, *New York Times* bestselling author of *The Lost Constitution*

"*Genesis* reads like Left Behind on steroids!"
—Douglas Preston, *New York Times* bestselling author of *Blasphemy*

"If you liked the Left Behind series, you'll love *Genesis*!"
—David Hagberg, *USA Today* bestselling author of *Dance With the Dragon*

"*Genesis* may be the best apocalyptic thriller ever written. It makes Left Behind look like *Rebecca of Sunnybrook Farm*."
—Junius Podrug, author of *Dark Passage*

"A unique plot, strong characters, and compelling writing turn *Genesis* into a powerful look at a disturbing future."
—Ed Gorman, Spur Award–winning author

GENESIS

Ken Shufeldt

A TOM DOHERTY ASSOCIATES BOOK
NEW YORK

This is a work of fiction. All of the characters, organizations, and events portrayed in this novel are either products of the author's imagination or are used fictitiously.

GENESIS

Copyright © 2009 by Ken Shufeldt

All rights reserved.

A Tor Book
Published by Tom Doherty Associates, LLC
175 Fifth Avenue
New York, NY 10010

www.tor-forge.com

Tor® is a registered trademark of Tom Doherty Associates, LLC.

ISBN-13: 978-0-7653-5849-3
ISBN-10: 0-7653-5849-2

First Edition: June 2009

Printed in the United States of America

0 9 8 7 6 5 4 3 2 1

To my granddaughter and my biggest fan, (Miss Cass) Casandra Bartram, for willingly reading the many early versions of the book.

In addition, I can never thank Mark Nair enough for all of his help, and for helping me believe in myself.

GENESIS

PROLOGUE

IRAQ 1991

The squad of rangers had been shadowing an elite detachment of the Republican guard for the last twenty-four hours. They were the best Saddam possessed, and the rangers' intelligence reports had led them to believe they were gathering their forces for a surprise attack on the coalition forces. When Captain Ellis watched them disappear into a tunnel in the side of a hill, he decided to call in a B-52 squadron for a preemptive air strike.

"CC1 this is CF1, over, SEB over, suppression direction 1820, distance 3000, mark direction 1860, distance 3500, over. Illumination mark continuous, over."

"CAS, TOT 1013, CC1 over."

"What do you think?" the sergeant asked.

The captain lowered his binoculars, removed his helmet, and ran his hand over his closely cropped blond hair. His face was tanned and a little sore from the windblown sand they had endured the previous day. At six foot six he was the tallest member of the squad, and the sergeant had seen him use his height to intimidate the fiercest Iraqi prisoner.

"I mean," said the sergeant, looking slightly uncomfortable at the captain's unflinching silence, "you think they've got something in there?"

Captain Ellis narrowed his eyes and turned his chiseled

face into the wind like a wolf sniffing for prey. "I don't know for sure," he said, "but I'm not taking any chances.

A few minutes later, a squadron of B-52's dropped a string of ten-thousand-pound bombs on the tunnels in the side of the hill. The massive explosions shook the ground under the rangers' feet, and the tunnel used by the Republican guards was vaporized.

One rogue bomb had fallen short, exploding in a shower of sand and dirt, and carving out an immense crater in the desert floor.

"Good God," the sergeant muttered under his breath, ducking slightly.

Captain Ellis, unflinching, waited until the dust had cleared. "All right men, it's time to go hunting."

As they made their way to the collapsed tunnels, the captain peered down into the crater left by the one errant bomb. A small piece of metal glinted at him from the bottom of the crater, but it was difficult to see any more detail through the blowing sand. He turned to his sergeant. "Take a couple of men down there and let me know what that is."

"Yes, sir," said the sergeant. "Murphy, Cusack, Lenard, you're with me."

The captain started to turn away, and then turned back to the sergeant. "Use the Geiger counter."

The sergeant scowled and looked like he wanted to say something, but he nodded and continued down the side of the crater.

They managed to make their way down the soft sand sides of the massive crater.

"It looks like a large metal coffin to me," the sergeant said.

Intrigued, the captain made his way to the bottom of the crater to get a look for himself. After he had examined the object, he reached into his pack and started to pull out a satellite phone. It wasn't an Army-issued phone, so he hadn't wanted his men to see it. He told the sergeant, "Take the men and check the tunnel areas for survivors."

"Do you want me to leave someone to make sure you can get back up?" the sergeant asked.

"No need. I'll be fine," the captain growled.

After his men left the area, he started to dial the satellite phone. He was not the sort of man who was easily excited, but in this case he had to dial the number twice before he got it right.

"Yes, this is Captain David Ellis. I must speak with the High Council."

"I'm sorry, the council isn't in session. I can put you through to Marvin Wilson."

"The chairman will be fine."

"Why are you calling me on the satellite phone? You know it's only to be used in an emergency. I know you're in Iraq, but we can't interfere in military matters," Marvin Wilson said.

"This isn't a military matter," Captain Ellis said. "I believe I've found Adamartoni's sarcophagus."

"Do you know what you're saying? Are you sure?"

"I can't be positive, but I think it's worth a complete examination."

"I'll dispatch Larry Sheldon to verify your findings. He's a Defense Intelligence Agency officer, and his presence in Iraq won't raise any suspicions. If you're correct, and it's Adamartoni, it will be the most important event in the history of the Logos. You need to secure the object, and don't speak of it to anyone."

THE ARTIFACT

When Larry Sheldon arrived in Iraq, he took a helicopter gunship to the site. As he stepped out of the helicopter and made his way to the rangers, Captain Ellis thought to himself, *He may be DIA, but he's definitely military trained, and I can see why the chairman sent him.* He was an imposing figure. Standing six foot four and weighing 250 pounds, he looked as though he could have taken out the Republican guard by himself.

When Larry Sheldon first saw the artifact, he wasn't quite sure what they had found.

"Do you have any ropes with you?" Larry Sheldon asked.

"Yes we do," Captain Ellis said.

Sheldon looped the rope around his waist and started down the crater wall. "If you'll have your men keep the rope tight, I'll go down for a closer look."

When he reached the artifact, all he could see was the one end sticking up out of the sand. He brushed the sand back so he could get a better look. He had spent a significant amount of time studying Logos history, and he immediately recognized the artifact as a significant find.

He couldn't be sure it was Adamartoni's sarcophagus, but he knew it was worth having it analyzed. Overcome by the enormity of what it could mean to the Logos, it took him a few seconds to compose himself. After he had gathered his thoughts, he motioned for the rangers to pull him back up, and he informed Captain Ellis.

"I want you to send some of your men down and finish digging the artifact out of the sand. You've done the right thing. As a member of the Logos, I know you understand the need for secrecy, but let me reemphasize that you must not speak of this to anyone. When you file your report, I don't want this mentioned."

Once again Captain Ellis understood why the Logos had sent him. He was used to commanding men, but when you heard him speak there was no question about what he wanted. "No problem. I won't explain, but I'll ensure my men keep their mouths closed."

Larry Sheldon contacted the Logos chairman, Marvin Wilson, to tell him what he had found. "Captain Ellis was right to call. There's a high probability he's found Adamartoni's sarcophagus."

"Unbelievable. We've been searching for thousands of years, and here it is. God does work in mysterious ways. Secure the artifact and I'll arrange for your transportation."

Eight hours later, he had it loaded on a DIA transport aircraft and on its way to the US. Sheldon rode in the cargo area with the artifact, and as he sat looking at it, he wondered whether it would prove to be what they thought it was. He had no way of knowing it was already intertwined in his life, or that it was going to prove to be pivotal to the survival of the human race.

GLEN EYRIE

Larry Sheldon was taking the artifact to Glen Eyrie, which was a DIA ultra top-secret research facility. As far as the public knew, the facility provided rest and relaxation for the government scientists stationed at the Sandia and White Sands, New Mexico, facilities.

Even though it was a cover story, the facility was a five-star hotel. The English Tudor-style castle had been built by General William Jackson Palmer, the founder of Colorado Springs, an entrepreneur, and a highly influential member of the Logos.

The castle had sixty-seven rooms, twenty-four fireplaces, and provided truly magnificent accommodations for the scientists. Even though it was near the Garden of the Gods and Pikes Peak, the scenic eight hundred-acre estate was secluded enough to allow them to conduct their research.

When Larry Sheldon landed in Denver he was met by a transport truck. He accompanied the artifact to Glen Eyrie, and turned it over to the DIA.

"Once again you've done a great job," Marvin Wilson said. "I don't believe anyone else is aware of the importance of the artifact."

"So you do believe it's Adamartoni," Larry Sheldon said.

"I do. The council has decided we're going to keep you updated on the status of our research. If it's what we believe, we'll need you to take over the planning and execution of what needs to be done. You've been highly effective in every assignment the council has given you, and we believe you've earned this chance."

"I don't know what to say, but you can count on me to do whatever is necessary."

The DIA began to gather a team to research the artifact. The DIA had been unaware that the new team were members of, and completely loyal to, the Logos.

The researchers had been unable to identify the metal, and had found it to be almost impregnable. While they were trying to open the sarcophagus they discovered there were laser-etched microscopic inscriptions covering literally every square inch of its surface. It took them almost two months to develop a process to enable them to magnify and capture images of the texts. Once they could actually see the texts they discovered they were in an unknown language.

After they made copies of the texts, the second team resumed their attempts to analyze the body in the sarcophagus. Even though they used the most powerful lasers available, it had taken over six months to penetrate the metal so they could begin their analysis.

ONE YEAR LATER

Larry Sheldon had been receiving periodic updates as the research teams worked, but he was surprised when he received a cryptic emergency message from the chairman. "We need you at Glen Eyrie immediately."

When he arrived at Glen Eyrie, Marvin Wilson met him at the entrance to the castle.

"Thank you for coming so quickly. We've finally been able to translate the language of the etchings on the sarcophagus," Marvin Wilson said.

"Great, but what was the urgency? You've told me the inscriptions were written thousands of years ago," Larry Sheldon said.

"We just finished translating the last passages, and they contained the full text of the final prophecy."

"You don't mean the one dealing with the end of the world, do you?"

"I do, and more importantly, it tells of our salvation. I would like for you to read the texts, and then we'll talk."

Sheldon spent the next six weeks reading the transcripts. As he read the texts, the story of Adamartoni and Evevette unfolded before him.

ADAMARTONI AND EVEVETTE

Just over a hundred thousand years ago, Adamartoni and Evevette's ship suffered a catastrophic accident. When their ship unexpectedly dropped out of FTL (faster than light) travel, it was unable to continue its resupply mission.

They had used one of the ship's shuttle craft to travel to the nearest planet in search of help. After they had made several orbits trying to ascertain where they should land, they decided to land where they had spotted signs of campfires. While they had been exploring the surrounding countryside, a massive earthquake struck, and damaged their shuttle beyond repair.

They discovered the first anatomically modern humans had just appeared on the earth, and they possessed no technology of any kind. Stranded on the primitive planet, they spent the next several hundred years trying to live their lives as fully as possible. Over the centuries, Evevette had given birth to thirty children. She had twelve girls and eighteen boys. They tried to learn how to coexist with the indigenous peoples, but they had grown frustrated at the lack of development in the locals. In an attempt to make all of their lives better, they had educated and trained them.

As Sheldon continued to read about their lives, he thought back to the historians who had believed the region where they landed to be the cradle of civilization. They had never known the civilization which evolved from Adamartoni's family predated the known rise of literacy by many thousands of years.

They had been members of the Theos race, and normally lived for hundreds of years. He marveled at their longevity, and he sensed that by today's standards they were immensely intelligent.

As he thought back to the sudden shift in human evolution which occurred during that period, he came to believe their family's interaction and eventual intermarriage had accelerated the evolutionary development of man.

Toward the end of the texts, he saw the desperation in their words. Even before Adamartoni's death, the family and their descendants were coming under immense pressure from the surrounding nomadic tribes. As the tribes became more aggressive, Adamartoni had become concerned his family and all they had accomplished would not survive.

He and his wife spent the last five years of his life building a sarcophagus for his burial. They used the last of the available energy from their shuttle to construct his sarcophagus. In a final attempt to preserve their family's legacy, they had decided to etch their story into the sarcophagus's almost impregnable metal. The microscopic etchings had included a warning for their future descendants.

Over the years, they continued to scan the heavens for signs of passing ships. No one ever came, but during their searches they recognized an event which would, in the distant future, cause the destruction of their newfound home. A gigantic asteroid was circling the solar system far outside the outermost planets. Their tracking programs showed a comet was going to divert its path and cause it to strike the Earth in just over one hundred thousand years.

Shortly before his death, Adamartoni added a final message to his sarcophagus. The message was from a recurring dream he believed was a foretelling from God. It detailed the events which would lead up to the destruction of the Earth, and of a young couple who would save humanity.

As Sheldon read the final lines of Adamartoni's message, he wondered what had happened in those final years of their lives.

He would never know, but the nomads eventually overran their cities, and most of what they had built was lost. Several centuries after Adamartoni's death, the sarcophagus had been lost in a massive earthquake. As the generations passed, many of the physical traits passed on from the Theos began to recede, until they became dormant.

Adamartoni and Evevette had both been deeply religious, and their teachings were the inspiration for the original texts which formed the basis of many of the books of the Bible. Sheldon also knew their texts formed the basis for the Logos beliefs.

THE REALIZATION

When he finally finished reading, Sheldon leaned back and thought to himself, *I now know what I need to do with the rest of my life.*

As he tried to relax, he thought back on his life to that point. He had been recruited by the Logos as an undergraduate at Princeton. After receiving his Bachelor of Science degree in Foreign Service at the age of nineteen, he won a Rhodes Scholarship to University College, Oxford, where he studied government. He had fully expected to go into public service, but it hadn't turned out that way.

After graduation the Logos had arranged for him to join the CIA. After a couple of years in the CIA they made sure he received an appointment to the DIA, where he had been ever since. As he remembered those years he thought back to some of the things he had done. He had started out life believing God would take care of him, and people always did the right thing. He now knew it wasn't true, and if you needed something to happen a certain way you sometimes had to do things other people might view as extreme.

He tried to get some sleep before morning, but he wasn't successful. Finally, he got up, took a quick shower, and called to schedule a meeting with the Logos High council.

After the council heard Larry's assessment of the texts, Marvin Wilson told him, "We're going to place you in charge of our planning and research teams for the coming events. We still have several years, but 2012 will be here before we know it. I've studied your records and I'm satisfied you're up to the task. You need to begin assembling your teams, and we'll expect weekly briefings on your progress."

"I'm honored, and I'll do my best. What sort of resources will I have?"

"You'll have every resource we possess. There's noth-

ing more important than the tasks you are about to under-
take."

Dr. Billy Evans had been leading their DNA research
team, but the Logos had become concerned he was too
old for the job. Dissatisfied with his team's progress, they
decided to move the project from Glen Eyrie to Sandia
Labs, and force Dr. Evans to retire. The news he had to retire once the move was completed had thrown him into a
rage at the injustice.

Determined to ensure he would be properly rewarded for
his years of dedication, he took half the DNA they had extracted from Adamartoni's body and placed it in an old antibiotic bottle. After he had it safely hidden, he arranged to
sell it to one of his old classmates, who just happened to run
one of the largest drug companies in the world.

What none of them could know, was that in all of Glen
Eyrie's history, there had never been an event more meaningful than the one which was about to occur.

1

IT WAS LATE March of 1992 in the Colorado mountains. Ben and Mary West were returning from Mary's mother's funeral in Denver, Colorado. They were on I-25 not too far from Colorado Springs when they ran into an unexpected snowstorm.

"I can't see the road," Ben said. "Can you see anything on your side?"

Mary rolled down the window and leaned her head out to try to see the side of the road.

"We're still on the road, but I can barely see the edge," Mary said.

He didn't want her to know he was starting to get worried.

"This old Chevy can go through anything. It's never let us down, and it's not going to now."

He leaned farther over the steering wheel trying to get a better view, but it wasn't working. The windshield wipers simply couldn't keep up with the snowfall.

"Can you still see the road on your side?"

"Yes, I can, but I'm getting cold. What are we going to do?"

He didn't have enough gas for them to pull over and try to wait it out, so he knew he had to keep going.

He glanced over at Mary to see how she was doing. She was due at any time with their first child, and they were anxious to get back to their home in Clayton, New Mexico, so their family doctor could deliver the baby.

He was trying to drive and look at a map to determine how far outside of Colorado Springs they were.

"Watch out! You're going to hit the post."

He tried to swerve, but instead of turning away, they skidded into the road sign.

When they hit the post, it pushed the radiator into the fan, stalling the motor. The impact ripped the post out of the ground, and wedged it into the front grille.

When they slammed to a stop, Ben hit his head on the side of the window. The impact threw Mary off the seat and wedged her between the seat and the dashboard.

As his head started to clear, he cried out, "Honey, are you all right? Are you hurt? Please get up."

She struggled, trying to get her pregnant body back into the seat, but as she did, she went into labor.

"I don't feel very well. Please help me, I'm scared."

His mind raced ahead to all the things that could go wrong, and then he remembered what his dad had always told him about worry.

He would say, "Some people waste their whole lives worrying. But the truth is eighty percent of the things they are worrying about never happen, and the other twenty percent they couldn't have done anything to prevent anyway."

He started to calm down and asked again, "Are you hurt?"

"My shoulder hurts, and I'm having cramps."

"Those aren't cramps. It's the baby."

"It can't come now. What are we going to do?"

He tried to make her as comfortable as possible, and then he tried to start the car so he could get it back up on the road. As the engine tried to turn over, the fan made a horrible noise as it hit the radiator.

Now he was worried. His young wife was in labor, and

his car was lying wrecked in the bottom of a ditch in the middle of a blinding snowstorm.

He wasn't sure how far it was to the nearest help, but he knew it was probably too far to walk in the snow. Not wanting her to worry, he told her. "I'll get the post out of the radiator, and we'll be on our way in just a minute."

As he worked to pull the signpost out of the grille, he noticed it said, GLEN EYRIE 2 MILES.

Once he removed the signpost, he used a tire tool to pry the radiator back from the fan as far as he could.

He got back in and tried to start the engine again. This time it started, but it was still making an awful racket.

He decided even if he burned the motor out, he was going to try for the town on the sign.

"We're going to Glen Eyrie and get some help. I don't know how big of a town it is, but they should at least have a phone."

This was their first time through the area, so they didn't know Glen Eyrie wasn't a town. It was a luxury hotel.

He gunned the Suburban backward out of the ditch and onto the access road which ran along I-25. Once on the road, he turned down the narrow two-lane road toward Glen Eyrie.

As he powered around the corner, he was praying. "Lord, please let me get Mary to this town, and let the baby be all right."

It was only two miles to Glen Eyrie, but it seemed like forever as the Suburban labored through the drifting snow. The wind was blowing at least forty miles an hour, and some of the drifts were already more than a foot deep. As he was straining to see through the blinding snow, he spotted the lights of Glen Eyrie.

"We made it, honey, and everything is going to be all right."

As the lights became clear, he could see it wasn't a

town, it was a guard shack with two Marines inside. He pulled in, stopped beside the guard shack, and shut the Suburban off.

A Marine sergeant stepped out into the blowing snow to find out what they wanted. Ben recognized the Heckler & Koch P9S nine-millimeter automatic on his hip and the Heckler & Koch MP5 machine gun on his shoulder. When he was in the Marines, the SEAL teams they trained with carried them.

The Marine stepped up to the running board and said, "This is a restricted area, and I'm going to have to ask you to turn around and go back to the main road."

Ben didn't know what to say, but he knew his old Suburban wouldn't make it to Colorado Springs.

"My wife's in labor. We were just in an accident. My car's running hot, and it won't make it to town."

The sergeant leaned in the window so he could get a better look. He saw Ben was telling the truth. Even though it was no more than ten degrees out, he could see the sweat rolling down her face, and it looked like she was in pain.

The sergeant wasn't sure what to do. His orders clearly stated he was not to admit any civilians to the facility without prior clearance.

He turned to the guard shack, and called to the other Marine on duty with him. "Get the lieutenant on the intercom. I need to ask him what to do."

He looked at Ben and said, "Please wait here. I'm going to find out what I can do with you two."

The lieutenant had just gotten an update on the weather forecast. There was a massive arctic weather system moving into the area, and the weather was only going to get worse for the next eight hours.

They were supposed to have finished moving the facility today. Due to the worsening weather, he had put off the closing and the transfer of the artifact back to the Sandia facility until the weather system had passed.

When the sergeant called, he already knew the weather conditions were bad and getting worse by the minute.

"We have a couple of civilians at the front gate. Their Suburban is in bad shape, and the lady is in labor," the sergeant said.

The lieutenant quickly made up his mind to allow them to enter.

"Send them up. No, wait. You lead them up so they don't get lost."

The sergeant hung up the phone and told the other Marine, "I'm going to lead these folks up to the castle. I'll be back as soon as I get them checked in.

"Follow me, and I'll take you up to Glen Eyrie."

"I can't tell you how much we appreciate this," Ben West said.

The Suburban was still making horrible noises, but they managed to cover the mile or so to the castle.

2

MOST OF THE staff had already left for the new facility at the Sandia National Laboratories. The lieutenant knew he needed someone to look at the pregnant woman, so he called Dr. Billy Evans, the lead scientist on the DNA research portion of their project.

"We have a situation, and I need your help," the lieutenant said.

"What's the problem?" Dr. Evans asked.

"I have a couple of civilians outside, and I think the woman is in labor."

"I've been doing genetic research and haven't practiced in years, but I guess I can deliver a baby."

The lieutenant walked out the front door and called to Ben and Mary West.

"Come on in, folks, and get out of the cold."

As he helped her from the car, Ben West noticed the seat was soaking wet where Mary had been sitting.

"Honey, are you all right?"

"Yes, I am, but I think my water broke as we pulled up."

The doctor greeted them as they entered the hotel lobby.

"I'm Dr. Billy Evans, and who might you two be?"

"I'm Ben West, and this lovely young lady is my wife, Mary. We were on our way back from Mary's mom's funeral, when we had a small accident on the highway. We saw the sign to Glen Eyrie, and we thought we could get some help here, but it has turned out to be, well, I'm not sure what it turned out to be."

"Glen Eyrie is a luxury hotel."

"I don't ever remember seeing a luxury hotel with a Marine checkpoint."

"The government has been leasing the facility for the last several years to provide our scientists a place for rest and relaxation. We're in the process of moving, so there's not much to tell. Now if you'll follow me, I'll get you situated."

He led them into a small examination room. "Help her lie down on the exam table while I get some blankets so we can get her warm."

After Ben removed Mary's shoes and socks, she swung her feet up onto the table. She groaned in pain and said, "Damn that hurts."

He knew she must be hurting, because she hardly ever cursed.

"Are you all right? What can I do?"

"Nothing, but that hurt."

The doctor returned with the blankets, and began covering her.

"Thanks, that's much better," Mary West said.

The doctor pulled the diagnostic equipment cart over to the bed so he could take her vital signs.

"I'll do the best I can, but it's been a long time since I delivered a baby."

"We appreciate you helping us out," Mary West said.

The machine beeped and displayed her vital signs.

"Your blood pressure is fine, and your pulse rate is all right, considering."

He moved to her stomach and a few seconds later he

commented, "The baby's heartbeat is good and strong as well. We don't have any females here, so I'll have to do the delivery by myself. Are you going to be all right with that?"

"I understand, and we're just glad you're here to help us," Mary West said. "I was afraid I was going to have the baby on the side of the road in a snowstorm."

"Help her get undressed and put on this gown. I'll be right back," Dr. Evans said. "I need to get a tray of supplies. I think I'll get a cup of coffee on the way. Would you two like a cup?"

"I don't want one, but I know how Ben loves his coffee," Mary West said. "You two go ahead. I'll be fine."

"Are you sure?" Ben asked.

"It's not a problem. I can get undressed by myself."

"Are you sure she's going to be all right?" Ben asked as he and Dr. Evans left the room.

"They both seem to be doing fine. What do you take in your coffee?" Dr. Evans asked.

"Just black is fine with me."

Dr. Evans poured a cup of coffee and handed it to him.

By the time the doctor had his own cup poured, Ben had already finished his. "Get you another cup? There's plenty more where that came from," Dr. Evans said. "I'm going to get the supplies I need, and then I'm going back to check on your wife. Why don't you sit out here for a few minutes and relax. If anything changes I'll come and get you."

"Thanks, I think I will. Is it all right to smoke out here?"

"Sure, there's no one else around."

He had finished about half the cigarette when he heard, "Come quick. I think the baby is coming."

As he entered the room, she cried out, "Oh my god it hurts. Please make it stop."

He reached out and took her hand. "Honey, it's going to be all right."

"Would you bring the big light in the corner over here? I need some more light," Dr. Evans said.

Ben pulled the light up to the foot of the bed and turned it on.

"How are you doing?" Dr. Evans asked.

Mary let out a moan and said, "Fine, but I think he's ready to come."

"Why do you think it's a boy?" Ben asked.

"Because he's in such a hurry to get here, that's why."

Dr. Evans pulled back the sheet and remarked, "Oh no, I can see the top of the baby's head. Just hold on a minute, don't push yet. I'm not ready."

She screamed, "You'd better get ready, because I think he's coming right now."

She screamed again, and the baby started to come.

In less than two minutes, the baby was in his hands.

"What do you need?" Ben asked.

"Bring me the tray of supplies on the counter."

Dr. Evans clipped the cord, clamped it, and then swabbed the whole area with iodine.

He examined the baby, cleaned it up, and placed it on Mary's chest. "The baby has a fever and is congested. I'm going to give him a shot of Levofloxacin. It's a broad-spectrum antibiotic, and it should take care of his symptoms. I have to go next door to prepare the shot." As he started to leave he asked, "Have you already picked out a name?"

"We don't have one yet," Mary said. "I guess we're going to have to decide."

"There's no hurry. You two take a few minutes to enjoy the baby, and I'll be right back."

Ben moved to the head of the table to hold Mary's hand and to get a better look at their new son.

"He's a fine looking boy," Ben said.

"He sure is! We did well, didn't we?"

"We sure did."

They spent the next couple of minutes enjoying their once-in-a-lifetime moment.

3

DR. EVANS WENT next door and unlocked the drug cabinet. They had already moved most of their supplies, but they still had a few drugs left. There were two locked cabinets in the room. One contained the drugs for their small infirmary. The other was a classified enclosure where they stored the results of their work.

When Dr. Evans received his notice that he had to retire by the end of the year, he had been supervising the preparation of the DNA they had extracted from Adamartoni's sarcophagus.

Infuriated at being forced to retire, he decided to sell some of the DNA to fund his retirement. He took half their available recombinant DNA solution and stored it in an antibiotic bottle. He placed it in the back of the classified storage cabinet. He had been sure it would be safe in there since he and his boss were the only ones with keys.

As part of the closing procedure his boss had taken an inventory of the two cabinets before he left for the Sandia location. When he found the antibiotic bottle in the classified cabinet, he assumed it was a mistake and moved it to the drug cabinet.

Dr. Evans opened the drug cabinet, selected the correct bottle, and filled a syringe with the Levofloxacin. As he walked down the hall, he thought about what he would do with the money he would get from selling the DNA to the drug company. The DNA had been prepared to be used in a recombinant DNA experiment, but that had all changed.

As he thought back to events which had occurred in the previous months, he remembered the day they were going to try to open the sarcophagus. Just before they made their first cut, they discovered it was covered with text. The etchings were almost microscopic, and required extreme magnification to be able to copy them. By the time the linguistics team finished copying the text they had over ten thousand pages of text. They detailed Adamartoni and Evevette's lives, teachings, and described how Evevette had entombed him in the sarcophagus almost a hundred thousand years ago.

They were members of a race called the Theos, and an earthquake had damaged their ship stranding them in what would someday be Mesopotamia. There were several references to a ship and someone or something called Xylon. They had assumed the ship to be a sailing ship, until their field team unearthed the remains of what they believed to be a spaceship. There wasn't much of it left, so they were never completely sure.

The final section of the text described an event which would occur in what then was the distant future. It described how a passing comet would alter the path of an immense asteroid and cause it to strike the Earth. In the final few paragraphs, it described how a young couple would be the salvation of humanity.

By the time they finished analyzing the text, they had come to believe the text detailed some of the events described in Second Peter. Like many of the original Biblical texts, the message was somewhat altered as it had been translated and retranslated over the centuries.

He hated to miss seeing how it all played out, but at least he was going to be able to retire in comfort.

He gave the baby the shot of antibiotic and asked, "Have you thought of a name yet?"

"Yes, we have," Mary West said. "We've decided to name him Billy Wayne West. We decided since you were so nice to us, we wanted to name him after you."

"Thank you both, but I was just doing my job," Dr. Evans said. "I'm going to go call the officer of the day and let him know we have one more visitor."

"I'm so excited, and the baby is so cute," Mary West said.

"He sure is," Ben West said. "It sure was lucky we turned down the road. We could have been in real trouble if we had stayed on the highway."

"You know what my momma always said," Mary West said.

" 'Everything happens for a purpose.' "

"I guess she's right for sure this time."

"The lieutenant says the roads are all closed, and you'll need to stay the night with us," Dr. Evans said. "I've had one of the suites on this floor prepared for you to stay in tonight. The kitchen will bring your dinner in an hour or so.

"We're going to roll the exam table down the hall to your room. I don't want you to have to walk any more than necessary. If you'll grab the other end of the table we'll get Mary to her room.

"Make yourselves at home, and try to get comfortable. I'll be back with your dinner," Dr. Evans said.

When their meals arrived, he took them to their room.

"Here's your dinner and a pot of coffee. If you need anything during the night, I'm down the hall in room ten."

"Thanks, we're both pretty tired, and with the day Mary has had, I don't think she will be moving around very much," Ben West said.

"I can't get over how nice the doctor was today. He has

tried to make us comfortable," Ben said after the doctor had left.

"He did well, but I was worried when he said the baby needed a shot of antibiotics."

"I know, but he said it was nothing but a fever and some congestion."

"Billy looks good, and he's nursing, so I think he's going to be fine."

The next morning the storm had blown through, and the sun was shining brightly when they awoke and looked out their windows.

"The sun is out, and it's a beautiful day," Ben said.

"Good, I wouldn't want to have many more days like yesterday."

"I'm going to find the doctor and see what we need to do to get into town."

He had just started down the hall, when he heard the doctor's voice.

"How are you two this morning?"

"We're great, but we're ready to get going."

"Great minds think alike. I had one of the Marines pull your Suburban over to the motor pool last night. He told me they should have it ready after lunch.

"Right now, I have breakfast for you two. I would also like to examine Mary and the baby if it's all right?"

"Sure, come on in."

"Good morning. How did you sleep?" Dr. Evans asked.

"I slept fine, except for caring for the baby from time to time. I think we're both fine, but come ahead and check us out."

He spent a few minutes examining her and said, "Everything looks fine so far."

"Great, when do you think we can go home?"

"As I was telling Ben, they should have your car ready right after lunch."

"We can never thank you enough."

"It's been my pleasure to experience delivering your baby and meeting you two.

"I'm going to examine the baby, and then I'll bring in your breakfast."

He checked the baby from head to toe, and when he finished he said, "The baby checks out fine. His temperature is a tiny bit high, but it's nothing to be alarmed about, the antibiotics should take care of it."

"Thanks, we'll have Dr. Moore check him out when we get home," Ben said.

"Where is home?"

"We live on a small ranch in New Mexico. It's about eight miles northeast of Clayton, New Mexico."

"I've heard of it, but I'm not sure where it is. How far is it from Amarillo?"

"It's about a hundred and thirty miles northwest of Amarillo, Texas."

"How long do you think it will take you to get back?"

"If the roads aren't too bad, it should take us three and a half to four hours. If we get out of here by one o'clock, we should be home just about dark."

"I'm going to have the staff bring your breakfast in. Then I'll go check on your car so we can get you on your way."

They finished breakfast and Mary asked, "Will you hold Billy while I take a shower and fix my hair?"

"Sure, go ahead. You've had a rough time."

"It wasn't as bad as I had feared. He sure didn't put up much of a fuss coming. It seemed like he was ready to get started."

After her shower, she sat down in one of the chairs to rest and feed the baby. She had just finished when the doctor returned.

"Good news. We have your car ready, and they filled it

with gas. The restaurant sent some sack lunches and drinks for the ride home."

"They didn't have to go to all that trouble," Mary said. "Please tell them thanks for us."

"I won't have to. They're all waiting outside to say goodbye to you."

"Well then, let's go thank them."

As they came out, there was a cheer from the twenty or so Marines, cooks, mechanics, and technicians standing outside. They had been waiting for ten minutes on the snowcovered ground.

"Thank you so much for everything. We can't thank you enough," Mary said.

"You just take good care of the baby, and it will be thanks enough for us," the motor pool sergeant said.

"You can count on it, and we'll never forget all of you."

When Ben started the Suburban, the motor was running smoother than it had in months. He rolled down his window and said, "You guys did a great job fixing up the motor. It sounds great."

"We didn't exactly fix it. We put in a motor out of one of the staff vehicles. We'll put your old motor in it, and fix it up after you are gone."

Ben was speechless, but Mary rolled her window down again, blew them all a kiss, and said, "God bless all of you, and thanks again for all you've done for us."

As they began their journey back home, they had no way of knowing what their inadvertent stop had set in motion.

4

As THEY DROVE away, Dr. Evans was considering what he needed to do next. He decided to get the DNA he had hidden and deliver it to his friend at the drug company. When he opened the cabinet, he panicked when he couldn't find the bottle. After he had completely emptied the cabinet he sat down to consider what could have happened to it. As he pondered, he remembered the shot of antibiotic he had given the baby. He retrieved the empty bottle from the trash and took a closer look at it. He had put a small red dot at the end of the drug's name on the label so he could identify it. When he turned the bottle in his hand, he saw the dot.

He thought to himself, *Oh my God, what have I done? I've given their baby a full shot of Adamartoni's DNA.* He sat sobbing to himself for several minutes. Finally, he composed himself. He decided to tell the Logos and the family what had happened. He knew he would probably spend the rest of his life in Leavenworth, but he knew he couldn't live with himself if he didn't.

The next day they loaded the truck with the sarcophagus and the remaining bottles of DNA. He decided to drive the truck himself so he could have some time alone before he confessed. The roads were in good shape, but as he rounded a tight corner on the mountain road, he hit a patch of black ice. The truck spun out of control and crashed through the guardrail. He hadn't been wearing a seat belt. So when the truck hit the guardrail he was thrown clear, and the truck rolled over him as it went over the edge into the canyon below.

There were six trucks in their convoy, and the rest of them stopped to try to help. The truck exploded when it hit bottom, completely incinerating everything on board.

Larry Sheldon had been in a helicopter on his way to Sandia Labs when they notified him of the accident. He had the helicopter land on the highway. Seeing a crowd on the side of the road, he walked over to where they were working on Dr. Evans. He was barely conscious, but he recognized Larry Sheldon's voice. "I need to tell you something," Dr. Evans said. "I accidentally injected a young couple's newborn baby with Adamartoni's DNA."

Larry Sheldon was going to ask him how it happened, but Dr. Evans died as he made his confession. He said a quick prayer for him, and walked over to where the rest of the group was watching the truck burn at the bottom of the canyon.

"What happened?" Larry Sheldon asked.

"I think he hit a patch of ice and skidded off the road."

"Was that the truck with the sarcophagus?"

"It was, and what's worse, all of the DNA samples were in it."

"How did that happen? They were supposed to always travel separately."

"Dr. Evans wanted all of the research on the truck with him."

They had intended to try to replicate the advanced abilities of Adamartoni with the DNA, but they hadn't gotten far enough to know whether it was going to work. When Larry Sheldon was airborne again, he called Marvin Wilson to let him know what had happened, and that they were going to need to follow the young couple and their baby.

Larry Sheldon had been working tirelessly trying to

develop a plan to save the Earth. The Logos had known the end of the world was coming for thousands of years. The exact language of the warning had been lost over the centuries, but they had known a fire from the sky would destroy the Earth sometime in the twenty-first century.

When they placed him in charge of planning, Larry decided to try to verify the warning. He redirected the *Voyager 2* deep-space probe, and pointed it toward the coordinates given in the texts. The probe sent back long-range scans of a massive Apollo-class asteroid which was traveling with a swarm of asteroids which stretched almost 30 million miles. The probe tracked the asteroids long enough to verify its normal course around the outer fringes solar system had changed. The asteroid had been passing just outside the earth's solar system for millions of years, but now it was going to strike the Earth. The Logos had continued to monitor its path, and now they were sure it was going to intersect with Earth's orbit in the year 2012.

5

As BEN DROVE home, he would occasionally adjust the rearview mirror to take a peek at Billy, as he slept peacefully in his car seat. What he couldn't see was while he slept his body was rapidly changing. The DNA in his bloodstream was already beginning to change his body.

An hour into their return trip, Billy's IQ was well above any human who had ever been born. By the time they entered New Mexico, his IQ, if it had been measurable, was at least 250 and growing. By the time the transformation was complete, it was not measurable by any test ever devised by man. While Billy would look like a completely normal boy, he was in fact a new species of man.

When they reached the city limits of Clayton, Ben stopped at the Chevron station to get some gas. The attendant, Wilbur Wood, had gone to school with Ben, so while he filled the tank they struck up a conversation.

"I haven't seen you in a week or so. Have you two been on vacation, and what happened to the front of your Suburban?"

"We're just getting back from Mary's mom's funeral in Denver, and we had an accident on the way back."

"Aren't you two due to have a baby before long?"

"He was born yesterday. We ran into a snowstorm, and I skidded off the road just outside of Colorado Springs.

After the wreck, we ended up spending the night at a hotel by the name of Glen Eyrie. The government was using the hotel to provide R and R for their scientists. Luckily, one of them was a doctor by the name of Billy Evans, and he was able to deliver the baby. This morning when we got ready to leave, some of the men stationed there had repaired our Suburban enough for us to travel, and they even filled it with gas. They actually stood outside in the snow this afternoon waiting to see us on our way."

"It sure sounds like you two had quite an adventure on the way back."

"We sure did, but it all turned out all right. Mary and the baby are fine, and we're home safely."

Wilbur looked through the backseat window at the baby sleeping peacefully in its car seat and said, "You'll have to bring him by so I can get a better look."

He finished topping the tank off, and said, "That comes to fifty dollars."

"I can't believe gas is two dollars a gallon."

Ben counted out his money and said, "Here you go, and we'll bring the baby back so you can get a better look."

As he turned onto the rutted dirt road to their old run-down ranch house, Mary woke up.

"Are we already home?"

"Yes, we are, sleepyhead. Wait in the car while I get the house open."

"Take your time. We're fine out here."

He left the car running so they wouldn't get cold. When he had everything ready, he helped them into the house.

As he closed the front door behind them, she remarked, "It may not be much, but I sure am glad to be home again."

"I hope I can do better for you and Billy."

"I didn't mean you aren't a good provider. I love you, and we'll do better, you just wait and see."

She gave him a quick kiss. "I'm going to bed if you don't mind. Even though I slept the whole way back I'm still tired."

"No problem, you've had a rough couple of days."

After he got them settled in for the night, he slumped into one of the chairs around the kitchen table and sighed. He was thinking about the past few days, and thought to himself, *Well, everything turned out all right. Mary and Billy are doing fine, and we're safely back at home.*

They had married shortly after they graduated high school. Except for the two years he spent in the Marines, neither one of them had ever been farther away from home than Denver. Like most of the kids they grew up with, they were content to lead the simple life of rural New Mexico.

The next morning he awoke to the smell of breakfast.

"Woman, what do you think you're doing?"

He put his arms around her. "I was going to get up and cook your breakfast. You should be in bed resting."

"Don't be silly. I'm fine. Now hurry up and eat your breakfast. We need to get Dr. Moore to examine Billy."

"Yeah, and we'll get him to check you out too."

"I'm fine, I tell you."

"I believe you, but just because you are already up to cooking breakfast doesn't prove a thing. We're still going to let him verify it."

"Have you ever seen such a good baby?" Mary asked. "He never seems to cry, and I think he's already paying attention to us. I've never seen a baby do that so soon. I sure hope there's nothing wrong with him."

"He looks fine to me, but the doc will get him checked out."

They didn't talk much on the way to town. They were both thinking about their new son, and what sort of man he would grow up to be. Would he be athletic like his dad, and would he be as smart as they both hoped? They had no way of knowing he would be both, but to an extent they couldn't even begin to imagine.

They had known the doctor's nurse since they were kids. She greeted them with a hearty laugh and said, "You two bring the baby over here, and let me see him."

"Oh my, he sure is a good-looking boy. I heard you two had quite an adventure on your way back."

"We sure did. I'll have to tell you the whole story."

"You'll have to do it some other time. Dr. Moore came in special to see you two. He's due back in surgery in less than an hour. So go on back, and you can tell me the whole story this Sunday after church."

They went into the exam room, and Ben helped Mary up onto the table. "I remember the last time you helped me up onto a table like this, and it sure feels better this time."

"I would hope so."

Dr. Moore entered the exam room and asked, "How are you feeling? I'm disappointed I wasn't able to deliver Billy."

"So were we, but we'll have a great story to tell him when he's old enough," Mary said.

"Let's have a look at you two." He motioned to Ben. "Hold the baby while I examine Mary. There's a gown in the bathroom. Would you mind changing into it?"

"Okay, Doc, I'll just be a minute," Mary said.

"I heard you had quite a trip."

"Boy, Wilbur sure gets around," Ben said. "But we sure did. We had a wreck on I-25 just outside of Colorado Springs, and I was worried for a while we were in real trouble. We managed to find a hotel just outside of Colorado Springs by the name of Glen Eyrie."

"I don't think I've heard of it."

"I hadn't either. I guess they like to keep it quiet."

When Mary returned Dr. Moore said, "Hop back up on the table, and I'll get started."

It seemed like forever to Ben, but it was only ten minutes before the doctor announced, "You look fine. Your blood pressure and heart rate are good. The baby doesn't seem to have caused you any trouble.

"Let's get started on Billy."

As he began to examine Billy, Ben told him about Dr. Evans giving him a shot of Levofloxacin for his congestion and fever.

"That's a good broad-spectrum antibiotic. I probably would have used something else, but it should work fine."

When he finished, he weighed and measured the baby. "He weighs eight pounds, eight ounces and is twenty-one inches long. He has a bit of a temperature at ninety-nine-point-six, but I don't believe it's anything to be concerned about. I'll draw some blood so I can get his blood type, and check to make sure the point of temperature is nothing."

He drew the blood and said, "Well, that wasn't so bad. He didn't even cry. I'll put a Band-Aid on it in case he bleeds some more. You can take it off by the time you get home."

He handed the baby to Mary. "He's as perfect as any baby I have ever examined."

"I'm so glad."

"You can get him dressed. I have to get to the hospital. I'm supposed to take out Henry Ramos's appendix in a half an hour, and I don't think he would be pleased if I'm late."

"Take it easy, and we'll see you Sunday at church," Ben said.

They were driving home when Ben said, "I sure am glad that Billy is healthy. Did he stop bleeding yet?"

She removed the Band-Aid and exclaimed, "There isn't even a mark on him!"

"He took it like a trooper. It must be too small to see."

She rubbed off the spot of dried blood. "I don't see any mark at all."

"He's just a tough little boy. He takes after his old man."

"Sure he does. You're a real baby when it comes to shots."

They both laughed, and didn't say much the rest of the way home.

While mother and child both lay down for a nap, Ben went outside to check on the livestock.

He noticed all of the animals needed water, so he started to water and feed them. When he was done, he went back inside, planning to have a short nap.

He had just gotten inside the door when his neighbor Rob Bustamante pulled up. They had been friends as long as either of them could remember.

Rob had been looking after the animals while they had been gone. Ben walked out to greet him. "Thanks for taking care of the place."

"Hey no problem, I was coming over to check the animals to water and feed them."

"I just finished. Come in and have a cup of coffee."

"Sure, but I can't stay long. Beth wants me to hook up the new LCD TV we just got today. She wants it in time for tonight's shows. We got cable last week, but our old TV wouldn't work very well with it."

"A new TV and cable service, how much did that set you back?"

"Not too bad, I traded three yearling calves to Lucas at the feed store for it."

"Let's have one quick cup, and then you can get back. We're going to get us a new TV, but I spent most of my spare cash on the trip. I can't believe the cost of gas, I was hoping it would go down, since they have most of the Iraqi oilfields back on line."

"I know what you mean. It's been pretty tight with us too. What did you name him?"

"We named him Billy Wayne."

"Billy Wayne? I know Wayne was Mary's dad's name, but where did Billy come from? I thought you would have named him after you."

"We were going to, but at the last minute we decided to name him after the doctor who delivered him. He was such a nice guy, and I don't know why, but we both thought of it at the same time."

"Well you can name the next one after you, but I'm still surprised."

"In a way I am too, but it seemed like the right thing to do at the time."

As Ben was pouring the coffee, Rob shared his good news. "Beth is six months pregnant."

"Congratulations, but how come you are just now discovering she's pregnant?"

"You know how she watches her weight, and she has always had problems with her period. So we didn't think much of it when she was late. We've been trying for a baby ever since we got married, and now we are going to have one."

"That's great news, and the kids are going to be real close together. Maybe you'll have a boy, and they can be best friends just like us."

"That would be great, wouldn't it?"

6

LARRY SHELDON BRIEFED the council on Dr. Evans's death, and his confession.

"This is terrible news," Marvin Wilson said. "We may have lost our only chance to save the world. What are you going to do about the baby? Do you intend to tell the parents?"

"I don't think we should tell them. I believe we should monitor them closely, but nothing else for the moment."

"Let us know if anything changes."

Larry Sheldon immediately began to put people in place in order to monitor the baby's health, and to see if they could figure out what the effects of the DNA might be.

The next three months passed quickly, and Billy was growing like a weed. He was already recognizing them, and was trying to sit up. Before they knew it, Rob and Beth were stopping by on their way to the hospital.

Rob ran up to the door, and Ben opened it to greet him.

"What's up?" Ben asked.

"We're headed to town. Beth's in labor."

"As soon as we get cleaned up, we'll be up to wait with you."

"Thanks, buddy. I'll see you up there."

"We're right behind you. Get that girl to the hospital. You don't want to end up in the middle of nowhere like we did."

He closed the door and said, "Beth is in labor, and they are on their way to the hospital."

"Give me a couple of minutes to get cleaned up. Would you mind getting Billy ready for me?"

Rob met them in the hospital lobby as they walked in.

"Thanks for coming. They just took Beth down to the delivery room."

"Already?" Mary asked.

"It all happened very quickly. When we first came in they listened to the baby's heartbeat, and they took them straight down to the operating room. They said something about the baby being in some sort of distress, and they were going to do an immediate C-section."

"They're going to be all right, aren't they?" Mary asked.

"I sure hope so, I don't know what I would do if anything happened to her."

"I know what you mean," Ben said.

Mary tried to reassure him. "Dr. Moore has been doing this for many years, and I'm sure she'll be just fine."

"Boy I sure hope so," Rob said. "Let's go down to the waiting room. They said they would come and tell me as soon as they know something. I see you have Billy along."

"We didn't have anyone to watch him," Mary said. "Our normal babysitter isn't available."

They all laughed, since the only one who had ever kept him was Beth.

They had been waiting for over an hour when Dr. Moore came through the waiting room door. They had never seen him look so worried. They all jumped to their feet.

"What's wrong?" Rob asked. "Are Beth and the baby all right?"

"She's fine, but the baby's having trouble. As far as I can tell, the baby's bleeding internally. I think I can fix it, but there's a problem."

"What's the problem?" Rob asked.

"I don't have any O negative blood. We usually have plenty, but when the pickup crashed into the hospital yesterday it destroyed all of our blood and plasma. There are several pints in Amarillo, but I don't think the baby will last long enough to get there."

"Can't you just operate, Doctor?" Rob asked.

"Yes I can, but there's a real chance the baby won't make it without a blood transfusion."

"Can't we get someone here in town to donate?"

"I don't know of anyone else with O negative blood who's a donor. Mrs. Jones was O negative, but she died last year. The only other one I know of is Billy, and he's too young."

"Are you sure he couldn't give a pint?" Mary asked.

"No, I'm not sure. It's just I've never taken blood from a baby for a transfusion. Actually, a baby will replace blood even faster than an adult. Would you two be willing to let me take some blood?"

"As long as it won't hurt him," Mary said. "We have no problem with it."

"Okay then, let me have him, and I'll go and take care of the baby."

Mary handed him to Dr. Moore, and said, "Take care of him."

"Don't worry; I won't let anything bad happen to him."

He took him and rushed down the hall to the operating room. It seemed like forever, but it was only an hour and a half until he returned.

This time he was beaming from ear to ear.

"Well, folks, everyone is doing great now. The baby had a perforated bowl, just as I thought. It was easily fixed, and she'll be fine."

"She?" Rob asked. "It's a girl?"

"Yes, it is. I'm so sorry. I didn't even take time to tell you last time."

"It's fine, just as long as everyone is all right."

"The nurse is putting a bandage on Billy's puncture marks."

"Marks?" Mary asked.

"I'm sorry, but it took the nurse a couple of tries to set the line to draw blood. He's fine, and he won't be any worse for wear in a couple of days," Dr. Moore said. "I just want to tell you how proud I am to have people like you in our community. Not everyone would have let their child go through giving blood at his age."

"We are just glad our family could help our best friends," Ben said.

"We'll never forget this," Rob said.

"You don't need to thank us. We have known you guys our whole lives, and you would have done the same for us."

"Still, I'm grateful."

"Would you like to see Beth now?"

"You bet, let's go," Rob said. "Can we see the baby?"

"No, not yet. I'm going to keep her in the recovery room until I'm sure she's stable."

"How long do you think?"

"I don't know for sure, but I'll let you know as soon as she's stable. Now let's get you down to see Beth. She's in her room already, and she's feeling better now that she knows the baby is out of danger."

"You guys want to come along?" Rob asked.

"No, this time is for the two of you," Ben said. "We'll stay here and wait on Billy."

They had been waiting for about ten minutes when the nurse brought Billy in.

"Here's your brave boy. You know he didn't even cry when we were taking his blood. Most grown-ups would have been squealing like a stuck pig."

"I'm going to check his arm and see how bad it looks," Mary said. "We may want to bring him back tomorrow if it looks too bad."

"Okay, let's look."

She pulled back the tape and gauze to get a look, but they didn't see anything. She peeled it back some more and said, "I don't see anything yet, it must be farther in."

She continued to peel the bandage back until it was completely off.

"Where are the marks they were warning us about?" Ben asked.

"There doesn't seem to be any under the bandage, and his other arm is fine as well," Mary said. "There's nothing there."

She wadded up the bandage and threw it in the wastebasket. They pulled his sleeves down and got up to talk to Dr. Moore.

They had just entered the hall when he came up to them. "The baby's doing great. In fact, they're taking her in to them right now. You can come on down to room five and see her. They asked for you."

"Sure, we will," Mary said. "The baby's already doing that well?"

"I know what I said before, but I've never seen anyone come around as quickly as she has. She sure is a strong little girl, kind of like her soon-to-be best friend Billy."

Everyone went in to see the baby. Rob was sitting on the edge of Beth's bed, and their new baby girl was in a bassinet beside the bed.

They had named her after Beth's mother Linda, and her dad Lou. Both had died on the night of Beth's high school graduation. A drunken friend of theirs had crossed the centerline and hit them head-on, killing all three of them. Beth had never been able to forget that night, but she and Rob wanted to honor their memories by naming their firstborn after them.

"You look good," Mary said. "But you look like you're still in pain."

"I had a few complications, and the doctor ended up tying my tubes. He said I shouldn't have any more babies. He told me he didn't know how I carried Linda Lou to full term."

"I'm so sorry."

"I'm just glad we managed to have one."

"You're right. We're both lucky to have fine healthy babies."

"We do, thanks to you two. I don't know how we can ever thank you for what you have done. Bring Billy over here. I want him to see the life he just saved."

Mary brought him over to the bassinet and held him up next to Linda Lou.

They were just going to let the babies be close to each other. The moment was for the adults more than the kids, but to everyone's surprise Billy reached out and touched Linda Lou's face, and he got a big smile on his face. Everyone laughed.

"Well, it looks like they are going to be as good friends as we all are," Mary said.

They had no way of knowing they already had more in common than any of them would ever understand.

The DNA injection caused Billy's changes. His blood caused hers. Her changes had not taken as long as his, but they were just as complete.

Even as they were talking, her brain and body continued to change. Her brain had already fused together, and every cell of her body had begun to receive the same regenerative powers as his. In fact, that was why she was recovering so rapidly from her surgery.

There were now two examples of a new species of human being.

"I don't know what we would do if we didn't have your family as friends," Beth said.

"You know we feel the same way," Mary said. "I sure hope our kids grow up as friends like we have."

"You never know, they might even end up being more."

"Here we are matching up our kids already. We're being silly. We're going to get going so you can get some rest," Mary said.

"Thanks so much for being here with us."

"No problem. We'll come over after you get settled in at home."

On their way home Mary said, "I don't think we could ever have better friends than Beth and Rob."

"I think you're right. They're special. I sure hope the kids grow up to be as close."

"I sure think they might. Did you see the smile on Billy's face when he reached out to touch Linda?"

"I sure did. I didn't think babies were aware at his age."

"I think they are all different, but he sure seemed pleased to see her."

What they didn't know was in addition to their other abilities, the kids possessed an innate ability to sense whether people were good or bad.

Over the next couple of years, the two families continued to enjoy each other's company while they watched the two children grow.

They got together as often as they could. Times had been hard, but at least once or twice a week they would take turns fixing dinner, and after dinner they would play cards. They would send the kids back to their room or outside to play, depending on the weather.

The kids never minded being together, and they were the best of friends. By the time they were old enough to talk, they were already discussing why they seemed to have nothing in common with the other children.

On Linda's fifth birthday, Rob and Beth had a hamburger and hotdog cookout for her birthday party. They were struggling to make ends meet, but they had managed to get her a new baby doll and a couple of new outfits.

Ben and Mary were having an even harder time, but they always brought a present for her birthday. They had managed to find her an electronic board game on sale in the Wal-Mart store. It was nothing special, but it did contain several games.

The kids took the game and went to their favorite tree in the backyard to play.

"Let's play a game," Linda said.

"Okay, what should we play first?"

"Your mom said it can play five different games. Let's play this one. The picture looks like there are several different figures used in it."

"There's one that looks like a horse, and this one looks like a castle."

"Okay, how do we start?"

She touched the question mark beside the icon for the game. It began a tutorial on how to play the game and the names of the pieces involved.

"It looks like one of us takes white, and the other will take black."

"Okay, I want white," Linda said.

"All right, I'll take black."

"What do we do next?"

"I think we take turns moving our pieces. It said we're supposed to capture each other's pieces when we land on the same space. I saw Mom and Dad playing a game they called checkers, and that's what they did when they landed on each other's pieces."

He pointed to the picture of the king. "When one of us can't move this piece where it won't be captured by the next move, the game is over."

"That doesn't sound too hard. Let's try it."

They had been playing for thirty minutes when Rob walked back to tell them the food was ready.

"What are you two up to back here? We haven't heard a peep out of you since you opened up the game. Are you playing chess?"

"Yes, I think that's what it's called," Billy said.

"Yes, it is. I used to play in high school. Dinner is ready, you two come on and eat."

"Can we finish our game?" Linda asked.

He saw they only had a few pieces left so he said, "Sure, go ahead."

As they played out their game, he was amazed to see they were moving their pieces in the proper manner, and they had a better than basic grasp of the game. He watched them play for a few minutes before he said, "Well you two, your game's a draw. That means neither of you is going to win. Let's go and get something to eat, and then you can play again.

"Did your dad teach you to play chess?" Rob asked.

"No, we don't have any games like this," Billy said. "We listened to the tutorial before we started."

"It must have been pretty good. You were playing correctly as far as I could tell from watching you, and that's simply amazing. It took me several months to master even the basic skills. No matter, you two come on and eat."

"Is there any ice cream?" Linda asked.

"Yes, there is. Ben just finished making it. We'll have some with your birthday cake when we finish eating."

They ate and had their cake and ice cream. "Can we go and play some more before it gets dark?" Linda asked.

"Sure, it's your birthday," Rob said. "You go right ahead."

As they turned to go, she said, "Thank you so much for my game. We're having a lot of fun playing it."

"You're welcome," Mary said. "I was afraid it was too old for you."

"Oh no, Billy and I figured it out."

After they had returned to their game Ben remarked, "Linda is such a smart little girl."

"Thanks, she is smart, but Billy is just as bright," Beth said.

"They're both exceptional children."

"Well of course they are. Look at who they have for parents."

They all laughed, and Rob said, "They learned to play chess from listening to the short overview and tutorial that's built into the console."

"Chess?" Ben asked. "How in the world could five-year-old children learn a game as complicated as chess that quickly?"

"I know how to play," Rob said. "But as far as I can remember I've never shown Linda how to play, or even talked about it. When I was back there earlier, they were playing, and they were playing correctly."

"Let's go back and ask them," Beth said.

They all got up and walked to the back of the yard where the kids were playing. "Where did you and Billy learn to play chess?" Rob asked.

"We watched the console's demonstration," Linda said. "It wasn't difficult to figure out. The pieces have a fairly limited ability to move, so it wasn't that hard."

"You two figured out all of that from watching what had to be a limited overview?" Mary asked.

"Yes we did. Have we done something wrong?"

"Not at all," Mary said. "We just can't believe you could figure out the object of the game, and how to play it that easily."

"I guess it doesn't matter," Ben said. "It's getting dark.

Pick up the game and go on inside. We have to get going. I've got to get up early in the morning for work."

After they had left, Beth was washing the dishes when Linda asked, "Would you play a game of chess with me before bed?"

"Sure, we should have time for one game before bed," Rob said.

Linda got the game ready while he poured himself a cup of coffee and got another piece of birthday cake.

"You go first," Rob said.

They had been playing for about twenty minutes when he announced, "Good game, you win. That was incredible. I was trying, and you beat me. That's the quickest I've ever been beaten. Let's play again."

Around midnight Beth came over to where they were playing.

"All right, you two, It's almost midnight. Go and get in bed, and I'll be right there to tuck you in."

Linda kissed them and ran off for bed.

"You didn't have to let her win every game," Beth said. "She needs to learn how to deal with disappointment."

"I wasn't letting her win. In fact I couldn't even give her a good game."

"Oh come on, you were runner-up at the state high school chess meet. You don't mean to tell me our five-year-old daughter can beat you so easily."

"That's exactly what I'm telling you. I couldn't come close to beating her. I think she may have been taking it easy on me the last couple of games."

"We'll talk some more tomorrow. I'm going to go and tuck her in for the night."

As she tucked Linda in, she told her, "You go right to sleep. It's very late. Did you have fun playing with Daddy?"

"Yes, I did. I hope he didn't feel too bad that I won. I tried to let him win a couple of times, but it didn't work out."

"That's what your dad said, but I didn't believe him."

7

THE NEXT WEEK the kids were in Linda's room playing chess, and the adults were sitting at the kitchen table playing cards.

"I still can't believe I can't even give Linda a good game," Rob said. "I may not be the best chess player, but I thought I was better than that."

"Maybe it's not you," Ben said. "Maybe Linda and Billy are just bright. When I talked with Billy, he told me they usually play to a tie, or split evenly on their games. He said it's difficult for either one of them to win a game."

"I've thought about that. In fact, Beth and I were discussing it last night. How can they both be that smart? I know we're all reasonably intelligent adults, but let's face it, none of us are rocket scientists."

"Mary was the valedictorian."

"But I'm not that smart," she said. "I tried to learn chess once, and while I can move the pieces, I never did grasp the game."

"Do you think we should get someone to take a look at them? There might be something wrong with them," Beth said.

"I don't think we need to worry," Ben said. "They both seem happy and well adjusted. Let's see how they do when they start to be around other kids."

They continued to play chess when Billy would come

over to her house, but she never played her dad again. It wasn't that either one of them planned not to play again. He was unconsciously ashamed he couldn't give his five-year-old daughter a decent game, and she didn't want to make her dad feel bad. So they never talked about it or played again. Rob didn't like change, and so it was just easier not to think about it.

Not too long after that, their parents began taking them to church on Sunday. They would join the other children in the church nursery during the prayer services.

After several weeks, they couldn't believe the other children their age wouldn't talk to them. The other children made fun of them and wouldn't play with them at all.

They tried to talk with some of the older children, but they weren't much better than the younger ones. When it came to the adults, they quickly learned what the adults expected from them, and it wasn't adult-level conversation or thoughts.

Because of their experiences, they learned to talk about meaningful things only when they were away from adult scrutiny.

Earl Williams was the pastor at their church. He had only been in town for two years. The previous pastor had died in a car crash coming back from a seminar in Amarillo. Earl had shown up the same week in search of a new church. He was one of the people Larry Sheldon had placed around Billy to try to monitor his development.

Earl Williams had been a member of the Logos for over ten years. They recruited him while he was still in the seminary working on his degree. Like all Logos he had been recruited because he was exceptional, and possessed a true love of God. He was a dedicated man of God, but he was also there to monitor Billy's progress.

Larry Sheldon had continued to develop a plan for dealing with the doom which was quickly approaching.

They verified the asteroid would strike in the year 2012, and he had thousands of people working on different technologies they believed might have some use.

They were attempting to develop either an escape plan or a way to divert the comet, while they continued to guard the secret of the asteroid. They had briefed no one outside of the government or their organization. They were limiting the number of people who were fully aware, because they realized the world would not respond well to the threat.

Shortly after the children began attending church, the pastor overheard one of their conversations. The Logos had briefed him on the need to observe Billy's behavior, but he was amazed to observe similar tendencies in Linda Lou.

The kids were having a conversation on how they should interact in public so they wouldn't upset anyone.

They heard a noise, and there was the pastor standing behind them. He had the funniest look on his face, as if he couldn't believe what he had just heard.

Linda looked up at him with her big brown eyes and said, "Please don't say anything."

He thought to himself, *No one would believe me anyway. These two children are less than six years old. What could I possibly say?*

"You two aren't doing anything wrong. Why haven't you let anyone know how well you can talk?"

"We don't want people to make fun of us for being different. We just want to be treated like all of the other kids," Linda said.

"I won't tell anyone. If you'd like, you can come by and talk with me anytime you want."

"Thank you."

"It's part of my job, and I'm constantly trying to help young people work through their problems. I do have to say, I've never had a chance to start with two so young."

"We appreciate being able to talk with you," Billy said.

"You're welcome, and this will be our secret until you both tell me it doesn't need to be. Now I have to go earn my keep and give today's sermon."

"I think he'll be a good source of information for us," Linda said. "Don't you?"

"I agree. I've been worried we would never find an adult we could talk to."

"Do you still agree our parents aren't ready for us to be this grown up?"

"I do. I still remember how many questions we got at your last birthday party, over just being able to play a silly game. So while we're not grown up, we do seem to be quite a bit different from all the other kids."

That night Earl Williams called Larry Sheldon to report his observations. After verifying his identity, the switchboard operator transferred his call to the High Council where Larry was meeting with Clayton Edwards, the new leader of the Logos.

"What do you have to report?" Sheldon asked Pastor Williams.

"I've been observing Billy West's actions as you instructed. His intelligence and thought processes are unquestionably more advanced than anyone I've ever met."

"We're already aware of his potential. That's why we posted you to watch his development. Do you have anything new to report?"

"Yes, sir, I believe his friend Linda Bustamante has the same type of abilities as he does."

"Are you sure?"

"I'm as sure as I can be at this point."

"I'll put a team on it. For now you need to follow the same procedures for Linda as I laid out for observing Billy. Continue filing weekly reports on your findings, and I'll let you know what we find out about Linda."

After he hung up, Larry Sheldon told the rest of the council, "We need to verify Earl's observations as soon as possible. Howard, I need you to put your best research team on this. If he's right, it may fulfill the prophecy of a young couple coming forward to save the human race from extinction."

It only took Howard's team a few days to discover the link between Billy and Linda. They had followed Billy since he was born, and once they searched the hospital records they knew the connection.

The Logos had no way of knowing what effect, if any, the DNA would have on Billy, but they hadn't even theorized he might be able to pass along the changes.

During the next few months, Billy and Linda talked with the pastor as often as they could. Pastor Williams would report the kids' activities for the week and Larry Sheldon would give him instructions for what to share next with them.

Pastor Williams and the kids spent a lot of time together. He taught them the philosophies of the Logos to ensure they learned their beliefs and the word of God.

They continued to try to interact with the other children from time to time, but they never managed to gain acceptance from any of them. Their parents continued to ignore the differences in them, and even though they all realized the kids were different, they simply didn't want to recognize them for what they were.

The Sunday morning before they were going to start school, they were talking with Pastor Williams.

"You start school this year, don't you?"

"Yes we do," Linda said.

"I hope your teachers will be able to keep up, but I doubt it. We've talked about this before, but I think it's time you start to talk more openly with your parents."

"I've tried a couple of times in the last month or so, but

I always seem to confuse my parents," Linda said. "They simply don't know how to respond. They're still trying to talk to a six-year-old."

"I know, kids. I don't know how to advise you on how to talk with them. I'm aware they haven't responded well to how far advanced you both are."

"No they haven't," Billy said. "That's why Linda and I have agreed to not ever show anyone what we are thinking, or what we're talking about."

"Well, you've succeeded so far, but it's going to get a lot harder as you start school."

"I know it is," Linda said. "But don't you believe we need to continue hiding how different we are?"

"Yes, you probably do. I just hate that you're not getting to enjoy being children. I'll continue to help you in any way I can, but you're going to have to start depending on your parents and teachers to help you along."

"We understand," Billy said. "We can't tell you what our Sunday conversations have meant to us."

As they left the pastor's study, a chapter in their lives closed, and another was about to begin. They were going to start the first grade.

8

THROUGHOUT THE YEARS, their parents had continued to ignore how truly gifted and different the kids were. Even when they noticed the kids never seemed to be sick, and their normal childhood injuries healed at an amazing pace, they just couldn't force themselves to admit how different they were.

Their parents were all sitting at the kitchen table playing cards as they so often did. "I can't believe the kids are ready to start first grade," Rob said. "It seems like yesterday when they were born."

"I know what you mean," Ben said. "I need to ask you something. We rarely discuss the kids, but they're quite different from the rest of the kids their age. I have trouble even understanding Billy at times. Do you two have the same problem with Linda Lou?"

"You know we do. I still haven't gotten over the chess incident on her fifth birthday. Do you know we've never played again? I guess I have been too ashamed to admit I can't even give her a good game."

"How do you think they're going to do at school?" Ben asked. "Mary and I were talking last night, and we're afraid the other kids are going to make fun of them and they'll not be able to fit in. You know they've never been able to interact with other children."

"It's funny you mention it," Rob said. "We were talking about the same thing. We believe they may have a difficult time in school. I don't know whether you've noticed it, but they go to great lengths to hide their intelligence from everyone, including us. I'm so ashamed they feel the need to hide their abilities from us."

"It's the same with us," Ben said. "I can't believe we've all been in denial for this long."

"What do you think we should do?" Mary asked.

"It's way beyond me," Beth said. "I guess we're going to have to see how it plays out in school. We'll talk to Linda tonight and see how she feels about it."

"That sounds like a good idea to me," Mary said. "We'll try to do the same with Billy. We haven't done a good job dealing with this, have we? We probably should have already contacted somebody to help us with them. I just hope we haven't waited too long."

"I don't think there's any real danger of that," Beth said. "They seem to have taken good care of themselves. It's amazing to me how quickly they adapt to their surroundings. When they saw we weren't capable of dealing with their abilities, they tried to protect us. It's sad our six-year-old children feel like they have to protect us."

They had finally realized they should have been doing something, but it wouldn't have mattered. There wasn't anything they could have done to alter the coming years.

As they planned, they talked with the kids, but the kids ended up assuring them they were fine, and they didn't need them to do anything different.

None of them could believe the maturity of the kids, and even though they all believed they were still failing them, they agreed not to change anything.

Linda Lou had grown into a beautiful girl, with dark brown hair and brown eyes which seemed to look right through you. She was taller than other children her age and already possessed an athletic elegance.

Billy was only average in size, but extremely athletic. He had almost-white hair and gray eyes which were just as piercing as Linda's.

Their IQs were immense, but the thing that would always truly set them apart was the bond they had between them. It continued to grow ever stronger as they matured, but even at the age of six, they always seemed to know what the other was thinking and feeling.

They were on the same bus route, so they sat together on the way to school. It made sense since they didn't know any of the other children on the bus. Their parents didn't have any friends other than each other, so the kids didn't either.

When they got to school the first day, they went straight to their classroom. They had been to school the previous Friday with their parents to register, and their teacher had shown them where their room would be.

Mrs. Robinson was their teacher, and this was her twentieth year of teaching first grade. She never had any children of her own, but she truly loved kids, and they loved her. All the parents tried to get their kids into her class. Everyone has that one teacher they remember, and she would be the one for most of them.

As they entered the room, Mrs. Robinson greeted them.

"Kids, your seats are up here by me. Please hurry, we're late getting started."

She began their first day of school as she had all of the others before.

"Good morning, students."

"Good morning, Mrs. Robinson."

They enjoyed their first day in school. They had colored papers, and cutout animals to paste in their workbooks, but most of all they enjoyed Mrs. Robinson talking with them. During the last part of the day, Mrs. Robinson was reading the class a story. She had just started when the principal came by and called her out into the hall.

While she was out, Billy got curious. He picked up the book from her desk to see what it looked like. As he looked at it, he began to read the story out loud to the class.

She finished her conversation with the principal, and turned to go back into the room. As she was about to enter, she heard Billy's voice. She hesitated before entering, so she could hear what was going on.

At first, she thought he was just talking and was going to reprimand him for not being quiet. However, as she continued to listen, she recognized the story she had been reading on the first day of school for the last twenty years.

Fascinated, she stood for a good five minutes and listened. She had long since memorized the words, so she knew Billy wasn't missing a thing. She was amazed a six-year-old could already read so well.

Satisfied she had heard enough, she went in to talk with him. He saw her enter, stopped reading, and said, "I'm sorry, I was looking at your book, and it just seemed right to tell the story to the class."

"I didn't know you could already read! We don't usually cover this book until you're in the second or third grade. I don't remember your parents telling me you could read."

"I haven't ever read a book before."

"You've been reading on the Internet then?"

"No, we don't have Internet. We don't even have a phone."

"I find it hard to believe. You didn't hesitate or miss a single word."

"I'm sorry. I didn't mean to upset you."

"I'm not mad at you. I'm pleasantly surprised."

The final bell rang, and everyone rushed to the door. On the bus ride home, Billy and Linda were talking.

"I think I messed up today," Billy said.

"You might have, but sooner or later they're going to figure out we're way ahead of the other kids in our class."

"How did you know how to read Mrs. Robinson's book?"

"I don't know. The words just seemed to come to me. I can't explain it."

"I know what you mean, I've looked at mother's Bible a couple of times, and the same thing happened to me."

"You never told me you've tried to read."

"It didn't seem important. It's like a lot of things we just seem to be able to do."

"I guess I brought the attention we've always tried to not bring upon ourselves," Billy said.

"Yes, I think you have."

Meanwhile Mrs. Robinson decided she would go out to Ben and Mary's to discuss Billy's actions in class.

After dinner, she asked her husband Lawrence, "Would it be all right if we make a trip out to Ben and Mary West's?"

"Sure, but what's up?"

"While I was out of the room talking to the principal, Billy West picked up the book I always read to the class the first week of school, and was reading it to the class."

"So, his parents already taught him to read. That's good, isn't it?"

"Sure it is. But when I asked him, he told me he had never read a book before. I want to find out if he was telling me the truth, or if he's going to be one of those kids who can never tell you the truth."

"No problem, but let's go before it gets too late."

"Okay, I'll be right out."

"So what do you expect to find out from Billy's parents?"

"I'm not sure, but it bothers me that he would lie to me. He seems like such a nice boy. I would hate for him to grow up thinking it's all right to lie."

Ben saw them coming up their road, so he stepped out onto the front porch to greet them.

"Barbara, Lawrence, what are you two doing way out here?"

"Barbara wants to talk to you about what happened at school today, and she didn't want to wait."

"Come on in. What did the boy get into?"

"Can you get Mary before I tell you about what happened today?"

"Sure she's in the bedroom sewing. Would you like me to get Billy as well?"

"No, I'd like to talk with the two of you alone. If it's all right with you?"

"No problem, have a seat and I'll get her."

"It's good to see you two, but what brings you all the way out here?" Mary asked as she greeted her guests.

"I'm sorry if I worried you, but I want to talk about what Billy did in class today."

"What did he do?" Ben asked. "Get in a fight?"

"It's nothing like that. Let's sit down, and I'll explain."

She told them the story, and as she finished, she told them, "When I asked him if you had taught him to read, he told me he had never read a book before. It's troubling he would lie to me about something he knew I wouldn't believe."

"But we've never worked with him," Mary said. "In fact, he doesn't even have any storybooks. We've had some hard times the last couple of years, and we haven't been able to afford any books for him."

"You mean you haven't taught him to read?"

"No, we haven't, and in fact I'm ashamed to say we

never even read to him. Ben will tell him bedtime stories sometimes, but we haven't ever read a book to him."

"How can that be? He was reading the book I always read the first week of class. If I had to say, it's probably a second- or third-grade reading level."

"I don't know," Mary said. "But he wasn't lying."

"I'm so sorry. I was so sure. I can't apologize enough."

"No problem, I'm just glad you cared enough to come and talk to us about it."

"I like Billy and his friend Linda Lou. I didn't want him to get off to the wrong start in life. How is it he can read as well as he does?"

"I don't know," Mary said. "Let me get him to come in here, and we'll ask him. Billy, come in here for a moment. Your teacher is here."

"Hello, Mrs. Robinson. I'm so glad to see you. I was afraid you were mad at me for touching your book today."

"I'm not mad, and in fact I would like to apologize to you for doubting your word."

"It's okay. I shouldn't have touched your book."

"Would you mind reading some more of it for your parents?"

"I would love to. Where should I start?"

"Just start at the beginning."

He had read the entire first chapter when Mrs. Robinson asked him to stop.

"Do you have any other storybooks?"

"No, we don't," Mary said. "Like I said, we haven't been able to get him any. I think the only other thing we have to read is a Bible, and maybe an Old Farmer's Almanac."

"I think the Bible is too hard, but let's let him try."

She told him, "Why don't you start at the beginning, and read until I ask you to stop."

After he had read the first fifteen pages, she stopped

him. "I've never seen anything like this in my whole career. As I was listening to him read, I was thinking how truly amazing it is he can read so well. I wish I had some tests for a child his age but I don't. If you don't mind, I'd like to give him some new tests we just got in. The state sent them to us so we can test high school students' intelligence and make recommendations on what they should take if they continue on to college."

"Do you think he's going to be able to take tests meant for high school students?" Mary asked.

"I don't know, but I would like to find out. If he can't do any of the tests, I'll talk to the principal about sending off for some more age-appropriate tests. We normally don't try to judge this kind of ability until the students are much older, but I'm intrigued by the abilities he has shown so far."

"We don't have a problem with it," Mary said. "But don't you think it's too much for a first grader?"

"It's probably a waste of his time, but I won't do it long enough to frustrate him. If it looks like he doesn't understand, we'll stop immediately."

"You do what you think is best," Mary said. "But will you let us know how he does?"

"Of course I will."

After they left Billy asked, "Did I do something wrong?"

"No dear, Mrs. Robinson just wants to see how smart you are."

After Billy was in bed, they sat down to talk about Barbara's visit.

"I'm worried," Mary said. "What if there's something wrong with Billy? It's not natural for him to be able to do that. Is it?"

"What would you call normal? I do believe he and Linda are both gifted children. As we discussed the other day, I think we've all been guilty of being in denial about them."

"I just hope we haven't held them back by not admitting we're not up to helping them."

"I hope so too, but it's too late to worry about that now. Let's see how Mrs. Robinson makes out when she tests him."

9

THE NEXT DAY Billy was up and dressed before Mary even came in to wake him up.

"You're up awfully early!"

"I know, I just woke up and wanted to get to school."

"Well, come eat breakfast. It'll be another forty-five minutes until the bus gets here. Are you ready for school? Where is your schoolbag?"

"It's right here."

He spent the time on the way to school telling Linda about Mrs. Robinson's visit.

"What's Mrs. Robinson going to do today?"

"I don't know. She didn't say what the tests were."

They went straight to their classroom, and a couple of minutes later Mrs. Robinson came in with her regular greeting. "Good morning, students."

"Good morning, Mrs. Robinson."

"All right, class, we're going to color for first period."

She walked around the room to make sure everyone was on the right page.

"All right, you can all start now. Billy, will you come with me?"

"Okay, should I bring my workbook?"

"No, you won't need it today. Class, I'll send Miss Hunter in to look after you."

When they reached the library, Mrs. Robinson asked

Rachel Hunter to teach her class for the rest of the morning, and then she told Billy, "Let's get to work. I'm going to take you to meet Mr. Willis. He's the high school counselor, and he has come over to work with you today."

Jim Willis was in the back of the library. He had already set up the testing area, and greeted them as they approached.

"Good morning, Mrs. Robinson. This must be the young man you were telling me about."

"Yes, it is. I would like for you to meet Billy West. Billy, this is Mr. Willis. He's going to ask you several questions. I'm going to be here the whole time, but I'm going to wait over there so I can watch while you and Mr. Willis work."

"Let's get started," Mr. Willis said. "If you need a drink or a bathroom break just tell me."

They spent the first hour doing association tests. Mr. Willis didn't say anything at all until they took a break.

"Why don't you go and use the restroom," Mr. Willis said. "Then you can get yourself a drink of water while I talk with Mrs. Robinson.

"Who's coached this child?" Mr. Willis asked.

"No one, why?"

"Someone has to have worked with him. He didn't miss any questions. In fact, he found an error in the test I hadn't noticed before. Let me do this next section with him, and then we'll talk again. Normally I would only give this section of the test to high school juniors and seniors. You have to read at a high school grade level or above to take it. I'll read it to him, and then tell him the possible answers."

"Tell him what he has to do, and let's see if he can do it."

"You've got to be kidding. I'll admit I haven't seen anyone of any age ace the first part of the test, but he hasn't even had reading yet, has he?"

After she shared the experiences of the previous day with him he said, "Okay, I'll let him try for a couple of minutes, and then I'll read it to him."

When Billy came back in, Mr. Willis said, "I want you to look at this screen and see if you can answer the questions at the end of each section. All you have to do to answer the questions is touch the icon beside the answer you believe is correct."

"Okay, I'll try."

"Would you like a cup of coffee while we wait?" Mrs. Robinson asked Mr. Willis.

"Sure, but let's go together. That way he won't think we are watching him the whole time."

They were gone longer than they intended.

"I'm sorry I left you alone for so long. I'll read you the questions if you need me to," Mr. Willis said to Billy.

"It's okay. I'm finished with the test."

"You're what?"

"I'm through. I did the sections just like you showed me."

Willis thought to himself, *He just went through and selected a random answer in each section, so it would look like he had finished the whole two-hour test.*

The fact was most students weren't able to complete the test in the two-hour period.

"Why don't you talk with Mrs. Robinson while I take a look at your test?"

She looked at her watch and saw it was lunchtime.

"Let's go eat lunch while Mr. Willis grades your test."

When they returned from lunch, they saw Mr. Willis at the end of the table staring straight ahead at the computer monitor.

"Why don't you wait here at the table for a few minutes? I'm going over and talk with Mr. Willis.

"What's wrong? Didn't he get any right? I mean, it wouldn't be a real surprise."

"It isn't that. He didn't miss any again."

"Huh?"

"I said this first grader just aced the first two parts of the test. As far as I know, no one has ever done it before."

"We need to give him the last part of the test."

"We can't give him the final section."

"Why can't we give it to him? It seems like a shame to quit now."

"It's all math problems. Everything from simple math and logic problems to advanced high school calculus."

"I didn't realize it was all math formulas."

"I misspoke. It isn't all math formulas. There are some math logic problems, such as the old, 'If a train is traveling sixty miles per hour . . .' questions."

"Do you think we could let him try those?"

"We can if you want, but I don't think it's realistic."

"We've gone this far. Let's let him try."

"Bring him over and I'll try to explain how to do at least some of the test questions."

Billy was brought over.

"I'm going to try to explain how to take this part of the test," Mr. Willis said. "Have you ever heard of math?"

"Some, I've watched Mother work on her budget, and I've watched Dad fill out the bills for grain."

"Good, you kind of know what I'm talking about then."

"I think so."

"Let's get started."

After about ten minutes of explanation Mr. Willis said, "I don't think I can explain it any better. Just skip the other questions, and don't worry if you can't do one. They're intended for much older boys than you."

For at least the first five minutes, Billy just looked at the first screen of questions. Mr. Willis was about to go over and stop him from getting frustrated, when he started to tap the screen to mark the answers on the test page. He tapped it to turn the page, spent less than thirty seconds studying it, and began to select the answers on the second page. He continued glancing at the pages and then he would select the answers or write them down with the electronic stylus.

In less than sixty minutes, he finished the test and looked over at the two teachers. "Billy, it's all right," Mrs. Robinson said. "We didn't think you'd be able to do this part."

"It sure is," Mr. Willis said. "You've already done far better than we could have ever hoped."

He walked over to the table, and tapped the screen to allow him to review what Billy had done. He opened it to the first page, fully expecting to see nothing but a few meaningless numbers and scribbles. Instead, he saw perfectly formed numbers.

He had the computer grade the test selections, and then he graded the manual portion of the test. It only took him about twenty minutes to finish grading the test. When he was done, he again stared off into space thinking about what he was witnessing.

Mrs. Robinson walked over and asked him the same question as before. "Did he get any right? I know it was too much to expect, but I thought he might get one or two right."

"He didn't get one right."

"Oh, well."

"Not one. He got them all right again."

"You're pulling my leg, aren't you?"

"No, I'm not. I was unsure whether anyone has ever aced the first two parts, but I know no one has ever aced all three. In fact, there has only been one other person to ace the math section. He now holds a doctorate in advanced mathematics from Harvard, and is the head of the mathematics department."

"This just can't be right."

"If I hadn't witnessed it with my own eyes, I would have called anyone who told me the story crazy, or a liar."

"What do we do now?"

"I think we should get the principal, tell him what has happened, and let him decide what comes next."

"I'll take Billy back to class. I'm going to let Rachel Hunter continue to teach my class while we go to talk with the principal."

They found Mr. Estep in his office. Mr. Willis tapped on the doorjamb. "Come on in," Mr. Estep said. "What are the two of you up to?"

Mr. Willis began, and as he shared their day's activities Mr. Estep didn't say a word. When he was finally finished, there wasn't a word spoken for several seconds.

Mr. Estep finally broke the silence. "Mr. Willis, it sounds like you and Mrs. Robinson have had quite an adventure today. Are you two trying to pull my leg, or are you serious with this unbelievable story?"

He knew quite well what they had discovered was possible. He just didn't want them to realize he was already aware of Billy's potential.

"I wouldn't have believed it if I hadn't just spent most of the day watching it take place," Mrs. Robinson said.

"I don't honestly know what to say. I haven't ever heard of this happening before," the principal said.

"Neither had we and it's why we've come to you."

"The first thing I want us all to do is not tell anyone, not even his parents, until we sleep on it. I want you to put a security code on the computer so no one can access the results. Let's meet in my office first thing in the morning and talk this through."

Mr. Estep took the next few minutes to mull over what he should do next. He was upset he hadn't followed Billy and Linda closer on their first days of school. When Pastor

Williams had briefed him on the kids, he had warned him they were progressing quickly.

His good friend Stephen Brownmuller had just taken a job with IBM in Oklahoma City. Larry Sheldon's original plan had been for him to move to Amarillo, Texas, so he would be close enough to help monitor the kids. Unfortunately, IBM had closed the branch in Amarillo, so the closest branch he could relocate to was in Oklahoma City.

Stephen held multiple doctorate degrees from MIT and Stanford, and was the smartest person Estep had ever known. Before joining IBM he had served as President George H. W. Bush's science advisor. As he picked up his phone to call, he remembered their last conversation. Stephen had explained to him that an Apollo-class asteroid was about to make its latest pass by the solar system, allowing the Logos scientists to confirm the prophecy on the sarcophagus.

In reality it wasn't a prophecy, it was a warning. Adamartoni and Evevette had plotted the asteroid's and the comet's path, and had determined when their paths would intersect. The resulting collision would alter the asteroid's path enough to cause it to intersect Earth's orbit. However, they hadn't considered the possibility that the sarcophagus would be lost and their language forgotten over the centuries.

When Stephen answered the phone, he asked, "Lee, what can I do for you?"

"I need to ask your advice on Billy West and his friend Linda Bustamante. Our high school counselor and their first-grade teacher just gave him an intelligence test."

"You let them test Billy?"

"I didn't let them, they did it all on their own. He aced all three parts of the test."

"You're telling me he aced an IQ and college-placement test?"

"Yes, that's exactly what I'm telling you. I have no idea what to do now."

The phone was quiet for at least a minute. Finally Lee Estep asked, "What are you thinking?"

"I'm not sure yet. Let me talk with Larry Sheldon, and I'll get back with you tomorrow."

10

WHEN BILLY GOT off the bus, he ran to tell his parents about his day.

"Billy, slow down," Ben said. "Did Mrs. Robinson say when she would talk to us again?"

"No, she didn't."

"Go put your school things in your room, and we'll eat supper," Mary said.

"I sure am hungry."

"You're always hungry."

When they had finished with dinner, Billy took his bath and got ready for bed.

"Is there anything new I can try to read?" Billy asked.

"It just so happens there is," Ben said. "Mr. Carpenter gave me his morning paper when I dropped off his feed this afternoon."

"Can I try to read it to you and Mom?"

"Sure," Mary said. "Just give me a few minutes to do the dishes, and we'll let you read to us."

When she finished she told him, "Okay, let's hear you read the paper. Don't feel bad if you can't read much of it."

He started with the headlines, and then he found the lead article on the first page and read it to them. He turned to page two and finished the article.

The lead story dealt with a farm subsidy bill just passed

in Congress. It detailed the specifics of the subsidies, and the formulas necessary to compute the payments.

"We'll get an extra eleven thousand dollars for the summer wheat crop," Billy said.

"How would you know what the amount is supposed to be?" Mary asked.

"I watched Dad sign for the wheat crop at the elevator."

"You couldn't have had more than a glance at the paper," Ben said. "You couldn't possibly remember that much detail."

"I do, honest, and please don't be mad."

"I'm not mad at you."

"Why don't you go and get the receipt?" Mary said. "I want to see if he's right. I couldn't do the math in my head. Could you?"

"You know I couldn't," Ben said.

Ben handed her the receipt for the wheat crop, and she took the newspaper, the receipt, and computed the extra payment.

It took her about ten minutes to do the math. The subsidy payments had several rates, depending on the type of wheat, the moisture, and several other factors such as the average wheat price for the month it was stored.

The paper printed the average prices for all of the summer months, as well as the daily prices for each month.

"You were close, but the subsidy would have only been nine thousand and fifty dollars," Mary said.

"That's not right," Billy said. "I'm sure it should be eleven thousand dollars."

"I used the average price for the month of July when we finished the harvest and stored the grain," Mary said. "Unless the paper got the average monthly prices wrong, I'm sure I did it right. It was pretty involved, but I was careful when I did it."

His face told her she should at least check the monthly

averages. She spent a few minutes recomputing the monthly averages. When she was done, she realized the paper had printed an incorrect monthly average. She used the corrected number in the calculation, and sure enough, it was eleven thousand dollars exactly.

"You're right, the paper made an error—"

She stopped in midsentence. Her six-year-old had just read a newspaper article dealing with farm subsidy formulas, remembered the details of the wheat harvest, done the math in his head, and had the answer within seconds of finishing the article.

After composing herself, she continued. "I'm sorry I doubted you. It's getting late, and you have school in the morning. Why don't you go get in bed? I'll be right there to tuck you in."

"Thanks for letting me read to you and Dad."

"How can this be possible?" Mary asked. "It was all I could do to understand the article, and figure what the payment would have been, and he does it in his head."

"I don't know, but he sure seems to be smart," Ben said. "This is just another reason we should have been working with him."

"I know, but it doesn't seem to have hurt his development."

"No, it hasn't, but we still should have done something."

Just then, Billy returned. "Don't forget. We can pick up our check next month at the extension agent's office."

"The subsidy just passed," Ben said. "We'll have to see how we do next summer."

"The article said it was retroactive for this year. As long as the wheat was placed in a state-certified elevator, and ours was, we'll get paid."

"Are you sure?" Ben asked.

"Yes, I am. It was covered in the last paragraph on the

second page. I know the elevator is certified, because I remember seeing the state certificate on the wall."

Mary reread the article, and reported, "He's right. We'll get paid for this summer's crop."

"That's unbelievable. This will make it so much easier this year."

She took Billy's hand, and walked him back to his room to tuck him in for the night.

When she returned, she asked, "What are you doing?"

"I just reread the article, and I still don't understand how Billy did what he did."

"I don't, either, but maybe Mrs. Robinson will have some answers."

11

THE NEXT MORNING Mrs. Robinson and Mr. Willis met Billy as he got off the bus.

"Linda, dear, you go on to class. We're going to take Billy again today."

"Is he in trouble?"

"He's not in trouble, dear. You just go on to class. Everything is fine. We're going to talk with the principal for a few minutes."

Mr. Estep was waiting for them outside his office door.

"Let's go into my office and talk. I'm expecting a call about Billy this morning. I heard about how well you did on the tests they gave you. Is it true your parents never had you read before?"

"Yes, it is," Billy said. "But they let me read a newspaper to them last night."

"You read the newspaper? What part, the comics section?"

"I read the article about the new farm subsidy bill Congress just passed."

"Were you able to understand any of it?"

"Yes, I was. I figured out we were going to get eleven thousand dollars back for our summer wheat crop."

"I don't think the bill was retroactive."

"Yes, it was."

"That's good news for almost everyone around here. I read the article last night, but I completely missed the part where it said it was retroactive. The formulas in the article were complicated. Did it take your father and mother long to figure out how much they would get back?"

"Actually, I told them what we were getting after I read the article. It took Mother several minutes to figure it out. Then she had to go back and redo part of it, because the paper had the average monthly price wrong."

"She caught the error, did she?"

"No, I did."

"You did! How did you know?"

"I just knew what the number was supposed to be."

"So you added the daily numbers up and then did the average?"

"Well, sort of. I just knew the number I needed after I read the article."

"You just knew?"

"Yes, I just knew."

As they were talking Mr. Estep's secretary, Eli Swift, came to the office door. "Mr. Estep, there's a Dr. Stephen Brownmuller here to see you."

"You mean he's on the phone?"

"I mean he's standing outside waiting to see you."

"Tell him to come on in."

"Let's get to the reason I drove all the way down here," Dr. Brownmuller said as he sat down. "This must be the young man you have been telling me about?"

"Dr. Brownmuller, let me introduce you to Billy's teacher, Mrs. Barbara Robinson, and our high school counselor, Mr. Jim Willis. Mr. Willis is the one who administered the tests to Billy."

"What have you learned about our young friend here?" Dr. Brownmuller asked.

"All I know for sure is he managed to ace a set of intelligence and placement tests which are intended to be administered to high school juniors and seniors," Mr. Willis said. "The tests give an IQ score, and provide general guidance on what sort of curriculum a student might want to take when entering college."

"What were his results?"

"The test only goes to a rating of one-fifty on the IQ portion."

"What do you mean, 'only goes to'?"

"All I can tell you is his IQ is at least, according to this test, a hundred and fifty. The test isn't capable of assessing IQs above that. We'll need to use a more specialized testing procedure to accurately gauge his intelligence. The recommendations sections were worthless. They recommend he majors in everything."

"I see what you mean. Is there an open room and a projector with a Bluetooth connection we can use?"

"There's one in the empty classroom across the hall," Mr. Estep said.

"Good, let's go over and get started."

"Eli, would you please bring us some water, coffee, and some soft drinks from the cafeteria?" Mr. Estep said. "You might see if they have some cake or cookies; little boys are always hungry."

"Big ones too," Dr. Brownmuller said.

"What would you like to do first?" Mr. Estep asked.

"I would like to show Billy a series of math questions on the screen and see if he can answer any of them. I'll continue until we get to a level he can't answer," Dr. Brownmuller said. "It won't be completely accurate, but I spent most of the evening working with some of the IBM scientists in Armonk, New York, to come up with the correct sequence of questions. Are you ready to get started?"

"Yes, I am," Billy said.

"I'll show you a math problem on the screen. Then you can either enter your answer on the terminal in front of you, or you can just tell me the answer."

"I understand. If it's all right, I'll just tell you the answers."

Dr. Brownmuller began by showing him three simple addition problems on the screen. A second or two after the numbers appeared he answered, "Twenty-three, forty-seven, and one-eleven."

"Good. Now here are some more." He selected the next problem, which was a more complex addition problem. He continued with progressively larger sequences of numbers, and each time Billy called out the answers as the numbers appeared on the screen.

"This is truly amazing. Would you like a soft drink, water, or a cookie?" Mr. Estep asked.

"I would like a cookie and some milk if I may."

"Certainly, I believe Eli brought milk."

"Thank you for the snacks."

"Let's keep going while you eat your snack," Dr. Brownmuller said. "I'm going to move on to multiplication problems."

He continued with more and more difficult problems. He didn't stop when he shifted to algebra, and finally to all of the calculus problems he brought with him.

When he had run through all of the math problems he had brought, he looked at his watch and saw it was one in the afternoon.

"I've worked you right through your lunch. Mrs. Robinson, would you mind taking Billy to the cafeteria?"

"Sure, aren't you going to eat?"

"I will in a minute," Dr. Brownmuller said. "I want to talk with Mr. Estep for a few moments."

"He's everything we had hoped," Dr. Brownmuller said. "I would like to take him to New York to work with the whole team."

"I don't know if his parents will let us, but we can ask. Let's eat lunch with the group, and then we'll go to talk to them."

After they finished lunch, Mr. Estep asked, "Barbara, would you and Mr. Willis mind riding along to visit Billy's parents?"

"Mr. Estep, I have to pick up my wife from work," Mr. Willis said.

"That's okay. I don't think we need to have both of you. Mrs. Robinson should be enough."

Mr. Estep got a small bus for them to use. As they were boarding, the class bell rang to let out the first-grade class.

"Can we bring Linda with us?" Billy asked.

"Sure, I'll go and get her," Mr. Estep said.

The bus stopped in front of Linda's house, but the kids didn't notice. "We're at your house, dear," Mrs. Robinson said.

"Okay, see you, Billy."

A few minutes later they pulled up in front of Billy's house. "Okay, let's go talk with Billy's parents," Mr. Estep said.

Ben spotted the bus coming down the road as he was coming out of the barn, and he started toward the house to meet them.

As Billy reached the front steps, Mary opened the door to greet him. "How was school today?"

Just then, she noticed the group of people coming up the walkway. She recognized Mrs. Robinson and Mr. Estep. "Mrs. Robinson, what are all of you doing here?"

"We've come to talk about the results of the tests Billy has been taking."

"We were wondering how he did on the tests."

"I'm sorry I didn't talk with you yesterday. I had intended to. But after Billy's test yesterday, we decided to talk to Principal Estep. After talking with us he decided to call his friend Dr. Brownmuller to see what he would recommend as our next step. We didn't intend to do more testing. But Dr. Brownmuller came down from Oklahoma City, and he wanted to give Billy some additional math tests."

"This is Dr. Stephen Brownmuller," Mr. Estep said.

As Mary was about to reply, Ben came around the edge of the house.

"Dr. Brownmuller, let me introduce you to my husband, Ben. Ben, this is Dr. Brownmuller, a friend of Principal Estep."

"We're here to talk to you about some tests we have been giving Billy," Dr. Brownmuller said.

"How did he do?" Mary asked.

"If you don't mind, can we go inside and talk?"

"I'm sorry, sure we can," Mary said. "Come on in. Would anyone like something to drink? I have coffee, tea, and milk."

Anxious to hear what they had to say, she quickly returned with a tray of drinks.

"Mr. Willis and I gave Billy the test I told you about the other night, and he aced all the sections," Mrs. Robinson said.

"What does that mean?" Ben asked.

"The test is structured to recognize an IQ range up to one-fifty, and his IQ is somewhere above that."

"That's pretty high, isn't it?"

"Let me put it this way. I don't believe there have been more than a handful of people who have ever scored above this range. We'll need to use a much more advanced test to be able to properly evaluate his IQ. Since we weren't sure what to do next, we decided to consult with Mr. Estep. After he heard our story, he placed a call to his friend Dr. Brown-muller to ask his advice on what we should do next."

"Dr. Brownmuller was supposed to call me back today with his recommendations," Principal Estep said. "Instead, he spent several hours on the phone with PhDs all over the United States, discussing how they could assist. When he finished, he got in his car and drove down here to work with us today."

Everyone turned to look at Dr. Brownmuller.

"When I got here this morning, we decided to let Billy take the battery of questions I brought with me. To make a long story short, I went all the way through the advanced calculus questions, and he never even asked for an explanation. He never missed giving almost immediate answers to the questions. He never stopped to consider or work through the problems, he just gave the answers."

Out of breath, he paused and then continued.

"He didn't miss any questions, which was not even a scenario we discussed. To better judge his abilities, I would like your permission to take him to New York for further testing."

"What are you asking for?" Ben asked.

"I would like to take him to New York for a period of time, and let him do further tests and interviews with our entire team," Dr. Brownmuller said.

"We're poor people. We can't possibly afford to send him to New York," Mary said.

"Let me assure you it will not cost you anything, and if one or both of you would like to come along, we'll pay all of your expenses as well."

"Who would that be?" Ben asked.

"IBM has a program we call the IBM fellows. The pro-gram is normally used for IBM employees, but from time to time we'll recruit a truly outstanding person from out-side of IBM."

"You do realize he's six years old, don't you?"

"Yes, of course I do. What do you think? Can I borrow him for a few weeks?"

"What about his schoolwork?" Mary asked.

"I don't think you need worry about his first-grade work. He'll more than likely never attend another day of public school," Mrs. Robinson said.

"What do you mean, never attend another day of public school?"

"If I understand Dr. Brownmuller correctly, someone like an IBM or the federal government will take care of the rest of Billy's education," Mrs. Robinson said.

"I don't know whether we want him not going to public school," Ben said. "Can we have the night to sleep on it?"

"Of course you can," Dr. Brownmuller said. "I can't even imagine what's going through your minds. Two days ago you had a normal first grader, and today we're telling you your child is one of the smartest people ever."

"Let's do this," Mr. Estep said. "We'll leave you for now, unless you have more questions. If you'll both bring Billy to school tomorrow morning, we'll talk about this some more."

"That sounds good to me," Ben said.

When they were gone Ben asked, "What are we going to do?"

"I have no idea," Mary said. "This is all happening too fast for me. Tonight after Billy is in bed, we'll talk it over."

They hadn't intended to discuss the offer until Billy had gone to bed, but as soon as they began to eat, Billy surprised them.

"I don't want to go anywhere. I just want to go to school like all the other kids, and I don't want to be separated from Linda Lou."

"If you don't want to go we aren't going to make you,"

Ben said. "I do think you ought to reconsider. They can teach you an awful lot."

"I don't care about what they have to offer. I just want to stay home."

"Well, it's settled then," Mary said. "We won't let Billy go to New York."

"No problem, I didn't like the sound of what he was saying. I felt like they were trying to take him away from us for good, and I'm not sure I trust Dr. Brownmuller."

"I feel the same way," Mary said. "But are we being fair to Billy? They could teach him so much, and maybe this is what we should have been doing all along."

"None of what they are offering matters to me. I just want to stay here. I can learn all I need to learn right here. The library is full of books for me to read, and there are plenty of computers with Internet access."

"Finish your dinner and we'll let them know our answer tomorrow," Ben said.

After dinner, they continued to talk about their decision.

"Do you think we're doing the right thing by not letting them keep working with Billy?" Ben said.

"I think so, and he doesn't want to go."

"Then that's what we are going to tell them."

The next morning when they walked into Principal Estep's office everyone stood up to greet them. "Come on in and we'll get started," Mr. Estep said. "Are you going to let Billy go to New York with Dr. Brownmuller?"

"We talked it over, and then we talked it over with Billy, and we're not going to let him go," Ben West said.

There was a stunned silence for a few seconds, and then an ashen-faced Dr. Brownmuller said, "I'm surprised, and quite disappointed. Are you thinking about what's best for him?"

"Yes, I think we are. Are you and your group? Billy is

six years old, and you want to take him out of school and away to New York. You even said he probably wouldn't ever go back to public school. We don't want that for him, and we're not going to let you take him. In fact, we don't want you running any more tests on him, and we want him treated as a normal first-grade student."

"Please don't do this," Dr. Brownmuller said. "You're depriving him of the chance of a lifetime."

"We don't agree."

"It sounds like you have made up your minds," Mr. Estep said. "I know you're doing what you believe is right, but I do wish you would reconsider."

"I'm sorry but our decision is final," Ben said.

"Then I assure you we will treat Billy as a normal boy, as you have requested," Mr. Estep said.

"Thank you," Ben said. "I would ask you and Mrs. Robinson to let Billy use the library and the school's computers."

"Of course, and we'll help him get any book he would like from the high school library as well."

"I'll make sure he's exposed to anything he wants," Mrs. Robinson said. "I don't know whether I would have had the courage to turn down what was being offered, but I truly respect you for it."

"Let me second those thoughts, and let me make you this offer," Mr. Willis said. "I have access to the University of New Mexico's library, and I'll get anything he wants from their library. I also have a high-speed Internet connection at the high school, and I would be happy to show him how to use a computer and the Internet."

"Thank you all," Ben said. "We're grateful for your understanding. I guess we'll go on home, and let you get back to your day."

12

WHEN BILLY RETURNED to the classroom he took his seat next to Linda, and she was smiling from ear to ear.

"You're back," Linda said. "I'm so glad you came back. I was afraid you were going away."

"I promise you I'll never leave you."

His simple statement, from one six-year-old to another, would be a promise he would never forget and never break.

"I sure wish they would have let him come with me," Dr. Brownmuller said.

"I know, but we'll do our best to make sure he gets what he needs," Mr. Estep said.

"I'll get you anything you need," Dr. Brownmuller said. "We can't afford for him to take too long to grow up. That child may be our only hope of saving humanity."

"It's not that serious, is it?"

"I can't tell you more, but yes, it is. You have to take over guiding Billy, and Linda, if she's as bright as we think. I'm sorry to put all of this on you, but I'll get you anything you need to help them."

"I just hope I'm up to the task."

"You'll be fine. You're a member of the Logos, and you have all of us behind you. When you have doubts, remember your training, and always remember you can ask God for help, and He will be there for you."

Over the next few years, Billy and Linda Lou continued to progress through school, but they were still not fitting in. No matter how hard they tried, the other kids didn't relate to them.

They had learned to help each other hide how truly brilliant they were from everyone, but even then the other kids sensed they were different, and wouldn't have anything to do with them.

Mr. Estep and Mrs. Robinson were constantly coming up with new ways to challenge them. Mrs. Robinson was not a member of the Logos, but she was a gifted teacher.

Mr. Estep took advantage of Mr. Willis's commitment to get help from the university and used it to expose them to more and more advanced material.

At the end of their sixth-grade year, Mr. Estep decided to see if he could convince Billy's parents to allow him to give Billy some more advanced assistance. Billy and Linda were outside playing while their parents were preparing dinner when he caught up with them. "It's good you're all together," Mr. Estep said. "Thank you for allowing me to come by and visit with you."

"No problem," Ben replied. "Has Billy or Linda had some sort of problem at school?"

"In no way has either one of them ever been a problem. I've come to ask if you'll allow us to install high-speed Internet access in your homes. I know neither of your families can afford to pay for it, and that won't be a problem. The school district is going to cover the cost of the lines and the computers."

"Thank you, Mr. Estep," Ben said. "We've been trying to save up enough to get the kids computers of their own, but it's been tough these last few years. Between the drought and the wind storms, we just can't seem to get any money saved."

As they were talking, the kids came in.

"Mr. Estep, what are you doing here?" Billy asked.

"I was just asking your parents if we could install Internet access, and give both of you a computer so you can study some more advanced subject matter."

"Thank you so much. We'll definitely make use of them. We have been bored. The teachers are trying, but the classes are just too easy."

"I know. I'm sorry we haven't been able to keep up with you, but I promise we'll do better."

Mr. Estep was feeling the pressure of guiding the kids. Larry Sheldon had instructed him to use whatever methods were necessary to move the kids' education along at a faster pace. The time was growing short, and they still didn't have a solution to their problems.

The Logos had even discussed having the kids removed from their parents' care if they didn't begin to go along with their plans. Luckily, they had come to understand the kids needed more specialized assistance.

As they accelerated their progress, Billy and Linda discovered they were slightly different in their areas of intelligence and interests, but they were equals in raw intelligence.

Mr. Estep and Dr. Brownmuller had been communicating on a weekly basis with Larry Sheldon on the kids' progress. Larry had taken a position at the University of New Mexico to ensure the kids continued to get whatever they needed.

Meanwhile, the asteroid was about to make another pass by the solar system. It had been passing close enough for a few of the more powerful terrestrial-based telescopes to track it.

The Keck telescopes on the peak of Mauna Kea in Hawaii were the first to discover the asteroid. The twin telescopes were the world's largest optical and infrared telescopes. Working in tandem, they were unsurpassed in their capabilities.

As the asteroid approached, Larry Sheldon had made the decision that they couldn't allow the rest of the world to discover its existence.

He dispatched a team to Hawaii. The team arrived at the Keck Observatory just after midnight. All of the observatory's scientists were present for the big event. They weren't quite sure what the object was, but they knew it was going to be close enough to make a positive identification.

Just as they recognized what the object was, the team entered. They didn't say a word. They simply killed everyone in the room with their silenced automatic weapons. It took less than a minute to exterminate the twenty-eight people who made up the entire staff of the observatory. Once they were all dead, the team placed plastic explosive charges throughout the facility. They had captured the charges from an Iranian terrorist cell, so when the FBI investigated, they would believe the Iranians carried out the attack.

When the team finished planting the charges, they retreated to a distance of a half a mile, and detonated the charges. One minute the observatory was there, and the next it seemed to explode and collapse in on itself.

An hour later, they were back on their Gulfstream jet on their way back to Denver. In addition to the explosives, they planted an evidence trail to ensure the authorities believed an Iranian terrorist cell had carried out the attack. Identical teams struck the other two facilities they believed would spot the asteroid, leaving a similar trail of evidence at each location.

The next morning the world believed terrorists had carried out simultaneous terrorist attacks on three observatories. The Logos hierarchy was in turmoil over Larry Sheldon's decision to carry out the attacks.

They all knew if the world had discovered the truth, the ensuing chaos would have resulted in an immense death toll. But it had been difficult to accept the sacrifice of almost a hundred innocent lives.

By the time the kids were ready to start the eighth grade, they were mature for their ages. Linda Lou was now a beautiful young woman. She had grown to five foot ten and 135 pounds. She had the figure of a fashion model and moved like a cat. Her long dark brown hair complemented her dark brown eyes and almost olive complexion.

All of the boys in grade school had tried to become her boyfriend, but she wouldn't have anything to do with anyone other than Billy.

Billy had grown to be six foot tall and 195 pounds. Had he chosen to become an athlete, he would have been world-class, but he had never played any sports.

When he had to participate in PE classes, the teachers were always in awe of his natural coordination and strength. The coaches tried each year to talk him into playing sports, but he always declined.

They had never been close to any of their fellow students. The boys all resented Billy because he wouldn't play on the sports teams with them, and Linda would only hang out with him.

One group of boys had been particularly aggressive toward them, and one day their leader, a large young man by the name of Pablo Navarro, decided he was going to kiss Linda Lou. They waited for her to come out of her afternoon PE class, and they surrounded her when she came out of the gym.

Pablo grabbed Linda and tried to kiss her. She struggled, but he was almost fifteen and quite a bit bigger and stronger than she was. He managed to kiss her a couple of times before she finally bit his lip. He screamed and slapped her, busting her lips and causing them to start bleeding.

"I'll show you, you're not too good to kiss me!" he screamed. As he tried to grab her again, he accidentally ripped her blouse most of the way off, and the others started to egg him on.

"Come on, Pablo, let's see what she looks like."

Growing braver by the moment, he ripped the rest of her blouse off. Linda tried to slap him, but he slapped her again, and the blood really started to flow.

Billy came around the end of the gym as he did every day to meet Linda. When he saw what was going on, he realized they were trying to hurt Linda Lou.

He sprinted over to them and knocked two of them to the ground. Then he grabbed Linda Lou and put her behind him.

She had never seen him even raise his voice, and certainly had never seen him mad at anyone. He screamed at Pablo, "You want to hit someone, try me."

"I've always wanted to do this!" Pablo bellowed. As he moved to hit him, Billy slapped his fist aside and drove a powerful punch into the center of the chest. He hit him so hard he broke two of his ribs, and Pablo dropped to the ground gasping for air. The others surrounded Billy and started punching and kicking him.

He managed to push Linda out of the way, as they took him to the ground. They were in a tangled pile, and he was hitting them about as many times as they managed to hit him.

One of the boys crawled free from the pile, and grabbed a piece of two-by-four lying nearby. He ran back over to the fight, and when Billy rose up from the pile to strike another blow, he hit him across the back of the head. He hit him with so much force the board splintered and broke.

Billy immediately fell to the ground unconscious. The other boys continued to kick and punch him while he was on the ground.

By the time the gym teacher came out the door, Billy was a bloody mess. Pablo was still on the ground moaning in pain, and when the gym teacher arrived, the others ran.

Linda had been trying to help Billy as much as she could, but one of the boys had thrown her down and was punching her. As he hit her, he was trying to get the rest of her clothes off.

When the teacher saw what was happening, he began to yell at the boys as they ran off. When he bent down to see how badly Billy was hurt, he was horrified. They had hit him with the board, kicked him, punched him, and pretty much beaten him half to death.

The gym teacher left to get help, and Pablo managed to get up and began to move off. He turned back to Linda and said, "We'll finish with you later."

Then he scurried away as fast as his injured ribs would allow.

Linda gently picked Billy's head up and held it to her chest, as she quietly cried.

During the five minutes it took the gym teacher to find help, she never moved from his side. As she cradled his head to her chest, she felt the blood stop running from her busted lips and eyes. The horrific injuries the boys had inflicted on them were already beginning to heal.

By the time the teachers returned with the school nurse, Billy was awake. As the school nurse began to wipe the blood off his head, she found nothing but smooth skin underneath.

"It's okay. I'm fine now," Billy said. "How are you, Linda Lou?"

The nurse turned and began to wipe the blood from Linda's face. She found the same thing: nothing.

"Where did all of this blood come from?" the nurse asked. "You two don't seem to have any injuries. Mr. Scroggins, I thought you told me Billy was badly hurt?"

"He was, or at least he seemed to be."

The nurse turned to Linda. "You look fine, dear, but again, where did all of this blood come from?"

"We don't know. Maybe it's from Pablo and his friends."

"Were they the ones who attacked you?"

"We're not sure. It all happened too fast. We didn't see who it was."

"Are you sure? You're not trying to protect those boys, are you?"

"No, we're not. Why would we?"

"I don't know, dear, but it sure seems like you are."

"Mr. Scroggins, I guess we've had enough excitement for today. Let's get everyone back to their classes. Linda, you and Billy need to go home and get cleaned up before you can come back to class. On second thought, why don't you just go on home for the rest of the day?"

"I'll take them."

"Thanks, Mr. Scroggins," Linda said. "Give me just a minute to put on a T-shirt out of my gym bag, and I'll be ready to go."

The next morning on the bus to school they discussed what they needed to do to protect themselves from the gang of boys.

"I'm going to deal with them one or more at a time," Billy said.

"What are you going to do?" Linda asked.

"They're all bullies, and they'll hurt you one of these times when I'm not around, and I'll not let that happen. So I'm going to have a discussion with them to make sure it will never happen."

"You're going to get in trouble."

"No, I won't. I'll be careful."

"How did we heal up so fast yesterday?" Linda asked.

"I'm not sure. We've always healed much more quickly than anyone else. It's just we had never been hurt so severely before."

"You were hurt pretty badly, weren't you?"

"Yes, I believe I was. I think I had a fractured skull and jaw. It hurt, but I don't think we feel pain quite like everyone else either."

"Do we do anything like anyone else?"

They were careful to stay away from Pablo and his gang of thugs for several weeks. Billy wanted to be sure Pablo had healed up from their previous encounter before he confronted them.

When he was sure Pablo had healed, he made sure they saw him leave the gym on his way to the bus barn. Pablo and his friends saw their chance, and they rushed after him.

When they came around the corner of the barn, he was waiting for them.

"What do we have here?" Pablo said. "Are you ready to get your ass kicked again? When we're through with you, we're going to see the rest of that little girlfriend of yours."

"Since you bring it up, that's why I wanted to talk with all of you. When we're done here, if I ever even see you look at her in the hall, you'll get the same thing you are going to get today."

"And what would that be?"

"As you would say, I'm going to kick all of your butts."

"Oh yeah?"

They all rushed Billy. Instead of them taking him to the ground as they expected, he smoothly sidestepped them, and the fight was on.

Billy hit Pablo squarely in the middle of his chest, and broke a couple of ribs on each side this time. Then he hit him right between the eyes, and knocked him out cold.

Once he had Pablo out of the way, he went to work on

the other five. As they continued to try to attack him, he flipped, kicked, hit, and generally beat the daylights out of them. This went on for at least ten minutes until none of them could get up.

When the last one had fallen, Billy knelt down to wait for them to come to their senses. It took them several minutes before they were able to sit up and look at him.

"You jerks just stay down on the ground," Billy said. "We're going to have a talk. I don't understand why you hate us so. Linda and I have never caused you any harm. However, as I told you, if you do want to continue to cause us trouble, I'll do this every day if need be. I don't want to fight you, but if you continue to threaten us, I will. I think you see I'm more than capable of taking care of any or all of you."

As the six boys listened, they didn't say a word until Pablo broke the silence. "Look, we didn't mean any harm. It just got out of hand the other day. We always knew you could probably take care of yourself, but I had no idea. I've never seen anyone fight like you did today. I think you broke my ribs again, and I'm still seeing stars."

Pablo gave his head a couple of shakes to try to clear his senses and then he continued. "I give you my word. None of us will ever bother you or Linda again."

They all spoke up to agree. "Yeah, Billy, we won't bother you anymore. We're sorry."

"Billy?" Pablo said.

"Yes, Pablo? What is it?"

"Can we keep this between us? I don't want the entire school knowing you kicked all of our asses."

"Yeah, that's fine. You guys go and get cleaned up before you go home."

"Thanks, and I mean it. None of us will ever cause you or Linda any more problems. If you ever need anything from any of us, you just ask."

From that day forward, Pablo and his boys were good to their word, and they actually became decent kids from then on.

On the bus ride home, Billy and Linda were talking. "I watched you fight Pablo and the boys this afternoon, and it was amazing," Linda said. "I know you can fight, I saw that the last time. But how did you fight all of them and not even get hit?"

"I'd read a couple of books on martial arts before the first encounter. After that, I got all of the books I could find on karate, and a Korean martial art called Tae Kwon Do. I used them to teach myself the two forms of martial arts. Once I had them mastered, it wasn't a big deal to handle them. It seemed as though they were moving in slow motion. It's hard to describe the feeling, but I was never in any danger of them hitting me."

As they finished their last year of grade school, they had managed to hide most of their true abilities from their fellow students. What they hadn't managed to do was fit in. They didn't have any real friends other than each other, and for them it was enough.

Billy had never forgotten his first experience of being recognized for what he could be, and he didn't want any part of it. Even though they had been attending grade school, they had made the bulk of their progress studying at home via their computers. Their computers had secure access to every facet of research that existed in the world. They believed they were on the World Wide Web, but they had actually been on specially constructed servers that allowed them to have unfettered access to the data they needed.

13

THE SUMMER BEFORE they were to start high school, Larry Sheldon orchestrated the next step in their education.

He was now the head of administration at UNM, so it had been a simple matter for him to arrange for them to have complete access to the campus library, and the labs. They could also attend any of the classes offered during the summer session. To make sure they could afford to come, he arranged for them to have the use of a small three-bedroom house near the college at no cost.

At Billy's urging, Mary got Rob and Beth to let Linda Lou accompany him to the university for the summer.

Linda Lou spent most of her time attending as many of the biology, pre-med and medical school classes as she could.

Billy spent his time attending math, engineering, and physics classes.

By the sixth week, all of the professors on campus had noticed them. They couldn't get over how the two were eager to learn, and how brilliant they were. Larry Sheldon had been quietly planting the thought that maybe the university should do something to help the kids.

Several of the professors got together to talk about the youngsters, and how truly exceptional they both were. The head of the math department, Dr. Richard Blevins, was the first to speak. "I haven't worked with Linda Lou, but I've worked with Billy for the past few weeks. He's a personable young man, and I've never in my career met a young man as brilliant as he is."

Dr. Melissa Spain, the head of the medical school, was the next to speak. "I've worked extensively with Linda Lou, and she's equally brilliant. She already has a better grasp of science and medicine than any student I've ever had graduate from our medical school."

"What is it you two propose?" Larry Sheldon asked.

"I haven't thought about us doing anything," Dr. Spain said. "However, now that you mention it, I was reading an article about a nineteen-year-old sophomore at Harvard. The university allowed him to take achievement tests to receive his Juris Doctor degree from their law school."

"If Harvard can do it," Dr. Blevins said, "why can't we?"

His challenging comments set off a heated discussion.

After several minutes of conversation, Larry Sheldon guided them to an agreement on what to do. They agreed to administer achievement tests in any subject the kids chose. They would structure the tests to allow them to achieve up to doctorate degrees in any of their selections.

"It's agreed then. Dr. Blevins will contact Linda and Billy to present our offer. Once the kids make their selections, I'll take care of setting up the testing schedules. I'll notify you when I have the schedules prepared so you can get your test plans together. I'll get started tomorrow. It shouldn't take me more than a week or so to get this put together. Let's plan on meeting next Thursday night for a status check and to make sure we are all still on board with the plan."

Later that night, he used his computer terminal to establish a video link with the Logos High Council.

Clayton Edwards, the leader of the Logos High Council, appeared on the screen.

"What's up?" Clayton Edwards asked.

"I need to update you on what's happening with the kids."

"Good, we just finished a council meeting, and everyone was wondering how they're progressing."

"I've been following them their entire lives, and even now I never cease to be amazed at their abilities. We're going to administer achievement tests in any subject they want, and allow them to receive up to doctorate degrees in the subjects."

"Are you sure that's a good idea? We've been careful not to allow anyone outside of the organization to become fully aware of their abilities."

"I think so. We need to get them started on the real mission as soon as possible. We can't afford for them to spend any more time in school. This should give us the opportunity to accelerate the process."

"I see your point. I'll brief the rest of the council in the morning. Let me know if you need anything."

The Logos have had almost limitless resources and people embedded at the highest levels of society and government. But they hadn't made any significant progress on a plan to deal with the asteroid, and they were running out of time.

The next week Dr. Blevins caught up with Billy and Linda in the library café.

"How are you doing this morning?" Dr. Blevins said.

"Good morning," Linda said. "What are you doing here? Don't you have a class?"

"Why yes, I do, but I had my assistants take over the class for me this morning. I would like to talk to both of you about a plan the other professors and I have come up with."

"Sure, professor, what have you got for us?"

"We've arranged with Larry Sheldon, the head of

administration, for you to take achievement tests in any area of study we offer. You can take as many tests as you would like, and the tests will allow you to complete up to a doctorate degree. If you're interested, just let me know which areas you would like to pursue."

"Let me see if I understand correctly," Linda said. "You're saying if I want to take an achievement test for a medical degree, you're going to let me?"

"That's exactly what I'm saying."

"We haven't even started high school yet," Billy said.

"We'll take care of your high school diplomas as well. What do you think, or do you need to think about it?"

Billy looked at Linda, and they grinned at each other.

"I think I can speak for both of us when I say, yes, yes, yes," Linda said. "We were actually talking about this the other night, but we couldn't decide who to approach about it. We've already talked about the degrees we wanted to earn."

Linda reached into her purse and pulled out their list of degrees. "Here you go, professor."

He took a few seconds to scan their lists. "Larry Sheldon will have your schedules ready by next Friday. Be at the Administration building next Friday by nine A.M., and we'll give you your schedules. You'll have your first tests and interviews at ten A.M. and then every day the next week."

"Professor, we can't thank you enough for this," Billy said.

"This isn't just me. All of the professors are helping."

"I can't believe we're getting this kind of opportunity," Linda said.

"It's more of an opportunity than you can possibly know," Dr. Blevins said.

"What do you mean?"

"If you're as successful as we believe, you two will have your pick of opportunities."

"Opportunities, what sort of opportunities?" Billy asked.

"I couldn't tell you the specifics at the moment, but things like grants for research, and access to any type of technology you need. But we're getting the cart before the horse. You two have to do well on the tests. Though from what I have seen so far, you will."

"I don't want to sound smug, but Linda Lou and I will do fine on these tests."

"All right, kids, I'll see you next Friday morning."

He left them to give their lists to Larry Sheldon so he could prepare their schedules.

"What do you think?" Billy asked.

"I'm excited and scared all at the same time. I don't know how to explain it."

"I know, me too. I have the sense our lives are about to change in ways we can't even imagine."

"You're right, but we have started now, and I do believe we're doing the right thing."

The next Friday when they arrived at the Administration building, Dr. Blevins met them at the front desk.

"Good morning. Let me introduce you to Mr. Larry Sheldon. He's going to help you throughout the tests, and he can answer any questions you may have."

"It's definitely my privilege to be involved in this endeavor," Larry Sheldon said. "Let's get started. Billy, your first stop is upstairs in the physics lab, room two-oh-five. Linda Lou, your first stop is on the third floor, Room three-twelve by the biology lab. When you're finished please come by my office, and I'll give you your schedules for next week. We have a busy schedule laid out for you, so you might try to rest up over the weekend."

That night after dinner, they were on the front porch talking.

"How did you make out today?" Linda asked.

"I only covered the first part of physics today, but I did pass the exams necessary for a Bachelor's degree. How did you do?"

"I made it through the tests for a BS in biology."

"I guess we did all right then?"

"Yes, we did. Let's tell your mom."

"No, let's wait until we get home, like we talked about. Once we're home, we'll tell all of our parents at once."

"Okay, but I don't know if I can wait," Linda said.

"Yes, you can, you just like to tease me. You have more willpower than I, and you know it."

"Well, that's true."

The next week they were busy, as Larry had warned them. But they passed each test, interview and, at times, it seemed inquisition with flying colors.

When the professors gathered to summarize the week's activities, they were surprised at their achievements.

Linda Lou had scored a 100 percent on all of the exams she had taken. She successfully completed a Bachelor of Science degree, a Master's degree, and her medical degree. Once she has completed her residency work she would be able to practice medicine and perform surgeries.

Billy had worked on a different set of degrees, but had also scored 100 percent on all the exams he had taken. He completed a Bachelor of Science degree in physics, and a Master's in mathematics, as well as physics.

In addition, he had completed doctoral degrees in mathematics, physics, and electrical engineering.

As they read the summary of their accomplishments, there was not a word said for at least ten minutes. Finally, Larry Sheldon broke the silence. "I'm not a professor like the rest of you, but I can't even imagine this has ever been accomplished before."

His comment set off a buzz of conversations all over the room. Finally, Dr. Blevins called for quiet. "Quiet, please. All right, one at a time."

Without exception, they agreed they had never heard of such successes even once, let alone twice. As the comments started to slow down, Larry Sheldon took charge. "Thank you all for coming tonight, and if there are no other comments the meeting is adjourned."

The next day Larry Sheldon briefed Billy and Linda. "I would like for you to finish out the summer at the university. I'll arrange for you to have access to everything you need to continue your studies."

"We'll definitely finish out the summer," Billy said, "and we appreciate your help."

14

LARRY SHELDON SET them up with a room in the Administration building. He had the computer department install several computers and Web access via an Internet2 connection.

Billy had already learned several computer languages. He started with an assembly language so he would understand the low-level functionality of a computer. Then he moved on to C, C++, Java, and several scripting languages. He wasn't interested in programming per se, but he knew he would need to develop his own software to achieve the things he needed to do.

They were both having premonitions of some upcoming event, but they didn't yet know what it might be. Linda was using her time to continue her medical studies. Larry Sheldon had obtained access to the Mayo Clinic's computers so she could continue her studies.

With complete access to their systems, she was able to study their archived case studies and research papers. She was even able to observe the daily operations of the clinic via webcam. Within the first week, she was participating as a remote learning student.

Larry Sheldon was close friends with the head of the hospital, Dr. William Robbins, and he was the one who had granted Linda access to the remote learning facilities.

Dr. Robbins was also a member of the Logos, and Larry had briefed him on both Linda and Billy. But he had taken particular care to brief him on Linda Lou. Larry Sheldon hadn't briefed him on the approaching asteroid. But he made it clear to him the Logos needed Linda to receive every consideration and his complete attention.

Dr. Robbins had quickly recognized that Linda was exceptional. He couldn't believe she was just fourteen years old. He had worked with some of the most outstanding students in the world, and he had never seen one with more potential.

After the first few operations she observed, she was asking questions most students never got around to asking.

During one particularly difficult heart surgery, she asked a question of the doctor moderating the surgery. After he answered her question, he asked her for an opinion to test her understanding of what was taking place. Her answer caused the surgeon performing the operation to modify his procedure to her recommendation.

The next day Dr. Robbins called Linda at the college.

"I'm Dr. William Robbins, and I'm with the Mayo Clinic in Rochester, Minnesota. I'm the head of surgery and in charge of the residency program at the hospital. I observed your interaction yesterday during the heart surgery. I was impressed with your grasp of the procedure and your intuitive questions and suggestions. I would like to offer you a place in our surgical residency program. I've talked at length with Larry Sheldon, and you come with his highest recommendations."

"Dr. Robbins, could I have some time to discuss it with my parents?"

"Certainly, but I need your decision no later than August fifteenth. After that date, I'll need to offer the position to someone else."

His statement wasn't quite true. His instructions were to ensure Linda entered the program, but he wanted to make sure she started as soon as possible.

"That should be more than enough time, and I truly appreciate the opportunity."

When she hung up, she turned to Billy. "I just talked with Dr. William Robbins, who's the head of surgery at the Mayo Clinic. He wants me to come to Rochester to do my surgical residency."

"It sounds like a tremendous opportunity. Are you going to do it?"

"I don't know. I want to, but I would miss you and my parents."

"How long would you be gone?"

"It varies, but from what I've read, it would be from two to four years."

"That long? I'll miss you."

"I know, but I think I should do this."

"Then you'll do it. I've been having the same sort of feeling. I just don't know what it is yet."

"I don't want to tell my parents until we get back home."

"No problem, we've already agreed not to tell them about our testing out of college. All of this is going to be quite a shock."

"You're right, but it won't be the first time we have surprised them. They've all been struggling with how to deal with us since we were born."

She continued to use the distance learning to advance her medical studies until they were ready to return home.

Billy continued to study everything he could on physics, computers, and robotic manufacturing. The remainder of the summer passed quickly, and before they knew it, it was time to return home.

The professors and Larry Sheldon threw them a going away party. When they arrived, all of the professors were crowding around them to let them know how impressed they were with their achievements.

Without exception, each one offered his or her assistance in the future. Larry Sheldon had been hanging back, letting everyone else congratulate and visit with them. As the party was beginning to wind down, he walked over to them and said, "I would like to congratulate both of you on a job well done."

He handed them each a metal business card. "The cards have all of my contact information on them. You can always reach me at the number on the card. If I'm not around, leave me a message, and I'll get back with you. I know all of the professors offered to assist you. Even though I'm not a professor, I have many contacts and resources that can be of assistance to you."

"It has been our pleasure to work with you. Linda and I can't thank you enough for what you have done for us," Billy said.

"No thanks needed. I value the time I've spent around you. What do your parents think about your achievements?"

"We haven't shared anything with them yet."

"You haven't told your parents? You haven't even told your mom yet?"

"No, we haven't. We wanted to share the news with them all at once."

"Okay, then, be sure and call me if you need anything, and I mean anything."

The next morning Mary was driving, and Linda was in the front seat. They talked steadily for the first hour they were on the road. Finally, Mary looked in the rearview mirror and asked, "Is there anything wrong? You haven't said a word since we left."

"There isn't anything wrong. I've just been sitting back here thinking," Billy said.

"Thinking about what, dear?"

"I would like to build a lab in back of the barn."

"I don't think there's enough room in the barn for you to have a lab."

"I want to build it out back, not in the barn."

"You know we don't have any extra money for supplies to build a lab."

"Don't worry, I won't need anything. I'm going to call Larry Sheldon when we get home, and talk to him about my plans for a lab."

"I've heard you and Linda Lou talk about him, but why would he help you build a lab?"

"I don't think I know the answer to that, but he took a real interest in us. He made us promise if we needed anything, we would give him a call."

"I know your father won't mind, but we'll ask him first thing when we get home."

When they dropped Linda Lou off at her house, they talked with Beth and Rob for a few minutes before they continued on home. As they pulled up in front of their house, Ben came running up to the house from the barn.

"Hi, you two! It sure has been lonely around here."

He grabbed Mary, picked her up off the ground, and gave her a big kiss and a hug.

"Dad, I'm glad to see you, but please don't hug and kiss me."

"All right, no kiss, but at least give me a hug."

"Sure, I missed you too."

Ben gave him a big hug, and said, "All right, let's get these bags in the house."

As they were carrying the bags inside, Mary said, "Billy wants to build a lab in back of the barn."

"I would love to let him, but I need the barn."

"I don't want the barn. I'm going to build it behind the barn."

"How in the world are you going to build a lab all by yourself?"

"I'll show you. If you say it's all right."

"I don't have a problem with it, but you know we don't have any extra money for equipment or materials."

"That's all right. I'll take care of all of that."

"Let me know if I can help."

"I will, and thanks. Linda Lou and I will do all of the work."

"Linda Lou? She isn't strong enough to help."

"I think you'll be surprised at what we can get done."

When Ben carried in the last bags, he told Mary, "You don't know how glad I am to have you home. I'm tired of my own cooking."

"So all you missed was my cooking, was it?"

"No, but we'll talk about that a little later."

They both giggled as if they were kids again. The next morning, Mary was fixing breakfast when Billy came out of his room and said, "Well, Mom, Dad really missed you, didn't he?"

"Oh, Billy!"

"It's okay. I'm not that young anymore, and I do know some things, you know."

"I know, but I just don't want to admit it."

"You and Dad have always been open to answering my questions, and I have appreciated it."

"You sound twice your age this morning."

"I spent most of the night thinking about that fact."

"What do you mean?"

"Can we go over to Linda Lou's house this morning?"

"Sure, I can take you over in a few minutes."

"No, I want us all to go. Linda Lou and I have some news we want to share, but we want to do it with all of you at once."

"Is Linda pregnant?"

"No, it's nothing like that."

"You had me going there for a moment. Are they expecting us?"

"Yes, they are. Linda is having this same conversation as we speak."

"You two seem to be plotting something," Ben said.

"Not plotting, planning."

When they arrived at Rob and Beth's, they were standing on their front porch waiting for them. Rob yelled to Ben as they were getting out, "Linda Lou said you would be here in a minute or two. I don't know how she knew, but she was right. It's good to see you two. We haven't been able to get together all summer, and we sure missed you."

"Us too. It was a long summer for all of us, except maybe the kids. What's the big news they are so anxious over?"

"I don't know. Linda Lou wouldn't tell us anything until you got here," Beth said. "Come on in, I have some tea ready, and I just baked some cookies."

"Cookies, I love your cookies," Ben said.

"I know you do; so does Rob. Come on in, and we'll hear what the kids have to tell us."

They all sat down around the cheap Formica kitchen table where they had spent so many happy times playing cards. What they were about to hear would change how they thought of the kids forever.

"Billy, would you mind starting?" Linda said.

"No problem. We have some news and we wanted you all to be together to hear."

"Go ahead and tell us then," Rob said.

"While we were at the university this summer, Linda Lou and I tested out of high school."

"What!" everyone exclaimed.

"Wait, there's more. As the summer went on, we both

realized we had moved far past what the high school could possibly teach us."

"But neither one of you has even started high school yet," Mary said.

"I know, but we knew we wanted to do other things."

"What do you mean, 'other things'?"

"I'll get to that in a moment. While we were there, Linda Lou also passed the exams for her bachelor's degree, a master's degree, and her medical degree. I passed the doctoral exams for math, physics, and electrical engineering. We could have taken more, but we didn't think it made sense to do more."

"I can't believe you and Linda Lou kept all of this from me," Mary said.

"It's about time Linda Lou and I let you in on several things about us."

"You haven't gotten Linda Lou pregnant, have you?" Beth asked.

"Oh no, Mrs. Bustamante, it's nothing like that, though Mom asked me the same thing."

"Well that's good. I would feel just terrible if you two had gotten in trouble. You're way too young for that."

"We've been keeping this secret since we were kids, and it's time to share it."

"Since you were kids? What in the world are you talking about?" Rob asked.

"We'll start at the beginning if you don't mind," Linda said. "When we were less than a year old, we understood everything going on around us. In fact, we both agree we were aware of everything going on around us from the first month we were born."

"Oh come on, that's impossible," Rob exclaimed.

"Give her just a moment to explain," Billy said.

"When you used to send us to our rooms, or outside to play, we were having long talks about what was going on around us. Even then we were aware we were different from the other kids."

"Different, what do you mean different?" Beth said.

"When we started going to church on Sundays we would listen to the other children, and they could only talk baby talk or less. The older children could talk better, but they weren't much better when it came to understanding. All they ever talked about was food, toys, and childish things. It was then we were sure we were different from the other children. Later, we started our Sunday conversations with Pastor Williams. He would answer our questions, and he would talk to us about what we were thinking. He helped us understand that even though we weren't like the other children, it was all right."

"You two weren't quite six years old when we started taking you to the church nursery," Rob said.

"That's right. We were only five years old at the time, but even then we were progressing at a rate way beyond our ages."

"How is that possible?" Rob said.

"I'm not sure we know ourselves, but for whatever reason it's the same for both of us. As far as we can tell, we tend to understand most things equally. Billy is stronger at math and science, while I tend to be better at all things related to biology and medicine. We've known for a long time how uncomfortable you've all been with how different we were from the other children. Do you remember how uncomfortable we made all of you when we taught ourselves how to play chess on my fifth birthday?"

"I sure do, and in fact we were so uncomfortable I don't think we ever talked of it again," Rob said. "We all unconsciously decided to believe it was normal, and you two were just smart for your ages."

"Your story is a perfect example of why we were forced to hide what we were becoming from everyone. We continued our sessions with the pastor until just before we started the first grade. "Billy, why don't you pick up our story from here?"

"Mom and Dad, do you remember the first week of my first-grade year?"

"How could we forget? Mrs. Robinson and Mr. Willis gave you those tests, and then that awful friend of Principal Estep's wanted to take you off to New York," Mary said.

"Yes that's right, and I asked you not to let them take me away, didn't I?"

"Yes, you did. You didn't want to leave us."

"True, but the main reason, which I didn't share with you, was I didn't want to have that kind of scrutiny on me, and eventually Linda Lou. I wanted us to be able to make progress on the plans we had started to lay out."

"Plans?"

"Yes, plans. We had long since decided we were going to educate ourselves. We knew we would gain access to the libraries at school, and the city library. We knew with those resources we could educate ourselves. By the time we reached the sixth grade, we were afraid we had miscalculated. We had exhausted all of the local resources by the time Principal Estep offered the computers and Internet access. We had already grown frustrated, but once we had the computers, we were able to accelerate our education. When you volunteered to take us to the university for the summer, we were well prepared to take advantage of the opportunity.

"After a few weeks at the university, several of the professors noticed how far along we were in our studies and how eager we were to advance our education. As a result, the professors we were working with got together to discuss what they might want to do for us. As luck would have it, Dr. Spain had just read an article about a young man at Harvard who had tested all the way out to a law degree. When they decided to give us the same sort of chance, they brought in all of the professors and staff they needed to administer the interviews and exams.

"When Dr. Blevins contacted us, he told us we could take as many exams as we wanted, as long as we continued to pass. Over a period of six days, we passed all of the criteria necessary for the degrees we wanted. That's pretty much a thumbnail sketch of our activities up to this point."

"That's the most amazing story I have ever heard," Beth said." But I don't think I fully understand what you two are saying. Can you explain it some more?"

"I'll try. I don't mean to sound like I'm bragging about us, but Linda Lou and I've come to the conclusion we're quite a bit smarter than anyone we've been able to identify. We've read everything we could find on precocious children, and we haven't found any mention of even one person like us, let alone two that are friends. Linda Lou did several tests on us while we were at college, and she found there are a few anomalies in our physical makeup. In addition, we both have normal temperatures of ninety-nine-point-six instead of ninety-eight-point-six.

"She gave us psychology tests to try to measure whether our brains were right or left hemisphere dominant. The tests showed our brains don't have a dominant side. We've taken all of the intelligence tests we could find, and not one could accurately measure our IQs. I guess to net out a convoluted story, as far as we can tell, we may be truly unique. Since we knew we aren't related in any way, we then tried to backtrack to find any common events in our past. We were trying to find anything which could have caused us to be so much alike, and yet so different from everyone else. No matter where we looked, we couldn't find any commonality between us."

"You two may be the smartest, but maybe you should

have asked your parents if there's a common bond between you two," Rob said.

"What do you mean?" Linda asked.

"You were born with a perforated bowel, and Dr. Moore
didn't know whether you were going to make it. He didn't
have any blood to use for a transfusion, and he was afraid
to operate without it. When Ben and Mary heard what was
needed, they let the doctor use a pint of Billy's blood to
give to you during the operation."

"You've never told us any of that," Linda said.

"No, we didn't, and I don't know why we didn't. Obviously you were too young at the time, and somehow it
never crossed our minds over the years to mention it."

"You never told me I gave blood to Linda Lou," Billy
said.

"No, we didn't," Ben said. "Like Rob said, it wasn't as
if we consciously withheld it from you. We just never
thought about it afterward."

"Could this be the bond between us?" Billy asked.

"Yes, I suppose it could be," Linda said. "But I've never
heard of a blood transfusion causing anything remotely
like what has happened with us."

"Is there anything else you might have forgotten to
mention over the years?" Billy asked.

"No, I don't think so, other than . . ." Mary began.

"Other than what?"

"We never did tell you everything about the day you
were born."

"Like what?"

"Ben, would you like to tell the story? You were more
coherent than I was."

"Okay, but you jump in if I leave anything out."

Ben spent the next twenty minutes relating the story
of the snowstorm, the wreck, and their stopover at Glen
Eyrie. He told them about Dr. Evans, the doctor who

delivered Billy, and how everyone had been so nice to them.

"Go on, Mr. West."

"Linda Lou, I think it's time you started calling me Ben."

"Okay, Ben, go on."

"The only thing even remotely disconcerting about the entire experience was when Dr. Evans gave Billy an antibiotic shot for his congestion."

"Do you remember what type of antibiotic it was?" Linda asked.

"It's strange but I do. It was called Levofloxacin."

"That's a broad-spectrum antibiotic. Normally you wouldn't use it for simple congestion."

"That's what Doc Moore said when I told him the story, and I haven't thought about it in years. I obviously don't have any way of knowing what was in the shot. Billy has been healthy all these years, so we never had any reason to think about it again."

"I don't think I've ever heard of Glen Eyrie," Billy said.

"We never knew much about it either," Ben said. "They were in the process of moving some portion of it when we arrived. The only thing Dr. Evans told us was they had been using the hotel to provide R and R for their research scientists. We tried to visit the hotel a few years later, but there was a padlock on the entrance gate."

They continued talking for several minutes, and then Billy asked, "Would you mind if I use your phone?"

"No problem," Rob said. "Who are you going to call?"

"I want to call Mr. Sheldon and see if he'll help me build a lab."

The phone rang twice, and Larry Sheldon answered.

"Hello, Billy, how can I help you?"

"How did you know it was me, Mr. Sheldon?"

"Please call me Larry. You're the only one who has this phone number. The card I gave to Linda has a different number. Now what can I do for you?"

Billy explained what he had in mind for the lab he wanted to build.

"No problem, I'll get you some help. Is there anything else you need?"

"No, I don't think so."

"I'll get to work and see what I can put together for you."

After they had hung up, Larry Sheldon contacted the Logos, and let them know what he needed to get Billy started. Next, he called Klaus Heidelberg. Klaus was the leading theoretical physicist in the world, and a good friend of Larry Sheldon. Larry didn't know how old Klaus was, but Albert Einstein had been his friend and mentor, and he even looked a lot like him.

"Klaus, Billy has called to ask for assistance building a lab on his dad's farm. Do you have the materials and equipment we talked about ready?"

"I do. Let me gather a few more things, and I'll be ready to travel."

"I'll see you in a few days."

Linda and Billy continued talking with their parents for another half hour, and then Ben said, "Kids, I need to get to work."

"Before you go, are you sure it's all right to build my lab behind the barn?" Billy asked.

"I suppose it's all right. Just make sure you're careful."

"We will be. Mr. Sheldon is going to send me some things to get started with."

The phone rang and Beth answered. "Billy, Mr. Sheldon is on the phone, and he'd like to talk to you again."

After he was finished talking he told them, "The university is sending a couple of truckloads of surplus electronic equipment, and some construction materials. Larry Sheldon said the military donated the equipment to them, and they never could figure out what to do with it. He said the trucks should be here tomorrow."

15

THE NEXT DAY two trucks showed up just as Billy was finishing breakfast. After they finished unloading, he started taking an inventory. He had just gotten started when Beth dropped Linda Lou off at the barn.

"It looks like you started without me."

"I just got started. All I've done so far is start taking inventory of our haul."

"What did we get?"

"I haven't looked at everything yet, but we have a real collection of stuff. There are six large Sun servers, several San Disc units, and we have the last Cray supercomputer ever made. It's supposed to be the largest and fastest machine they ever built. It was constructed to control all of the space-based weapons platforms they were about to launch. There's also a dozen or so Petawatt CO_2 lasers they were going to place on space-based platforms for missile defense. When they decided not to launch the weapons platforms they placed it all in storage. I haven't started cataloging the rest of the stuff, but I imagine it's all of the same quality."

"I didn't know we were going to place weapons in space, and I thought Larry Sheldon said this was junk which had been donated to the college."

"Some of it might have been, but I think they made a special shipment to combine with the donations."

"Why would they do that?"

"I think it was Larry Sheldon's doing."

"It's nice he has taken an interest in you."

"It isn't just me. He's the one who got you hooked up with the Mayo and Dr. Robbins, isn't he?

"You know he did. He is trying to help us. Isn't he?"

"Yes, he sure is. He's turned out to be our biggest supporter. I don't know why, but I sense he has our best interests in mind. I spent some of my time this summer studying lasers, so I think we can make use of them."

"Good, what else did you see we can use?"

"There's a huge army hospital tent in the supplies. I think we can set it up to work in until we can get our lab built."

"Excellent, let's get started."

They spent the rest of the day getting the tent unpacked and spread out. They finished putting the tent up just as the sun was going down. Mary called out to them, "Kids, come on in. Dinner's ready."

"Mrs. West, this looks good, I love fried chicken."

"I know you do, dear, and please, I thought we agreed you would call me Mary."

"Okay, Mary, but it still seems strange to me."

"I know, it does to me as well, dear, but it's definitely all right, so just relax."

"Let's eat. I'm starved."

There wasn't much small talk until Billy said, "We got a lot of great stuff, and we got our tent set up just before dark."

"I saw, but I didn't know you were going to use a tent," Ben said.

"We didn't either. But it will work out great until we can get our lab prepared."

"We have chocolate cake for dessert," Mary said. "Would either of you like coffee with your cake?"

"We don't want coffee tonight, but we will take a glass of milk."

"How do you know what Linda Lou wants?"

"I just do. We usually know what the other one is thinking."

"Your mom and I think we can sometimes, but not all of the time," Ben said. "Boy, you've outdone yourself this time, this cake is great."

"It sure is, Mom."

"Why, thank you. I didn't do anything different, but it does seem to be good tonight. It must be the company."

"I need to get home and get to bed. We have a big day tomorrow," Linda said.

"Ben, would you take Linda Lou home?"

"Sure I will. No, wait. Billy, why don't you take her home? You're a good driver, and you don't have to get on the highway."

"Okay, I will, and I'll be careful."

"I know you will," Ben said. "I just wish I had been as responsible as you are."

"Why, thanks."

"You're welcome, and before you two go, I would like you to know your mother and I couldn't be more proud of the both of you. I don't think we've completely grasped the enormity of what you two have accomplished, but just know we are proud of both of you."

"Thanks again."

"Yes, thanks," Linda said.

"Let's get you home," Billy said.

"Your folks sure were sweet tonight. They seemed to treat us differently tonight, didn't they?"

"They sure did. It seems like they got what we were trying to tell them yesterday. I believe it was a load off of their minds to finally admit they have never understood us."

"I think you're right. I'll let you know how my parents are tomorrow."

He pulled up in front of her house, and shut the car off.

"I'll see you in the morning. I'll get my dad to bring me over."

She reached for the door handle, but stopped, leaned over, and gave Billy a quick kiss.

"Linda?"

"Yes, Billy?"

"You've never done that before."

"I know, but it's about time one of us did."

"What do you mean?"

"We're more alike than any two people have ever been, and you know I care for you a lot."

"Well, of course I do, and I hope you know I feel the same."

"Yes, I do, and I think we're old enough to show it, don't you?"

"Yes, I do." He pulled her across the seat to him, and gave her a long kiss.

After a couple of minutes, they parted and she remarked, "That's a lot better, but we should probably work up to this boyfriend, girlfriend thing. It's not like we don't understand what we're getting into."

"That's true. We, for better or worse, understand all of the mechanics to almost anything. But we haven't ever allowed our emotions to come into play."

"We've always been able to control our emotions, to a fault even. Let's agree to continue this, but slowly."

"Okay, L, we will."

"L . . . you've never called me 'L' before."

"No, I haven't. Do you mind?"

"No, silly. I think it's cute."

"Okay, then, we'll talk some more tomorrow."

The next morning, Billy started inventorying the rest

of the equipment. As he did, he noticed a large crate on the edge of the supplies. He walked over to it, and he spotted a pouch on the front of it. The note inside was from Larry Sheldon: *Billy, the crate this note is on contains our closest attempt at fusion power. We haven't been able to solve the magnetic containment problem with the module. We've spent years and billions of dollars trying to get it to work, and we don't have much to show for it.*

I don't know if you can get it to work either, but you're the most brilliant young man I have ever encountered, so I hold out some hope. If you need anything else, just call the number I gave you, and I'll get whatever you need. Please destroy the note, and don't share the information with anyone other than Linda. I'm sorry to put this burden on one so young, but you're our last hope.

Billy took one last look at the note, placed it in a metal pan on the table, and set it on fire. As he watched it burn, he was thinking of Larry's words, and wondered what he might have meant by "our last hope."

He decided to leave the crate until last. He walked outside to get a breath of fresh air and wait on Linda to arrive.

"Hi, Mom brought me over on her way to town. She and your mom are going into town to shop for the day. Did you start without me?"

"I was going to start with the huge crate over there, but when I read the note on the crate, I decided to wait on you."

"What note?"

"Larry Sheldon sent me a note explaining what's in the crate. He said it's a prototype of a fusion reactor. They've spent billions of dollars on it, but they couldn't get it to work. He wants me to try to finish their work."

"It's quite an honor for him to send something like that to you."

"Yes, it is. But the last sentence in his note has me spooked."

"What did it say? I've never seen you spooked by anything."

"He said I was their last hope."

"What did he mean by that?"

"I have no idea. But I didn't like the inference."

"We've been having premonitions for several years, but we just can't figure out what they mean," Linda said.

"Yes, we have, but we don't have time to worry about it right now. We have a lot of work to do."

They spent the rest of the day cataloging the equipment. As the sun was starting to set, Mary called to them, "Kids, supper is ready. Come in and eat, and you can start again tomorrow."

"Okay, we'll be right there," Billy said.

"We had a good day. We have everything inventoried. All we have left to do is uncrate the fusion reactor," Linda said.

"We'll start on it tomorrow."

He took her hand and said, "Linda Lou, I've thought about last night. I've always known it, I guess, but last night made me realize how much I love you."

He pulled her to him, and they kissed for a minute or so.

"That was nice," Linda said. "I definitely think we're getting better at this. We still need to take this slowly. We have so much to do, and I don't think we have time for us to get serious right now."

"I know, but it was nice."

"Yes, it was, but we had better get going or your mom is going to come looking for us."

They were eating dinner when Linda said, "I talked with Dr. Robbins this morning before I came over."

"What did he have to say?" Billy asked.

"He wanted to know if I had made my decision regarding going to the Mayo for my residency."

"What did you tell him?"

"I told him yes, if they still wanted me."

"When are you going to leave?"

"I told him I had to check with you to see when I could leave. Do you think you can continue without me?"

"It will make it harder, but this is something you have to do. How long do you think you'll be gone?"

"I asked Dr. Robbins the same thing. He told me it normally takes three to four years, depending on the areas I'm working in."

"That long?"

"Yes, I'm afraid so. I can stay here if you think I should."

"I would love it if you stayed. But you know as well as I do you have to go. When are you planning on leaving?"

"I have a flight on Wednesday."

"That's only another four days. I sure am going to miss you."

"I'll miss you too. I'll call whenever I can."

The next four days flew by, and before they knew it, Rob and Beth were taking Linda to the airport. Billy and Linda were in the backseat, and they weren't saying a word. He had his arm around her, and she had her head resting on his shoulder.

Once Linda had checked in, they were standing beside the boarding gate talking. Rob and Beth finished saying their good-byes and stepped back so the kids could say theirs. Billy and Linda kissed, and as they did, he heard her voice in his head saying, *I love you too.*

He was startled and broke the kiss. "How did you do that?"

"I don't know. I heard you tell me you love me, and I just responded. Come here and let's try it again."

As they were kissing, they were again hearing each other in their minds. *How is this possible?*

We have always felt like we knew what the other was thinking. I guess we actually did, Linda said.

They had been kissing and talking for a couple of minutes. *We had better stop. Your parents are probably wondering what's going on,* Billy said.

I suppose you're right, but this is cool.

"I didn't think you two were ever coming up for air," Beth said. "Is there anything you would like to tell us?"

"I don't think so," Linda said. "Other than, you do know we love each other. Don't you?"

"We've sensed it. We've even talked about it with Ben and Mary. We just weren't sure you two had realized it yet."

"Yes we have, but we don't have time for any of that just yet."

"What do you mean?"

"We have been having premonitions since we were kids. We haven't been able to figure out what it is yet, but they are getting stronger all the time," Linda said.

"That sounds serious," Rob said.

"It's very serious."

"I think it could be the most serious event to ever happen," Billy said.

"I've got to get going. They just gave the last boarding call. I'll call you all when I get there."

She gave Billy another quick kiss, and hurried down the ramp. They stood and watched until her plane had disappeared from sight.

"We sure are going to miss her," Rob said.

"I am too," Billy said.

"I know you are, son. You don't mind if I call you 'son,' do you?"

"Of course not, Linda and I think of you and my parents as our parents."

"Why, thank you."

They dropped Billy off at home. He started to go into the house, but instead he went out to the tent to work for a while.

16

BILLY STARTED UNCRATING the fusion reactor prototype. A night breeze was rippling the sides of the tent and
as they did the tent poles were gently creaking. As he
worked his thoughts turned to Larry Sheldon. He had come
to the conclusion Larry Sheldon wasn't exactly who he
claimed to be. He was definitely in charge of the university's administration, but a normal university administrator
couldn't have arranged for them to get a shipment of high-
tech goods the government had spent billions of dollars developing.

It took him most of the night to uncrate the reactor and
its components. When he opened the last box, there was a
portfolio inside. He sat down, opened it, and began to read.
As he read their logs and notes, he began to understand the
frustration the team had felt. They had worked on the project for almost four years. By the second year, they believed
they were close to success. But when they attempted to initiate the fusion reaction, the magnetic containment would
fail. They spent another two years trying to solve the problem, but they were never able to maintain the magnetic
field long enough to reach ignition.

He finished reading the reports, and realized it was
morning. He decided to see if his mom had breakfast ready.

He walked into the kitchen. "Did you work all night?"
Mary asked.

"Yes, I did. I didn't intend to, but I got busy unpacking the last of the crates, and lost track of time."

"Sit down and we'll eat."

"What have you been up to?" Ben asked.

"I've been unpacking the equipment the college sent. I got some cool stuff."

"When you say you got cool stuff, it must be truly amazing."

"You're right. It's special."

"What are you going to do with all of it?"

"I'm going to install it in the lab when I get it built. Mom, do you want some help with the dishes?"

"No, I'm fine. Why don't you go lie down and get some sleep before you go back to work."

That evening Mary had to shake Billy to wake him. "It's time to get up and eat dinner."

"What time is it?"

"It's six o'clock, and your dad's hungry. So get up and we'll eat."

"I didn't intend to sleep all day. I must have been more tired than I thought."

After they finished dinner, Billy told them, "Thanks for dinner. I'm going out to do some work."

Around midnight he was studying the magnetic containment donuts surrounding the fusion reactor. The core was filled with a mixture of deuterium and tritium, which he knew was the most promising combination of elements they had tested.

After he finished his inspection of the core, he reread the notes from the team who had assembled the reactor. When he finished, he knew what he needed to do.

Their containment fields had continually failed before they could achieve the 40 million Kelvin's of temperature necessary to overcome the coulomb barrier. But that wasn't their only problem. The inductance coils they were using weren't powerful enough to generate the temperatures needed for fusion.

Their last attempt to generate enough heat had been to inject intense beams of neutral atoms into the core to increase the temperature. But even with the addition of the atoms, there simply wasn't enough heat to initiate the fusion process.

Billy spent the rest of the night compiling a list of supplies and equipment he needed to reconfigure the reactor. When he finished the list, he used one of the CAD computers from the shipment to redesign the reactor.

The shipment included a portable satellite communications system which allowed him to log into the secure Web site Larry Sheldon had provided. Once he was connected, he uploaded his supply list, the new design, and a short note to Larry Sheldon detailing the additional help he needed.

When he finished, he ate breakfast with his parents, and then he lay down for a nap. He had only been asleep for a couple of hours when Mary shook him awake.

"Larry Sheldon is on the phone for you."

"What's up?" Billy asked.

"I have a gentleman here whose name you may recognize. Klaus Heidelberg is here with me, and he would like to ask you a couple of questions concerning the design changes you sent me."

"Klaus Heidelberg, the physicist? I've read all of his papers."

"The reactor is my design," Klaus Heidelberg said. "We worked on it for years, but we couldn't solve the last few problems. When Larry briefed me on how brilliant he believes you to be, I hoped someone with a fresh perspective would see something new to try.

"I spent the last couple of hours studying the changes you sent, and the equipment you asked for. From what I see, you want to replace the magnetic containment donuts with donuts made from type-two carbon superconducting ceramics. You're also using the ceramic superconducting material to bring power to the magnetic containment, and deliver the generated heat for use."

"Yes, that's right," Billy said.

"I also see you intend to use three of the Petawatt lasers to add an additional heat boost. I ran a quick simulation before the call, and I think you're correct. You're right to change the donuts to a different material. We were having problems with them losing conductivity when they were exposed to the magnetic fields and extreme temperatures.

"From my quick analysis of your changes, I believe you may have solved our problems with the reactor. I looked through your list of materials and I see you've asked for quite a bit more of the ceramic-based superconducting material. What are you going to do with the rest of it?"

"Dr. Heidelberg?"

"Please, call me Klaus."

"Okay, Klaus. I believe with enough power I can generate a field which will repel virtually any material or force, even gravity waves."

"Are you talking about antigravity?"

"Yes, I am. It was your research that led me to believe gravity can be affected by extremely powerful magnetic forces."

"I remember that paper. The only reason I wrote it was Albert asked me to. He truly believed in the concept, and believed I could finish his work on the theory."

"Albert? Would that be Albert Einstein?"

"Why yes, it would. He was a close friend and my mentor. I finished the paper just a few weeks before he died. No one else in the scientific community believed it, but he truly appreciated the effort."

"I believe you were right on, and I intend to build a device that will prove it."

"You have no idea what it would mean to an old man. I've been afraid I wouldn't live long enough to see Albert's and my work proven."

"Do you have any other questions for Billy?" Larry Sheldon asked.

"No, I don't. I've enjoyed our conversation, and I hope to meet you in person one day."

"It would be my pleasure," Billy said.

"I'll get to work on your list," Larry Sheldon said. "It shouldn't take me too long to round up the materials you want."

Billy spent the next three weeks hooking up the rest of the computers, and disassembling the fusion reactor. On Monday of the third week he saw a cloud of dust coming his way. He walked out to the road where he saw the dust was a convoy of trucks coming up the road. When the first truck pulled up to the tent, he was surprised to see Larry Sheldon in the passenger seat.

"I wasn't expecting you," Billy said.

"I was gathering up the stuff you asked for, and Klaus asked if he could come along," Larry Sheldon said. "He wanted to meet you in person, and see if you can use his help."

Dr. Klaus Heidelberg came walking up to where they were standing. Billy was somewhat surprised at his appearance. He had seen pictures of Dr. Heidelberg but they didn't do him justice. He was a large barrel-chested man, and still carried himself like the prizefighter he had been in his younger days. As he got closer, Billy could see the age in his weathered features.

"Here he is now," Larry Sheldon said. "I would like to introduce you to Dr. Klaus Heidelberg."

"Dr. Heidelberg, I'm glad to meet you."

"Please call me Klaus, and it's my great pleasure to

meet you. Larry has told me some truly amazing things about you. I've spent some more time with the designs you sent over, and I'm convinced you've solved the fusion reactor problem. I also think you may be on the right path on the antigravity application as well. Would you consider allowing an old man to work with you?"

"I can't tell you what an honor it would be to work with you," Billy said.

"All right you two, enough of the mutual admiration society," Larry Sheldon said. "Let's get to work."

"I'll have to ask Mom and Dad if it's all right for Klaus to stay here. We don't have much room, but I'm sure we can work it out," Billy said.

"Don't worry," Larry Sheldon said. "We brought several double-wide modular homes for accommodations. If it's all right with your dad, we'll set them up out back."

"I know it'll be all right with Dad. We don't use the area out back for much of anything. It's almost solid rock and not much good for anything."

"Good, we'll get started then, if you're sure it'll be all right?"

"I'm sure, but if you like, we'll go in and ask him."

After Larry Sheldon and Dr. Heidelberg had met Ben and Mary, Ben quickly agreed to let them use the land out back.

"It's no problem, but I'm not sure we have enough electric service to handle all of the stuff you brought," Ben said. "We had to run the line to the house ourselves, and we didn't size it to handle that much load."

"Don't worry, we brought our own generators. In fact we'll hook the barn and the house into our generators so you can stop paying for electricity."

"Thanks, that'll sure help. Money has been real tight these last few years."

"You won't have to worry about money. We're going to pay you fifty thousand dollars a month for the use of your land."

"Fifty thousand a month!" Mary exclaimed. "That's more money than we made last year."

"We can't take that much money from you," Ben said.

"Don't worry for a minute about the money. We have complete government funding."

"I can't believe all of this is happening," Ben said. "First Billy and Linda skip through high school and college in one summer, and now all of this."

"I know this is hard to believe, but please trust me, I have to do this," Billy said.

"I trust what you say. It's just a little overwhelming to me and your mother."

"It sure is," Mary said.

"I need to get to work," Ben said. "I promised Rob I would help him cut his oats today."

The trucks continued to arrive all through the day, and well into the night. When they finally stopped, modular buildings and equipment covered the entire section of land behind the barn.

As the last truck left, Billy said, "This is a lot more stuff than I asked for."

"This is just the start," Larry Sheldon said. "We're going to buy up all of the land around your father's place. We're going to need a lot more room before we're done."

"What do we need all of the room for?"

"There are several thousand people coming to help on the project. Within six months, we'll have an entire complex of factories set up. Right now, we need to get the housing ready before the workers arrive. After the housing, the first building we're going to put up is a temporary lab for you and Klaus. You and Klaus need to get the reactor up and running. We're going to need a lot more power than we can bring generators for."

"Why are you bringing all of this stuff here to the middle of nowhere? Don't you have all of this stuff at the labs where you developed the original reactor?"

"We did. We had an incident a few months back, and we can no longer use the facility."

"What happened?"

"I can't tell you. You don't have clearance, and it's strictly need-to-know."

"If it's a problem, we need to get him the same clearances you and I have," Klaus Heidelberg said. "He's already developed designs we would've classified at the highest level."

"All right, I'll do it. I can grant him a temporary clearance until I can submit it and make it official," Larry Sheldon said. "What happened was a terrorist attack. We believe a Middle Eastern group, probably Iranian, was responsible for delivering a bacteriologic attack on our previous facility. We sent a team in to retrieve the prototype reactor, and it took them almost ninety days to sanitize it.

"We lost over eleven hundred people at the plant. Other than Klaus, who happened to be in Washington with me, everyone else in the country that's ever worked in this area of research is dead. There were simultaneous attacks on the British, French, Chinese, and Russian scientific teams. The attacks killed virtually everyone with experience in this area."

"How can that be? There hasn't been a single story on the TV or news services concerning any of those events. How did you manage to keep them out of the news?"

"We have our ways, my boy."

"You aren't just the head of administration for the university, are you?"

"Well, I am the head administrator, and yes I'm more than that. I'm in charge of all Top Secret and above research projects for the United States and the United Nations. I've been in charge for over ten years. We've never made the existence of the projects public in an attempt to preclude events like what happened. Somehow, the terrorists found out what we were working on, and they managed to locate our facilities.

"I don't believe they discovered the real purpose of our project, but I'm sure they'll try again. We're going to build new facilities here in New Mexico, starting with your dad's farm. We're still not going public, but this time we're going to assume they'll find us. We're using the African Division to set up a perimeter of a hundred miles around the facility."

"You're going to establish a hundred-mile circle around us?"

"We already have. They're moving into position as we speak. They'll stay in place until we can devise a better defense perimeter."

"We're in the middle of the United States. What do we need a defense perimeter for?"

"For the same reason we lost our previous facilities. The terrorists will attempt to destroy this one as well.

"We're going to offer to relocate anyone who doesn't want to stay. We'll buy their homes, land, and pay to relocate them wherever they want."

"I think you'll find most of them will stay. The people around here are used to hardship."

The next several months passed quickly, and for the first time in months Billy was at the breakfast table eating and talking with Ben and Mary.

"I can't believe how much you and your friends have accomplished in only nine months," Mary said. "How many buildings do you have built?"

"Dr. Heidelberg was telling me last night we have seventy-five manufacturing buildings up, and there's also housing for fifty-two hundred people."

"What in the world is all of this for?" Ben asked.

"I can't talk about what we're working on. All I can tell you is it's important."

"You've told us you can't tell us anything several times now," Ben said. "We're your parents; surely you can trust us with what's going on."

"I wish I could, but Larry Sheldon has sworn me to secrecy, and besides, there's no need for you guys to worry about it."

17

BILLY HAD JUST gone to bed when he felt Linda in his mind.

What's up? Linda asked.

How are you? I sure do miss you.

I miss you too. I'm taking a shower before I go back to the hospital, and I felt your presence. What happened?

Billy told her of all of the changes which had taken place since she'd been gone.

This is the first time we've been able to talk like this since I left, Linda said. *I guess it's because you're excited. I hope we'll be able to figure out how to talk like this whenever we want to.*

I sure wish I was there right now.

What are you thinking? I thought we weren't ready for that yet.

You know exactly what I'm thinking. You can read my mind, right?

Yes, I can, and we'll get around to it someday, but not right now. It's a pleasant thought though. Enough, my water is getting cold.

Okay, I'm about to take a nap. Love you.

I love you too. Sleep well, and we'll talk again soon.

They hadn't talked as much as they would have liked during the last nine months. Linda had been incredibly busy learning her craft as a surgeon. She had been making unbelievable progress, and had received her certifications in seven different procedures.

The senior surgeons were already asking her to assist whenever they had a particularly difficult procedure. She, like Billy, had the innate sense of what to do when an unexpected event occurs. Even if she had never seen the issue before, the right answer just seemed to occur to her.

As she began her tenth month at the hospital, Dr. William Robbins called her to his office.

"Please, come in and sit down," Dr. Robbins said. "I'm going to ask you to do me a favor. It's going to be difficult for you, but I'm sure you're up to the task.

"We're about to receive a group of survivors from an attack on a government research facility. You and I will be the only doctors allowed to treat the three patients who are about to arrive. I'm going to pull you out of the normal surgery rotation for the duration of their treatment."

"Of course I'll do whatever you ask of me," Linda said. "What's the big secret? We have the best doctors in the country, and as a group, they've seen pretty much everything when it comes to injuries."

"These patients aren't injured. They're infected."

"Infected with what?"

"That's what we have to find out, and quick. The three people they are bringing in are the only survivors of over seventy-six hundred people who were infected during the attack. From the time of the attack, to the first deaths, was just over twenty-four hours. After forty-eight hours, the only ones left alive were the men they are bringing in.

"The team leader of the rescue mission told me he had never seen anything like what they found. There was blood everywhere, and there were bodies scattered throughout the facilities. It took them several hours to find the survivors. They had been in an isolated area of the base and were some of the last to be infected."

"How could that have happened?" Linda asked.

"They found the wreckage of the six crop-dusting planes the terrorists used to disperse the virus. The base's security force managed to shoot down all but one of them, but not until they had sprayed the entire base. An Air Force F35 lighting from the local airbase shot down the last one.

"The team is using portable incinerators to cremate the bodies. After they've finished with the bodies, they're going to napalm bomb the entire base and quarantine it with a Marine contingent."

Dr. Robbins's phone rang, and when he finished the conversation he said, "They're here. Let's go down and see what we have."

They both donned hazmat suits before they entered the quarantined area. Linda was shocked at what she saw. The three men were in capsules that resembled glass coffins. Each tube had its own self-contained air supply and capture tanks to hold the used air supply.

All three patients had a blue hue to their skin, and there were droplets of blood covering the glass of their capsules. One of the patients had a coughing fit as she walked up to his capsule, and she saw even more droplets of blood speckle the glass as he coughed.

"These patients don't look like they're in good shape," Linda said.

"They weren't able to do much for them once they were sealed in the transport capsules," Dr. Robbins said. "We couldn't allow anyone to open the capsules to care for them. I'm afraid they won't live much longer if we don't figure out what the infection is."

"Can we open the capsules to get some blood samples?"

"Sure, the suits we're wearing will protect us."

They worked quickly, and in less than an hour, they

had moved all three of the patients to beds with oxygen tents over them. Linda drew blood samples from all three of the patients and began to analyze them.

As she studied the blood under an electron microscope, she thought back to one of the first studies she had read on pandemics.

The study had dealt with one of the worst pandemics of all time, the Spanish flu. The worldwide pandemic killed millions of people in the years 1918–1919. They named the outbreak the Spanish flu, even though it had not started in Spain. The pandemic had actually begun in the United States at Fort Riley, Kansas.

The virus had been an unusually virulent strain of the H1N1 Influenza A virus. As she studied the sample, she saw it was similar to the samples she had seen in the study. The scientists had recovered a body of one of the victim's buried in the permafrost of Alaska. They managed to re-create the virus from the preserved tissues. They finished cataloging the samples, and then they had supposedly destroyed them to prevent any accidents.

She captured the images of the slides to a file on her laptop computer. Once they were loaded, she did a digital comparison of the current slides and the ones from the study.

She almost immediately identified the new disease was a variation of the Spanish flu. The symptoms were identical, except the mortality rate was even higher with the new strain.

As she continued the comparison, she saw there were some subtle differences. The modifications to the new virus were enough to ensure the natural immunity of most people would not be able to deal with the new strain.

The virus was even more deadly than the original mutation due to their manipulation. The mortality rate from the Spanish flu had been around 5 percent of the entire world's population. She observed that with this strain, it could be 95 percent or more.

Like the original disease, there was a rapid onset of symptoms, but the progression was even faster. Over the next couple of hours, she worked to identify all of the modifications the terrorists had made to the original virus.

Finally, Dr. Robbins came over to where she was working. "I've got them as stable as I know how to get them. But I'm afraid they're not going to live through the night."

"I've identified the disease. It's an engineered variant of the Spanish flu. I've identified the modifications they made, but I haven't been able to engineer a vaccine yet. I feel sure it will respond to drugs, and I believe I can reengineer one of the existing vaccines to serve as a treatment."

"Is there anything you need?" Dr. Robbins asked.

"Not at the moment."

"I'm going to continue to monitor the patients, and I'm still attempting to keep them alive. Do you think treating them with an NAI like zanamivir will do any good?"

"It will probably help, but since it has been over forty-eight hours since they showed symptoms, it'll not help very much. But it can't hurt."

Dr. Robbins spent the rest of the day and all night working on the three men. He gave them the largest dose of the NAIs he thought they could tolerate. Even though he never left their sides during the night, by morning they were all dead. After the last one died, he walked across the hall to where Linda was still working on a vaccine.

"How are the patients they brought in?" As she asked the question, she saw the answer in his eyes.

"The last one just died," Dr. Robbins said.

"I'm so sorry. I'm getting close to a solution to the vaccine, but it wouldn't have helped them."

"Maybe we can save the next group."

"There's been another attack?"

"No, not yet. But there will be."

She worked straight through the day, and even though she had not slept in over forty-eight hours she continued working into the evening. Around midnight, she leaned back from the microscope and remarked to no one in particular, "I believe I have it."

She walked over to an intercom on the wall and called. "Guard, will you please wake up Dr. Robbins for me? Tell him I think I have a solution."

It only took Dr. Robbins about twenty minutes to get suited up and reenter the lab.

"I'm sorry; I didn't mean to sleep so long. You must be exhausted."

"Would you mind double-checking my work? I'm sure I have the vaccine figured out, but I'm so tired I would like someone to verify my work before we send it out to be produced."

"I would be honored. I can't believe you've already developed a vaccine. It normally takes our team months to find a solution when we get a problem like this."

It took him the rest of the night to verify Linda's work. Finally, he looked up and said, "You've done it. This will definitely work. I'll have the plant begin work producing the vaccine right away. It'll take a couple of months to produce a useful amount, but at least we can get started."

It took another couple of hours before Linda got to the room they had prepared for her. She decided to take a hot shower before she tried to get some sleep. As she stood in the shower, she felt Billy in her mind.

Hi, you've caught me in the shower again.

What's happened? Billy asked. *I can tell you're utterly exhausted.*

She let him see the events which had occurred over the previous two days. *I'm so sorry. At least you were able to develop a vaccine. I see now what Larry Sheldon was telling me today. He said one of their facilities had experienced another attack. Are you all right?*

I think so, but I've never seen people suffer like that.

I understand, and I don't know if I could've handled it as well as you did.

Yes, you would. You're stronger than anyone I have ever known. Thinking of you actually helped me get through it. I'm tired; I'm going to get some sleep now.

Sleep well. I love you and I miss you.

18

BILLY WALKED INTO their lab, and Dr. Klaus Heidelberg greeted him. "Hello, my young friend. I think we're ready to try the reactor. The technicians finished installing the last of the reengineered magnetic containment donuts last night."

"I was thinking," Billy said. "We're almost finished rebuilding the reactor, but we haven't put anything in place to make use of it. We'll have the fusion reaction held in place by the magnetic containment, but we have no way of utilizing it for power. I want to run a magnetic tube through the magnetic containment field."

"I believe with the magnetic projectors you've developed it's achievable, but to what end?"

"I want to flow liquid sodium through the magnetic tubes into the containment area. The heat will turn the sodium into superheated gas, and we'll use the tubes to transfer the heat into the power generation portion of the system."

"We need to test the magnetic containment tubes before we try this," Dr. Heidelberg said. "Superheated sodium will be extremely dangerous if the containment fails."

"I agree that it's dangerous, but it shouldn't take too long to develop a set of tests to ensure that the containment fields will work."

They spent the next three weeks working through the

tests. Once they were both satisfied it was as safe as they could make it, they scheduled the installation of the magnetic tubes. Once the tubes were active, they filled the system with liquid sodium. When he was satisfied the tubes were stable, Billy enabled the reactor's magnetic containment fields.

"The reactor's containment field is stable, and we're only pulling forty-five percent of the available power from the first reactor," Dr. Heidelberg said.

Since they had three commercial-grade fission reactors onsite to power their work, they had more than enough power.

"I'm going to activate the heating coil now," Billy said.

"We're at seventy-five percent of the temperature needed for ignition," Dr. Heidelberg said after an hour of observation. "This is already hotter than we ever managed to get the reactor. We have full containment, but we still lack several million degrees of temperature to achieve fusion."

"I'm going to fire the lasers," Billy said. "It shouldn't take more than a few seconds to reach ignition temperature. I'm firing now."

He fired the three lasers for a full six seconds before he cut them off. The magnetic containment area was now emitting a bright green glow. If the magnetic containment field had not been filtering the light, it would've been brighter than the sun. They could have adjusted the field so no light would escape, but they had wanted to see if there was a noticeable change when it reached ignition temperature.

"I believe you've done it," Dr. Heidelberg said.

"We've done it," Billy said. "The bulk of the work in the reactor is your work. I just helped with some of the details."

"Let's cut the reactor over, and take the other ones offline," Dr. Heidelberg said.

Billy switched the fusion reactor over to take control of the heating load from the three fission reactors. He verified the system was stable and initiated a power-down sequence for the fission reactors.

They spent the next ten days verifying the output and stability of the fusion reactor.

"As far as I can tell everything is working as planned," Billy said. "The only anomaly I've found so far is the reactor is putting out three times the heat we expected. I think it's time we add several more generators to the mix."

"We're already generating more electricity than all of the generation plants in the US," Dr. Heidelberg said. "We're running most of the electricity to dummy loads as it is. So what are we going to do with the additional capacity?"

"Let's call Larry Sheldon and see if he can get the Army Corp of Engineers to run transmission lines to the eastern, western, and the Texas interconnect points of the power grid. Once the transmission lines are in place, we'll be able to deliver power to the entire United States."

"It'll take years to build that many miles of transmission towers."

"Normally you would be correct, but I want to use power cables made from the ceramic superconducting material to carry the power. I've come up with a method to superheat the carbon steel outer covering to make it almost indestructible. We can lay the cables on top of the ground along the railroad right of ways. Since we can just lay it on the ground, we'll be able to cut the installation time to a fraction of building new power transmission towers. We'll be using the superconducting material so there will not be any measurable loss of energy in the transmissions."

"How are we going to manufacture that much ceramic cable?" Dr. Heidelberg asked.

"We have an unlimited amount of power, and Larry Sheldon can bring us whatever raw materials we need. I've been working on a design for an automated plant to produce the cable. We've been producing the ones we're using by hand, but we need to be able to make thousands of miles of cable."

"I'll call Larry Sheldon right now if you have your plans ready?"

"I have them on my laptop. Give me a few minutes and I'll e-mail them to you, and I'll copy Larry as well."

After Billy e-mailed the plans, he started work on his next project. He wanted to finish his plan to make Dr. Heidelberg's and Albert Einstein's vision of antigravity a reality. As he began to flesh out his thoughts, Dr. Heidelberg was laying out their plans to Larry Sheldon and his team. Dr. Heidelberg finished briefing Larry Sheldon, and sought out Billy to let him know what Larry Sheldon had told him.

He found Billy hard at work on his laptop.

"Larry says hi, and he says it'll take him at least ten days to round up all of the stuff you want," Dr. Heidelberg said. "The Army Corp of Engineers will be here in two weeks to begin the construction of the manufacturing plants. They're going to bring in prefabricated metal buildings so it won't take so long to finish the construction. He's also going to contact the two largest construction companies in the US to lock up all of their capacity so they can run the transmission cables. He said to tell you he would contract with the BNSF railroad to bring in the raw materials. He also said to tell you we need to work as quickly as possible."

"That's incredible. How in the world does he get things done so quickly?"

Dr. Heidelberg didn't say anything for several seconds, and had a tremendously sad look on his face. "What I'm about to tell you must stay between us. I need you to promise me."

"Sure, but I already have the highest level of security clearance there is, according to you and Larry."

"Yes, you do. But the full details of this are only known by a select group of people in the entire world. Do you remember hearing of the terrorist attack on the Keck Observatory?"

"Of course I do. It was horrible. Everyone was killed, and the observatory was completely destroyed if I remember correctly."

"You do remember correctly, though I doubt you've ever remembered anything incorrectly. Ten years ago Dr. Edwin Yates, who was the lead astronomer for the facility, spotted an anomaly far outside our solar system. It took him another year to identify what it was. He contacted Larry Sheldon shortly after he made the identification. They used the Hubble to boost the image to try to verify their findings, but they were unable to make a complete identification. The anomaly was about to reoccur, and they were all gathered to view it when the facility was destroyed and they were all killed."

A little exasperated Billy said, "For heaven's sake, just tell me what you're talking about."

"What they discovered was an Apollo-class asteroid. The asteroid is many times the size of the asteroid which caused the extinction of the dinosaurs. To put it in context it's roughly the size of the moon. We believe it's been passing far outside of our solar system for millions of years. Dr. Yates believed a large comet altered the asteroid's path, and it's going to intersect with the Earth's orbit. We've been tracking it ever since they verified its existence."

"Are you sure of your facts?"

"There had been some hope another event would cause it to divert enough to miss our solar system. We now know we have had a keyhole event, and the asteroid is going to strike the Earth. At its present course and speed, we have approximately two years before it reaches our solar system in 2012. Six weeks after it enters the solar system, it'll reach the Earth. When it does, it will mean the end of the Earth."

"How is it possible no one else has identified this threat?" Billy asked.

"We've been disabling any telescope powerful enough to spot the asteroid. We've been using the Arab terrorists as scapegoats, but it's actually been Larry Sheldon's operatives destroying them."

"What do you mean Larry's operatives? I know he's not who he seems, but how can he pull off activities like that without anyone knowing?"

"Larry Sheldon is definitely not what he seems. What I'm about to tell you is even more sensitive. He's also in charge of the Logos operations worldwide. The Logos are an ancient evangelical society which believes an event such as the asteroid will cause the end of the world. They have almost unlimited resources, and have representatives throughout the world. Larry Sheldon and I've spent years attempting to develop a plan to save the world from destruction as it was prophesized in their teachings."

"Then you're a member as well?"

"Yes, I am. I've been a member since I was an undergraduate at MIT."

"What have you and Larry Sheldon's teams worked out for a plan?"

"That's what Larry's comment in the note meant. We don't have a workable plan, and we're hoping you can come up with one. We've had even less luck developing a plan than we did trying to get the reactor to work."

"I'm overwhelmed with what you have just told me. Let me think on it overnight, and we'll talk again in the morning."

"No problem, I'm going to stay here and finish working on what you've laid out so far. I don't know whether we should bother laying the power cables, but we can talk about it in the morning."

"We haven't seen you in weeks," Mary said to him as he came through their front door. "I was beginning to wonder if you had disowned us."

"I'm sorry. Klaus Heidelberg and I've been working night and day, with just a nap here and there. I didn't realize it had been so long. How are you and Dad doing?"

"We're fine, but your dad still can't get over what Larry Sheldon is paying us. Rob and your dad bought the feed store in town, and they're having a ball running it."

"That's great. You and Dad have worked so hard all your lives. It's good to see you do some of the things you've always wanted to try. I've not been much help to you, but I promise what I'm working on is important."

"You've nothing to be ashamed of. We're both so proud of you. It's amazing what you've accomplished so far. You and Linda aren't even twenty-one yet, and you've already accomplished more than most people do in their entire lifetime. It should be us apologizing. We could have tried to understand you kids more. It's not that we didn't want to, we just couldn't grasp the enormity of your abilities."

Ben entered the kitchen. "Good to see you. What have you and Klaus been doing?"

"We got Dr. Heidelberg's reactor working, and we're now generating enough electricity to power the entire US."

"I knew you thought you could solve the problems with the reactor, but it didn't take long at all."

"I guess I got lucky and saw what the issues were when I first looked at the reactor."

He considered telling them about what Klaus Heidelberg had told him, and then decided not to. There was no need to cause them to panic about something there may be no way to prevent. They ate a great dinner, and caught up on what had been going on.

They continued talking until 9 P.M. "I'd better get busy and clean up the dishes," Mary said. "Why don't you take a nice hot shower and get some rest. If you've been working like you always do, you haven't had a decent night's sleep since we saw you last."

Billy was standing in the shower when he felt Linda in his mind.

I finally caught you in the shower, Linda said. *I was beginning to think the only time we were going to talk like this was when I was in the shower. What happened?*

He opened up his mind so she could see what Klaus Heidelberg had told him. She spent several seconds absorbing the events. When she was finished, she said, *Can this be true? I'm so afraid. Are we all going to die?*

I don't know for sure. What he shared with me has me concerned, but it's too early to declare we're all going to die. Klaus and Larry want me to devise some sort of a plan, but I haven't had a chance to consider what it might be yet. How have you been, young lady?

I've been working on what seems like a never-ending stream of germ warfare victims. The remnants of the waves of terrorists who got out of Iran continue to cause trouble. They seem to be everywhere, and they have access to some sophisticated technology to reengineer the viruses.

As he absorbed the thoughts from her mind, he saw some of the horrors she had been experiencing.

I'm so sorry, that was just horrible.

It's all right. I'm getting tougher, and someone has to do it. I see what you mean when you catch me in the shower, this is nice.

What are you thinking?

You know exactly what I'm thinking.

Yes, I do, and I wouldn't mind at all, but like you have been saying, we aren't ready yet. Besides, we have too much to do.

Yes, we do, but it doesn't make it any easier to wait.

No, it doesn't. How long will it be until you can come home?

I don't have any idea, but I do know it's going to be a year or more, Linda said.

Remember what I showed you. If I don't get a plan, we aren't going to have much more time than that. If it gets to the point where I know I can't come up with a plan, I would like to spend what time we have left together.

Tell me it's not going to come to that. It's not as if I don't want to spend the rest of my life with you. I just can't face the fact that everyone is going to die.

You know I'll try my best, but I don't know if anyone or anything can save us. It doesn't look promising at this point.

They spent a few minutes just sharing each other's thoughts. Finally, Linda said, *I can tell you're exhausted. So finish your shower and get some sleep. I love you, and one way or another we'll be together for whatever time we have left. I love you with all my heart, and good night.*

I love you even more.

He finished his shower and lay down to see if he could get some sleep. As he often did, he began to dream. As he dreamed, his mind was working through millions of possibilities.

His mind sorted through all of the various options. If the scenarios had been running through the world's largest supercomputers, it would have taken them years to sort through the data. By morning his mind had arrived at a solution he thought was their best chance of survival.

The next morning he entered their lab, and saw Klaus Heidelberg with his head resting on a workbench asleep. He tapped him on the shoulder, and said, "It's morning, wake up."

Klaus slowly raised his head off the workbench and asked, "Is it morning already?"

"Yes, it is. Did you spend all night sleeping on the bench?"

"I guess I did. I talked with Larry Sheldon and his team around midnight, and I was going to continue working. I laid my head down to rest for just a moment, and here we are."

"I didn't stir much myself last night," Billy said.

"We need to get to work on some sort of a plan. Larry Sheldon verified we have around twenty-one months before the asteroid reaches the edge of the solar system. Six weeks later, the Earth will cease to exist."

"I think I've formulated a plan," Billy said. "After I get it worked up in the computer, I would like you to review it. The plan depends on getting the antigravity concept up and running. After we get it working, I think we can build a series of large ships to save as many people as possible."

"That sounds like a pretty tall order."

"Of course it is, but the situation calls for an aggressive plan of some sort, doesn't it?"

"Of course it does, I just can't believe we can get it done in time. As soon as you get your plans together, we'll call Larry Sheldon and let him know what we are going to need."

19

IT TOOK BILLY almost nine weeks to develop his plans for the antigravity system and the initial plans for the ships. He was working on his CAD terminal when Klaus Heidelberg sat down beside him and asked, "How are you coming with the plans?"

"I think I have the initial designs done. I just transmitted a copy of the plans to Larry Sheldon, along with a tentative bill of materials. Let's go over to the communications building, so we can use their videoconferencing equipment to talk to Larry and his team."

When they reached the communications building, Larry Sheldon and his team were already on the video screen.

"I received your plans," Larry Sheldon said. "I have to tell you no one here understands what you've sent us."

"It's all right, we do, and I'm convinced the plans Billy has developed will work," Klaus Heidelberg said. "Do you think you can help us?"

"You know the answer to that question. You and I have spent the last ten years trying to get to this point. It has taken Billy what, a year and a half to solve what we couldn't figure out in ten?"

"That's why we took a chance and involved him. Isn't it?"

"If you can get me the materials to build one ship right

away, I think I can have the prototype built in a hundred and twenty days," Billy said. "It won't be a full-scale ship, but it'll be large enough to prove the concept."

"I've been stockpiling equipment and raw materials for the entire ten years we've been searching for an answer. I have everything on your list. It's only going to take me a couple of weeks to have the trains begin loading. It's only eight hours by train from Denver, so we should have it loaded and delivered to you by the end of the month."

"Great, we'll begin work on a smaller version of the fusion reactor. Now that we know how to get it to work, it'll be a simple process to scale them," Billy said. "I'm going to need two of the superconducting cable plants converted to manufacture sheets of the superconducting material. With the new process we've developed, the sheets will be stronger than titanium steel. The struts and the walls will be constructed from ceramic material, only they'll be blended to be a superinsulator instead of a conductor. We'll use the superconducting cables to run power from the central generators to the rest of the ship.

"I designed the outer hull so we can charge each plate to a different level of energy. The hull will provide a shield for the ship, as well as its means of propulsion. The fields will be capable of repelling or attracting any form of material, or energy, depending on the frequency and polarity we use."

"That's all in the plans you sent me?"

"Yes, it is."

"Good, once we have the prototype I'll have another request to make of you."

"What is it?"

"No need to bother you with it now. Just hurry and get the thing built. We don't have any time to spare."

"Okay, we're going to get to work. Give us a call if you need anything."

"You do the same. I'm coming down with the train, so I'll see you in a couple of weeks."

Billy and Klaus returned to the lab and called a meeting with the construction teams.

"Ladies and gentlemen, you did a great job assembling the fusion reactor," Klaus Heidelberg said. "I have a new task for you, and I need you to do whatever is necessary to ensure we finish in no more than three weeks."

The leader of the group was a brilliant young Stanford engineer named Nicholas Stavros. "What's the new task?" Stavros asked. "You know you can count on us to do whatever's necessary."

"I have the plans here for a smaller version of the fusion reactor your team assembled. Do you think your team can pull it off?"

Nicholas Stavros looked at his team of thirty-five of the brightest technicians in the world, grinned, and said, "You bet we can. What do you say, team?"

The room shook with their resounding, "Yes we can. Yes we can."

"There's your answer," Nicholas said.

Billy grinned and said, "You guys never cease to amaze me. Just let me know if you need anything. One other thing before we get started. I want you to build the reactor on skids so we can move it before we actually light it."

"Move it?" Nicholas Stavros asked.

"It's going to power a ship when it's done. We just don't have the ship yet."

"Cool, I'm looking forward to seeing the ship. If it's as neat as your other thoughts, it should be something to see."

"I promise you and your team will be some of the first to see it. In fact I'll want your team to finish out the inside of it."

The weeks passed quickly, and the team was almost

finished assembling the reactor. Klaus and Billy were at the station to meet the train bearing the equipment and Larry Sheldon.

"Good to see you," Billy said.

"It's good to see you too," Larry Sheldon said. "Klaus, how have you been feeling since I last saw you?"

"I'm afraid I'm not a young man anymore, but I don't feel too bad, I suppose."

"How old are you anyway? I've always wondered."

"Not that it matters, but I'll be a hundred thirteen in September."

"You're a hundred and thirteen years old, no way," Billy said. "I always thought you might be maybe eighty, but a hundred and thirteen never entered my mind."

"My entire family has been long lived, but I've already lived longer than I ever believed I would. Enough about me, have you brought our supplies with you?"

"Yes, I have and more. There are two more trains coming with another thousand men and women to help us with the construction."

"So that's why they built those new barracks last month?" Billy said.

"Yes, it is. This will bring our workforce to over seven thousand workers. I've also engaged every manufacturer in North and South America to help in the fabrication of the pieces we need. The South American plants will concentrate on manufacturing the ceramics. They have an extensive supply of the natural minerals we need, so I thought it would be easier to have it done there. We're going to run every air transport we can commandeer to bring the finished materials to us.

"I suppose you noticed we've taken over the municipal airport, and built new runways to accommodate the increased air traffic. We built twenty-six main runways and twenty-six cross-wind runways to enable us to land as many aircraft as possible. If that's not enough, we'll build more, but I believe they should be able to handle the traffic."

"I hadn't noticed, but I haven't been into Clayton in over six months," Billy said.

"You wouldn't recognize it, or anything around it," Larry Sheldon said. "We've pretty much surrounded the town with new construction. The entire facility probably covers twenty square miles by now."

"You're right, I wouldn't recognize it, but how are the townspeople holding up to all of this?" Klaus Heidelberg asked.

"From the reports I've been getting they have been supportive. The town is booming, and we've made a point to overpay for everything so they don't feel as bad about what's happening."

"I know my mom and dad still can't believe what you're paying them for using the farm," Billy said. "Let's get them started unloading this stuff. The team will have the reactor ready by Tuesday."

"They did work fast, didn't they? We've prebuilt the first airframe you designed. We have it on the last three flatcars. We will get it unloaded and start putting the skin on it. How are we supposed to join the ceramic plates together on the frame?"

"We built new welders that use ultrahigh voltages to fuse them together and bond them to the frame," Billy said.

"Great, we'll get started right away. How big an opening do we need to leave for installing the fusion reactor?"

"Let's see, the plates are twelve feet square, so two should be plenty."

"Okay then, I'll go and get them started."

"I'm going to spend the weekend with my parents if

you can spare me," Billy said. "I haven't said more than a few words to them in weeks."

"I think I'm going to try and get some extra rest myself," Klaus Heidelberg said. "I've been extremely tired the last week or so. I guess I'm just getting old."

Billy and Klaus attempted to unwind for the weekend in their own ways, but come Tuesday morning they were both back and ready to go to work.

As they walked into the gigantic new hangar where Larry Sheldon and their teams had been working, they were shocked to see them welding the last two plates into place.

Larry Sheldon spotted them as they were walking across the hangar floor to the ship. "How are you two? Did you both get some rest?"

"Yes, we did," Klaus Heidelberg said.

"I can't believe how much the teams have accomplished in such a short time," Billy said.

"It's amazing, but you've got to remember, we prebuilt most of the ship. I hope we can come up with a process that will allow us to mass produce the ships if they work."

"I haven't seen anything Billy designed not work," Klaus Heidelberg said. "So I have to believe this will as well."

"Let's go in and see how they're coming," Billy said.

They walked up the gangway extending from the door in the left front side of the ship. It was made of the same material as the rest of the ship, and engineered to extend and retract from the ship.

The ship was 250 feet long, with a diameter of 60 feet, and shaped like an old-style dirigible. It was resting in several half circles of metal to hold it up off the hangar floor. Its hull had a dull semimetallic gray look to it.

When they entered the control center, they noticed the ship wasn't completed on the inside. They had finished the three deck levels for the length of the ship, but they had only installed the bulkheads in the front of the ship. When they looked through the hatch leading to the back of the ship, they could see all the way to the far end. They saw the flashes from the men welding the last hull plate into place, and then the ship was dark except for the emergency lights every fifty feet.

They had installed the main lights throughout the ship, so Billy walked to the control console and turned on the main cabin lights. He could now see to the far end of the ship, but it was nothing but an empty shell. They walked through the bulkhead toward the rear of the ship. It was two hundred feet of empty space, and as they walked back to the ladder to the deck below, they could hear their footsteps echo throughout the ship.

Billy led them down two flights of stairs to the bottom deck. When they reached the bottom deck, they saw the familiar shape of the reactor. The power cables were running in all directions from the power center. When they were finished the cables would be under the deck, but right now, they were everywhere.

The group stepped over the cables as they walked around the reactor looking it over. The crew had used the high temperature welders to bond the skid-mounted reactor to the ship's deck, and the welds looked almost glassy. As he completed the circle around the reactor, Billy met Nicholas Stavros. "You and your crew have done an outstanding job."

"Thanks. We've just finished hooking up all of the power leads."

"Are you finished?" Billy asked.

"So far we only have the reactor and the equipment for the control room installed, so we still have a few things left to do."

"Have you installed all of the power leads for the hull plates?"

"Yes, we have, and we've tested all of the circuits to make sure we have good connections. We've also installed the hatches and ramps in the front and rear areas."

"Excellent. I think we'll go up and check out the controls. Would you like to accompany us?"

"Sure, I'm sending most of the team back to the barracks to get some sleep. We've been working twenty-hour days for the entire time. I'll keep a few of them, in case you want to power up the reactor."

"If your crew is too tired I'll understand."

"They won't want to miss anything. We can sleep anytime."

Satisfied with the reactor, they retraced their steps to the control center. The bridge was still bare except for the main control consoles and eight chairs. All of the chairs were on pedestals welded into the deck plates. There were two in front of the main console, and three on either side along the wall.

Billy sat down in the left-hand pilot's chair, and ran through a systems diagnostic test. After about twenty minutes, he looked up and declared, "Everything checks out. Would you please initiate a power-up sequence on the ship's reactor system?"

"Will do," Nicolas Stavros said. "Reactor one team initiate a five second reactor start."

"Reactor start sequence initiated."

Billy watched as the power gauges jumped to life. "We have full power. Please have your team remove the outside power cables, and when they are done, you might as well send them to get some sleep."

Ten minutes later Billy turned to Nicolas Stavros and said, "I'm going to close the hatches, and see if this thing will move. Please radio the hangar support team to open the main hangar doors, and evacuate the building just in case."

"We're ready," Nicolas Stavros said.

Billy tapped the pilot's control screen to power on the hull. The hull immediately received the voltage from the reactor, which was set to the lowest possible power level. Even at that level, the field had the energy to lift the ship from the cradles where it was resting. It was now hovering three feet above the cradles.

He checked the gauges, and verified the ship was hovering. Then he turned on the front cameras so they could see where they were going. The front of the ship seemed to disappear in front of their eyes. Nicholas Stavros blurted out a question.

"What's happened to the front of the ship?"

"The front is still there, it's a virtual reality holographic projection that makes it seem like the front is gone," Billy said. "I'm going to turn on the rest of the cameras so we can see in all directions."

He tapped the screen three more times to turn on the rest of the cameras. The views from the top, bottom, and rear of the ship sprung to life on three separate displays on the console. He glanced at each one to make sure the ship was not drifting.

When he was satisfied the ship was stable, he raised the power level to the rear of the ship. The ship began to move forward on its first journey.

The ship moved slowly through the hangar doors, and out onto the taxiway alongside of the hangar. Once it was about a hundred feet from the hangar, he brought it to a halt.

"What are you doing?" Klaus Heidelberg asked.

"I want to take the ship for a test flight, but I want to see if anyone would like to get off the ship before I do," Billy said. "I'm confident it's safe, but you can never know for sure."

All of them quickly agreed they wouldn't miss it for the world.

"Okay then, if you'll all take a seat, we'll get started."

He gave them a minute or so to get settled in. "If all of you are ready, we'll go in just a moment."

He turned to Larry Sheldon and said, "Would you please call the tower, and see if they will clear us for a test flight?"

Larry Sheldon tapped the console to activate the radio. "Tower, this is the . . . what should we call the ship?"

"Let's call it *Imagination*," Billy said.

"Why that name?"

"I know why," Klaus Heidelberg said. "Don't I, Billy?"

"I would guess you do. One of Klaus's closest friends, Albert Einstein, once said, 'Imagination is more important than knowledge.' "

"I thought so, and I think it's a fine name for our first test ship."

Satisfied they were ready, Larry Sheldon contacted the tower, "Tower, this is the *Imagination* ready for takeoff. We're at hangar X-One, and request clearance to climb directly to fifteen hundred feet. We'll hover in place for two minutes, and then we'll request further clearance."

"Did you say, 'hover in place'?"

"Roger that, Tower."

"Are you in a helicopter, or a balloon?"

"Neither, Tower. We're in an experimental craft."

"*Imagination*, you're cleared for takeoff and to hover at fifteen hundred feet. Call the tower for clearance before proceeding from your position."

"Thank you, Tower, understood."

Billy touched the screen to drag the power level upward ever so slightly to apply more power to the bottom plates. The ship immediately began to ascend. He again had only applied a small amount of power. The ship was climbing straight up at a speed of fifteen feet per second. As it approached 1500 feet, Billy slowed the ascent, and then brought it to a stop at exactly 1500 feet.

Billy had never seen Clayton from the air, and even if he had, he wouldn't have recognized the sight below him. There were buildings, roads, houses, runways, etc. for a twenty-mile circle around what was once a sleepy New Mexico town.

He glanced at the screen that showed the view directly below them. The group of six people, who followed them outside, had quickly grown to almost a thousand people. As Billy continued to look, he could see people running toward them by the hundreds.

"It sure didn't take long for the word to get out, did it?" Larry Sheldon said.

"It sure didn't," Billy said. "I guess that takes care of the need to keep it a secret, doesn't it?"

"We don't have time to worry about it. We have less than twenty months left," Larry Sheldon said. "Let's try her out."

"Just take it slow, we haven't hooked up the flight control computers," Nicolas Stavros said. "We installed them, but they aren't patched into the flight controls yet. So you're going to have to fly it manually."

"Thanks, I'll take it easy," Billy said. "Call the tower, and tell them we'll be leaving the area headed west."

"Tower, this is the *Imagination,* and we require clearance for a departure to the west," Larry Sheldon said.

"*Imagination,* hold your position. I'll have to check with command for authorization."

"Tower, this is Larry Sheldon, authorization code Lima Foxtrot, Lima 96587. I require clearance to the west. Clear all traffic to the west until further notice."

The radio was silent for several seconds, and then the tower responded. "Mr. Sheldon, sorry for the delay. We've diverted all traffic to the west, and you're cleared to go."

"Okay, we're good to go."

"Someday you'll have to tell me exactly what you do," Billy said.

"Yeah, someday I will."

Billy applied additional power to the bottom and rear plates to begin their test flight. He only applied a tiny fraction of the available power, but they were climbing at 35,000 feet a minute, and their forward speed was just over 2200 mph. As they ascended, there was no noise in the ship whatsoever. They were all silently watching the landscape rush by at incredible speed.

He let the ship continue on course and speed for four minutes. At the four-minute mark, he brought the ship back to a hover. They were just below the boundary of the stratosphere and the mesosphere, at an altitude of 141,500 feet.

"You're now officially astronauts," Larry Sheldon said. "I have to believe we're the first group to claim the honor this easily. How fast were we going?"

"We had a forward speed of just over twenty-two hundred mph, and we were climbing at thirty-five thousand feet a minute," Billy said.

"How much of the available power were you using?"

"It wasn't even registering on the gauge, so it had to be less than one tenth of a percent."

"That's incredible! How fast do you think this thing can go?"

"It's hard to say. As it approaches the speed of light, the power requirements go completely off the scale. That said, I believe we should be able to approach fifty to fifty-five percent of the speed of light."

"Unbelievable, but what's next?" Larry Sheldon asked. "While this is simply incredible, we still don't have a plan to save the human race. Will this allow us to journey into space to escape the asteroid?"

"I'm sure the ship is capable of space travel. How much oxygen do we have on board?"

"We filled the tanks with enough for fifty people for ten days," Nicolas Stavros said.

"Since there are only eight of us, we should have plenty for a short trip."

"What do you have in mind for a short trip?" Larry Sheldon asked.

"Let's just see how it goes. Then we'll decide how far we go."

He touched the screen to start the ship on its way. This time he set the power to the first mark, or one tenth of a percent power. The ship accelerated much quicker this time, and in less than a minute, it had reached full speed for the power level. He checked their speed. The monitor's readout was capable of measuring speeds up to ten thousand mph, but it was completely off the scale.

Billy swiveled his chair around and told the group, "I'm going to take us around the moon for our first voyage. The moon happens to be at perigee, so it's at just over four hundred thousand kilometers or roughly two hundred fifty-one thousand miles."

During the ten minutes it took him to recalibrate the system, they had moved well out of the atmosphere. The Earth was rapidly shrinking in their rear camera view. He finished the recalibration, looked at the speed showing on the monitor, and announced, "We're going fifty-two thousand miles per hour. It'll take us about four hours to reach the moon."

"That can't be right," Klaus Heidelberg said. "I haven't experienced any sense of motion at all."

"I wasn't sure before, but as I suspected, the antigravity field is not only propelling us, it's also acting as an inertial dampening field," Billy said.

Billy looked over at Nicholas Stavros and asked, "Would you mind taking a walk with me? I want to check the ship out to see how it's holding up."

"Sure, let's go."

They ended their inspection at the reactor.

"Everything looks great," Billy said. "You and your men did an incredible job."

They returned to the bridge to check on their progress. When Billy checked their position, he saw they were coming up on the halfway point of their first trip.

They sat marveling at the grandeur of space as the moon continued to grow in size as they approached.

While they were waiting, Nicolas Stavros connected the navigation computer to the flight control system. The navigation computer hadn't been fully programmed yet, but Billy added a couple of subroutines so it would be able to do some rudimentary preprogrammed commands. He programmed it to slow the ship as it approached the moon, and place it in orbit.

He told the group, "Please return to your seats, we're almost there."

The ship slowed and assumed an elliptical orbit around the moon. As they started around the backside of the moon, he focused his attention on the bottom cameras. None of the others could see the bottom view, but they were already completely enthralled with the view in front of the ship.

"I always wanted to be an astronaut, but they stopped space exploration and I never had the opportunity," Nicolas Stavros said.

"I can appreciate your disappointment," Larry Sheldon said. "I'm the one who had to make the decision to stop the space program. After we finally stabilized Iraq and Afghanistan, we didn't have enough resources left to restart the programs. Once we verified the threat from the asteroid, I've focused every resource we had left on trying to solve the problem. The ship we're in may actually make all of the sacrifices worth it."

"Asteroid? What are you talking about?" Nicolas Stavros asked.

Larry Sheldon hesitated for a few seconds and then responded, "There's an asteroid which will strike the Earth in less than nineteen months from now."

"How big is it?"

"It's just a little larger than the moon."

"How much damage are you expecting?"

"There won't be damage; there will be the total destruction of the Earth."

"That can't be true. I haven't heard anything about any of this on the news."

"Nor will you, if I have anything to say about it. Were this to get out, chaos would break out all over the world. The resulting panic could kill millions and serve no purpose. We're going to keep this quiet until we have some sort of story to tell the world."

There was complete silence in the cabin for several minutes, as everyone was thinking over Larry's words. While everyone was thinking, Billy was scanning the moonscape as it rushed by. As they came around to the front side of the moon for the first time, he spotted the wreckage of the Goddard moon mission.

Robert Goddard was one of the early rocket scientists, and they had named the first major attempt to settle the moon after him. It had been a multinational mission, and had the overly ambitious goal of establishing the first moon base.

The mission had crash-landed on the moon, and they lost most of their supplies. When the Iranian terrorists destroyed the NASA facility, they had not been able to resupply the team before the astronauts all perished.

President McAllister had attempted to get the Russians or the Chinese to launch a mission to save the team. The Russians were going to attempt an emergency mission, but the Iranians had coordinated with the Chechen rebels to destroy their space capabilities. Just before the Russians were to launch the rescue mission, they hit their launch facility with a tactical nuclear weapon. They didn't have any delivery system for the weapon, so they put it in a truck and drove it through the front gate.

It wasn't a particularly large weapon, but the results were what they had hoped. The entire facility was turned into a radioactive wasteland, and shortly afterward the Russians abandoned it permanently.

The Goddard crew managed to hold out for over a year before the last one died from lack of oxygen. Billy remembered the memorial services, even though he was only in grade school at the time.

There had been a tremendous backlash in America over the multiple attacks. President McAllister wiped out the Iranians the next day, with a series of neutron bomb–tipped missiles ending the threat. At the same time he coordinated a joint strike with the Russians to remove the Chechen threat.

Billy drew a deep breath and quietly wiped a tear from his eye.

"We need to get back or we're going to end up worse than they did," Klaus Heidelberg said.

"You're right, but what a waste of lives."

Billy reprogrammed the computer for the return trip and hit enter to start the ship back.

As they descended to the airstrip, the radio came alive.

"Tower to *Imagination,* please come in. It's good to have you back. We were worried you had trouble. You're cleared to land at your discretion."

Billy landed the ship and returned it to the landing bay. He brought it to a stop in the massive hangar, hovering six feet from the floor. He opened the front hatch and extended the gangway to the hangar floor.

The entire team who had assembled the *Imagination* was waiting at the foot of the gangway. They greeted them with cheering as they walked down the gangway. "Ladies and gentleman, you've built a real ship here," Nicolas Stavros said. "We've just been to the moon and back."

There was a moment of stunned silence from the crowd.

"If all of you will please gather over here in front of the ship I will try to explain," Larry Sheldon said. "What Nicholas just told you must stay a secret. We'll be continuing with the construction of ships, and each of you'll have your own team to lead. We're going to be attempting a construction project bigger than anything the world has ever seen. We'll all need to work pretty much night and day for the duration."

Stewart Hennessey, the lead electrician of the crew asked, "What's the hurry? We've already been working day and night. We're all looking forward to some time off."

"What I'm about to tell all of you has to stay a secret for the duration of the project. The urgency is that in just under eighteen months, an asteroid will destroy the Earth. We must use the time we have left to build as many ships as possible. Because the only people who are going to survive will be on board the ships we build."

Larry Sheldon waited for almost a minute for someone to make a comment. But everyone was in shock. Finally Larry said, "I know all of you are going to do your best, because that's why you are here. I want you all to take the rest of the day and enjoy your success. Tomorrow you'll receive the plans for your ships and meet your crews."

20

AFTER EVERYONE HAD left Larry Sheldon took one of the helicopters and flew to Glen Eyrie. The Logos High Council was in session, and he wanted to brief them in person.

When he arrived, he took the elevator down to the cavern below the castle. When he stepped off the elevator, he was once again awestruck, as he had been every time he had entered the cavern.

The cavern was immense. It covered an area equal to two city blocks and the ceiling was 179 feet below the surface. In the center of the cavern was the ziggurat where the council held their meetings. It was an exact copy of the Etemenanki of ancient Babylon. The ziggurat was seven levels high, and the meeting was taking place on the top level. The council was already in session, and they were sitting at a round table located in the exact center of the top level.

There were seven members of the council, and above their heads, the roof of the cavern looked like the night sky. It was a night sky, but not of this world. It was a perfect representation of the sky above the Theos home world as it was a hundred thousand years ago. Tens of thousands of years ago the original members of the Logos copied the scene from one of Adamartoni's texts, which predated the Bible.

Larry Sheldon opened a section of the table, walked into the center, and said, "As it was foretold, the chosen ones have appeared to lead us to safety and a new life. Billy has already solved our power problems, and today we took a test flight to the moon in his prototype ship."

The statement set off a buzz of conversation around the table. Clayton Edwards was the current chairman of the council and he called for quiet.

"So Billy was able to solve Klaus's problem with the reactor?"

"He was. An even more exciting development was his development of antigravity to power the ships. That's what enabled us to travel to the moon and back in a matter of hours."

"Hours? How fast can it go?"

"We were only using a fraction of the available power, and we were able to attain fifty-two thousand mph."

"Impossible. You would've been crushed by the acceleration."

"The ship's antigravity fields also act as inertial dampeners."

"You mean like what they used to talk about in science-fiction stories?"

"Just like that, only these actually exist. It effectively cancels out any feeling of acceleration."

"Are you going to be able to build enough of these ships to save everyone?"

"It's too early to tell exactly how many we'll be able to build, but there's no way we'll be able to save everyone. We would have had to start construction a decade ago."

"We'll contact President McAllister and brief him," Chairman Edwards said. "I'll work with him to develop a plan to select the people, and to ensure as many of the Logos are selected as possible. I suppose we owe Dr. Evans a debt of gratitude even though he was trying to steal from us."

"If it hadn't happened Billy wouldn't be who he is, and neither would Linda. I still believe God intervened and caused the accident. The events we're living are definitely following the ancient texts."

"I know we've asked you to do many things over the last few years, and that some of them have caused you great personal pain. But I must ask you to continue to do whatever is necessary to ensure Billy's plans are carried out."

"I've never questioned the council's orders, and I'll continue to do whatever is necessary to ensure the survival of the human race," Larry Sheldon said.

"You should be getting back. I need you to continue briefing us on a weekly basis, and I'll use our full resources to ensure your needs are met."

BACK IN NEW Mexico, Billy and Klaus sat down on a bench beside the *Imagination* to talk for a few minutes. "There's something I need to tell you," Klaus Heidelberg said.

"Sure, what is it?" Billy said.

"I'm dying."

"You're what?"

"I said I'm dying. I have at the most six months left."

"When did you find out?"

"A couple of weeks ago. I didn't want to tell you until we completed our first ship. I was hoping we would finish before I got too sick to work."

"What's wrong with you?"

"I have a bad heart. I've had several bypass operations, and they tell me I can't survive another. After I passed a hundred, I thought I was the one who would live forever. I guess no one wants to admit they're mortal."

"I'm so sorry. I wish you had told me sooner."

"There's no need to be sorry, my young friend. You've more than enough to worry about. I believe if the human race has any chance of survival, you and Linda Lou are that hope. I just wish I could have hung around a few more years to help the two of you get through this."

"I don't know what to say."

"There isn't anything you need to say. I've lived over a hundred years, and if it's my time, I've lived a full life. Everyone I have ever loved has been dead for many years. So don't worry about me.

"That's enough about that, I'll work as long as I can, but I don't think it's going to be much longer. I've noticed the last couple of weeks I don't have any real energy anymore."

They talked for a few more minutes, and then they each went back to their rooms. Billy had been staying in the facility for the last six months. He had been working long hours, so he had taken a room at the facility so he wouldn't bother his parents.

He showered and flopped on the bed to relax for a moment before trying to go to sleep. He almost immediately felt Linda's mind in his.

What are you up to? Billy asked.

I was about to ask you the same thing.

I guess this time is because of me. We still can't connect without one of us having some event first. Can we?

No, not yet, but I know we will someday. So what've you been up to?

He opened his mind so she could experience their test flight and the trip to the moon. As the images of the trip flashed into her mind she felt Billy's sadness.

It's too bad about the astronauts, but they understood the risks when they signed up.

I know they did, but that's not what I'm sad about.

She touched his mind again to see what was making him so incredibly sad.

I'm so sorry. I know you've grown close to Klaus. If you would like, I can have him checked out up here?

He said he's been looked at by the doctors at Walter Reed. They performed his last two bypass operations, and they're sure he can't survive another one. Do you think your group can give him a chance?

I think so. In between working on the various engineered diseases the world's terrorist organizations have been throwing at us, I've been working with the genetic engineering group. We've developed a new technique to clone organs from mature stem cells we harvest from the patient. Using this technique, we've solved the problem of organ rejection.

That's great. I'll have Klaus there tomorrow by noon. How long does it take to grow an organ?

We have it down to around six months.

I don't know if Klaus can last that long. He sure doesn't look good. I think they gave him six months to live a while back.

You get him up here right away, and we'll do everything we can for him.

They shared a few moments together, and then Linda said, *I have a surgery at four o'clock in the morning, and I need to get some rest.*

Good night, sweetie. I love you, and I miss you.

I love you too. We'll be together before too much longer.

The next morning Billy was knocking on Klaus's door before he even had a chance to get out of bed for the day.

"What in the world has got you up this early?"

"Pack a bag. You're going to the Mayo Clinic this morning. Linda has a group standing by to examine you, and begin cloning a new heart for you."

"Why are you babbling on about a new heart? That isn't possible."

"Yes, it is. They've developed a new technique to utilize mature stem cells from your body to grow any organ they want. Now get packed. I'll be back in about an hour."

He hurried across the base to Larry Sheldon's office so he could explain what was going on. "I'll have a medevac aircraft ready in thirty minutes," Larry Sheldon said.

Billy was going to fly out with Klaus, but Klaus told him, "You don't need to hold my hand to the hospital. You need to stay here and get the teams moving on the ships. I was thinking last night, and you need to scale up the ships some more. We're not going to be able to produce enough of the smaller ships. Besides, they wouldn't be able to carry enough provisions for our journey."

After Klaus's plane was gone, Billy hurried back to their lab and began work on a new ship design. He worked day and night for the next six weeks while he attempted to adapt the ship's design to a larger scale.

While he was working on the new designs, the team completed the *Imagination*. It was capable of supporting a crew of 150, and could carry enough provisions for a yearlong journey. Billy had originally intended to change the scale of the *Imagination* to make the larger ships. When he studied the larger ships' design, he realized the original design didn't scale well. He redesigned the ship so they could use the same construction techniques used to build the large oceangoing passenger liners. Unlike a ship with a keel, he designed them with a flat bottom. The flat bottom would allow them to be built on the ground without any support underneath.

He designed them to have amenities similar to those found on a first-class cruise ship. He had no idea how long they were going to be on board the ships, so he wanted to make sure they have everything they would need.

The ships would have fifteen levels. The top three levels would not have any walls, except the outer hull. The top levels were going to contain buildings, parks, schools, etc., which were going to be as realistic as possible.

The ceilings on these levels would have environmental systems, which could simulate day and night, as well as mimic the four seasons. The areas would even be able to simulate rain, snow, etc.

He knew some people would question why he didn't build them to hold as many people as possible. But he knew if they were going to survive for an extended length of time, they would need more than the bare necessities.

The ships would be just over 270 feet high, or roughly equal to a twenty-seven-story building. They would be a mile wide and two miles long. The dimensions would be completely out of the question for any normally powered vessel, but size wasn't an issue due to their new propulsion systems. The antigravity systems could lift the ship's weight with no problem at all. There wouldn't be any differing stress points on the hull to cause it to buckle because the hull itself provided the lift and the propulsion.

When Billy finished, he saved the plans on the main computer and walked across the street to Larry Sheldon's apartment.

"I just finished the plans and stored them on the server," Billy said.

"That's great, I was beginning to worry," Larry Sheldon said. "We're running out of time. I don't know how many ships we can complete in the time we have left, but we have almost fifty thousand construction workers ready to begin. We haven't totally wasted the six weeks. We've received and stockpiled an immense amount of materials and are receiving daily shipments of the hull and deck plates. The superconducting cable plants are running at full capacity, and have already produced enough cable to build several ships. I think we have enough capacity and time to build around a thousand ships."

"A thousand ships! That's great."

"It is, but it won't allow us to save a large percentage of the US population."

"I believe fully loaded the ships can carry around sixty-three thousand people each," Billy said. "If we have a thousand ships, we can save around sixty-three million people. That leaves two hundred thirty-five million people we can't save in the United States alone."

"I know, but it's a lot better than losing the entire population," Larry Sheldon said. "I'm also going to send your plans for the two classes of the ships to the other governments of the world. I'm not sure how many of them will be able to use them, but we have to give as many people a chance as we can."

"How are we going to select who gets saved?"

"We're still working on the plan, but I believe we'll hand select the first fifty thousand people for needed skills. After we select the first group, I believe there will be a national lottery to select the rest. I foresee the selection process, and getting everyone on board the ships, being a nightmare. We'll have to deal with all of that in due time, but right now we need to get the ships built. Have you heard any news on Klaus?"

"I haven't. But I'm going to try and talk with Linda tonight."

"Let me know how he's doing. I've known him most of my adult life, and I don't know what I would do without his wisdom."

"I know. I haven't known him nearly as long as you have, but I miss him too. I'll let you know if I find out anything new."

After he left, Larry was contemplating how Billy and Linda would deal with the reality of what had caused them to be what they were. He thought to himself, *I'll deal with it when I have to.*

Billy took a quick shower and had just laid down. *Linda Lou, are you there?*

Yes, I am. I just went to bed myself. Klaus is doing as well as can be expected at this point. We have him on complete bed rest, but I don't know if we're going to be able to keep him alive for another four and a half months. I don't think his heart is going to last. We've given him every treatment we can think of, but nothing seems to help.

I'm sorry to hear it, but I know you'll do the best you can for him. I've finished the plans for the ships, and we begin construction tomorrow.

That's great. How are you going to build enough ships to save everyone?

Larry and I were just discussing that. At best we're only going to be able to save around sixty-three million people.

What's going to happen to the rest of the people?

Billy didn't answer, but Linda saw the answer in his mind.

All of those people are going to die, aren't they?

I'm afraid so. We can't figure out how to go any faster. I just wish we could have started years earlier. We might have saved everybody. We're going to send the plans to every government in the world so they can start their own building programs. But I don't know how many of the governments can or will do anything. I do know Larry can be persuasive when he wants to be.

How soon do you intend to make the news available to the general population, and how do you think they are going to react?

We're trying to keep it a secret as long as possible. If we're successful, we'll make a general announcement of our plans ninety days before we must leave. We'll need to leave Earth no later than six hours before projected impact. With that amount of a head start, we'll be able to reach a position outside of the asteroid's path.

I believe once the news is out, there will be a period of a week or two where people don't believe it. After that, I believe it will get progressively worse. At first there will probably be riots, and panic. Sometime after the riots begin, people will try to rush the staging areas for the ships. They're going to want to force their way onto the ships. Once it begins, it's going to become truly awful. We'll have military units stationed to prevent the crowds from reaching the ships, but I don't know whether they will be able to stomach killing friends and family.

It can't get that bad, can it? This is the twenty-first century; we're more civilized than that.

You've read as much history as I have, and you know how fragile civilization is. It hasn't taken events nearly as serious as this to cause widespread riots and panic. I don't know for sure how bad it's going to be, but I believe it's going to be worse than anything anyone has experienced before.

I miss you, but I don't see how I can abandon Dr. Robbins and the team. When the time comes, can you make sure I can bring our staff?

If you'll give me a count, I'll make sure we allocate room for them on our ship. Larry Sheldon and I've talked, and not only are we going to include the selected best and brightest on our ship, we are going to bring their families. We're also going to ensure the original population of Clayton has a spot as well. I'll make sure our parents are on board our ship, so you don't need to worry. I miss you so much. I know we have agreed to wait until we have this worked out before we start thinking about us, but it sure is getting difficult.

I know, it's more difficult every day, but we have to finish

*what we've started. I'm completely exhausted, and I need
to get some rest. I love you. We'll talk again very soon.*

Good night sweetie, I love you too.

THE NEXT DAY Billy and Larry Sheldon met with
Nicholas Stavros and his team. "It's good to see all of you
again," Billy said. "I've finished the plans for the bulk of the
ships we're going to be building. I thought about it some
more last night, and I'll be working on a few more ship designs for you to manufacture. I'm going to prepare the design for water tankers, fuel ships, and a few specialty ships."

He looked straight at Nicholas Stavros and said, "I'll
be bringing you the design for our flagship. I'm going to
design it last, and when I finish I'll want you and two of
your best teams to concentrate on it."

"We've all been talking, and is there going to be room
on the ships for our teams and their families?" Nicholas
Stavros asked.

"Absolutely, in fact we're going to begin relocating
them to the facility," Larry Sheldon said. "I want to have
them all in place within the next ninety days. We want to
make sure you can focus on your work without worrying
about your families. We've also searched all of your family trees, and have identified all of your relatives so they
can be included. In addition, you can each name up to one
hundred friends to accompany us. I hope this helps set
your minds at ease, and it's the best we can do. If anyone
has any other concerns please let me know."

The last plans Billy had worked on were for the flagship,
and he had decided it needed some extras. He doubled
the size of the ship. It would be 540 feet high, two miles
wide, and four miles long. The prototype had been roughly
the shape of a dirigible, but this design looked an awful lot
like one of the original nuclear submarines.

It had the same rounded bow and stern as the submarines, though this one would have no need to cut through the water, or even the air. Other than the start of their voyage, the ship would spend the rest of its life in space.

Billy wanted to ensure the ship was capable of meeting their needs. So he designed it to have four separate reactors to ensure it would have almost unlimited power. Not only were there four reactors, they each would have fully five times more capacity than the original design.

The ship would also contain Petawatt lasers mounted every three hundred feet all along the sides of the ship. The lasers would be able to cover every possible angle of approach to the massive ship.

As an afterthought, he added four massively powerful magnetic field emitters to the front of the ship. Like the plates of the ship, they were capable of emitting extremely powerful magnetic fields. However, unlike the plates, they could emit highly focused magnetic fields. He designed them to be able to focus the beams in a range from as small as the size of a dinner plate, to as large as five miles wide. He hadn't finished his thoughts on how he was going to utilize them, but he felt an overwhelming need to have them installed in the ship.

When he finished the last of the design details, he called Larry Sheldon.

"I've finished the flagship's design. I've added several additional features to the ship. It'll be considerably larger than the other ships, which will allow me enough room to continue my research while we travel. The ship is also capable of carrying at least one hundred and thirty thousand people in relative comfort. Do you think we can make sure our handpicked people can be scheduled to be on board?"

"I'm creating all of the schedules and plans for the entire evacuation, and I can make sure whatever we need done happens."

"Great, can I still use Nicholas Stavros to head up the construction teams?"

"Absolutely. He called me yesterday checking to see when we were going to need him. His crew should be finishing the ship they're working on by tomorrow. That makes the second one they have managed to complete since we started."

"Great, I uploaded the plans to a separate folder on the design server; it's in a protected folder called Flagship. The password to get into the folder is XA124GB6. I'm going to take some time and work on some additional ideas for equipment I think we're going to need. If you need me I'll be in the lab, but I probably won't see you for a while. I'm going to need several days to complete the rest of my plans."

"No problem, we'll get started, and I'll make sure no one bothers you. If you wouldn't mind, check in from time to time, so I can keep you updated. Otherwise, I won't call you unless there is an emergency. I do have to ask, what's so important that you want to isolate yourself right now? You know we only have thirteen months before we have to leave."

"I know. I'd explain, but I'm not sure myself."

21

WHILE BILLY WAS secluded in his lab, Nicholas Stavros and the crew worked at a frantic pace to complete the ship. Larry Sheldon was true to his word and only contacted him twice in the weeks he was away to answer questions they had about the ship's design.

Linda had continued to work with Dr. Robbins as they tried to deal with the influx of diseased victims from terrorist attacks.

She had taken Klaus Heidelberg as her personal patient and was helping the stem cell research group grow him a new heart. He had been at the Mayo for eight weeks when his health hit bottom.

She received a call from the ICU at three-thirty in the morning. The doctor on duty had just resuscitated Klaus Heidelberg and was struggling to keep him alive. Linda got dressed and took a cab to the hospital.

When she arrived, she found him in a crisis. He was still alive, but after she examined him, she knew he wasn't going to live more than another forty-eight hours.

She went to her lab and began work on an idea that had come to her as she was traveling to the hospital. There had been many versions of artificial hearts since the first transplant in 1982, but none of them had proved to be reliable enough for more than a short-term assist.

She knew they would have a new heart for him in four

months, but it wouldn't matter if she couldn't keep him alive until it was ready.

She considered doing another angioplasty to try to increase the blood flow to his heart. The problem was his heart was so enlarged, that even if his arteries were completely open it still couldn't pump enough blood.

She knew Billy had perfected his superconducting ceramic materials and was able to cause them to attract or repel virtually any material, and that had given her an idea.

She had the staff bring a portable magnetic imaging unit to the ICU to do a detailed map of Klaus's heart. When they finished, she had them e-mail Billy a copy of their work.

She sat down at her desk and forced herself to relax so she could contact Billy.

Is that you? Billy asked.

Of course it is. How many people talk directly to your mind?

Well, that would be one, of course. How are you?

I'm fine, but Klaus is in bad shape.

He looked into her mind and saw how badly he was doing.

Isn't there anything else you can try?

That's why I'm bothering you. I have some thoughts on how we might be able to help him on a temporary basis.

She let him see her thoughts on the ceramic container.

I can make that. I'll construct it so you can recharge the power capacitor through the skin. It will be relatively simple to engineer it to compress the heart. Show me exactly how the compression sequence needs to work to cause the blood flow you need.

She painted the image in his mind.

That'll be easy enough to do. I'll begin work on it this morning, and I should have it to you late tonight. Will that be quick enough?

It will have to be. Thank you so much, now get to work.
Will do; love you.

He moved to his CAD/CAM computer and copied Linda's design into it. When he finished, he punched run, and the automated lathes began to work. The device wasn't very big so it only took a couple of hours to produce. While the lathes were working, he called Nicholas Stavros and got him to assemble the microprocessor and the capacitors he needed.

While they were working on the device, he wrote the programs to run the microprocessor. By late afternoon, they met in his lab to assemble the unit. While Nicholas assembled the unit, Billy constructed a magnetic transfer device that would charge the capacitors through Klaus's chest so there would be no batteries and no wires.

All Linda would have to do was snap it into place around Klaus's heart. As soon as they charged the device the first time, it would immediately start functioning.

It took them until 10 P.M. to finish the device. They called Larry Sheldon to pick up the device, and he took it to the airstrip where he had the *Imagination* waiting. He piloted the ship himself, and in less than an hour, he was at the Mayo Clinic.

The hospital had a helicopter pad on the roof, but the ship was much too large to land there. He brought it to a stop about five feet above the pad, opened the door, and extended the gangway down to the roof. As he walked down the ramp with the briefcase containing the device, Linda came out the door to the roof. She waved to him. "Thank you so much for bringing it yourself," Linda said. "Is Billy with you?"

"No, but he sure wanted to come. I wouldn't let him. I made him lie down and get some sleep. I need him rested enough to work on some automated construction devices for me. We're not going to meet our goal of a thousand ships if we can't figure out how to build them faster. Once he scaled up the designs, we have found we don't have the right equipment to build them. Nicholas Stavros's crew is the only one that has completed more than one ship. But enough about our problems. How's Klaus?"

"He's still alive, but barely. I have the team working on him right now, so I need to go. They should have him ready to receive the device by the time I get back down to the operating room. Thanks again, and tell Billy I love him."

"I'll do that, young lady. Now go and save our friend."

She rushed back down the stairs to the operating room.

"We have him ready to go on bypass while you install the device," Dr. Robbins said.

"Proceed."

"We've stopped his heart, and he's ready."

She placed the case on the surgical tray, and removed the device from the case. She snapped it open and placed it around his heart. The device fit precisely, so it only took a few minutes to complete the procedure.

"You can close him up," Linda said. "I have the device in place."

It took Dr. Robbins about twenty minutes to sew him back up, and then he stepped back. "All right, I'm done. I sure hope this works."

She unfolded the power transmitter's antenna up and out of the case. She extended it and placed it against Klaus's chest, directly over the newly installed device. She pressed the button to initiate the charge, and thirty seconds later the transmitter clicked off.

As they watched the heart monitor, they saw the effects as it started to work. The device had Klaus's heart beating at seventy beats a minute and his blood pressure stabilized at 118/86. His skin colorization had an almost gray tint to it, but it quickly returned to a nice pink hue.

"Let's start to wake him up," Linda said.

It was a couple of hours before he was ready to leave the recovery room. When the nurses had him back in his room, Linda went in to check on him.

"How are you feeling?" Linda asked.

"I feel good. I hurt like heck, but I already feel stronger than I have in a long time."

"Let me take a quick look at you, and then if you feel up to it, I'll let you talk to Larry Sheldon and Billy on the phone."

It only took her a couple of minutes to check his vitals, and then she put the phone on speaker and dialed the number Larry Sheldon had given her. It rang once and Larry Sheldon answered.

"How's Klaus?"

"I'm feeling much better, thank you."

"Is that you, old friend?"

"Yes, it is. Is Billy there with you?"

"I'm here. It's good to hear your voice again."

"It's good to be heard. You and Linda did an amazing job with whatever is in my chest."

"I don't think we named it, but it doesn't matter as long as you're feeling better," Billy said.

"His vitals are excellent, and his color is good," Linda said. "He's going to be sore for a few weeks, but I think he's in good shape considering."

After they had talked for several minutes, Linda cut them off.

"All right, that's enough for today. We need to let him get some rest. We'll get him up in the morning to start walking, and he can give you another call."

Turning to leave, she said, "I'll be back in the morning to check on you. If you need anything at all, just ring the bell for the nurse. We have you on a full set of monitors, so if you have any problems we'll know immediately. I believe with the aid of this device, you'll be able to make it until your new heart is ready."

"I'm rarely at a loss for words, but in this case I am. This morning I had accepted I was going to die, and now it looks like I might hang on a while longer. Thank you again for caring so much."

Linda returned to her office to reflect on the day's activities. She had only been relaxing for a few minutes when she heard her page.

"This is Dr. Bustamante. You paged me?"

"Yes, we did. Dr. Robbins wants you to meet him on the roof in ten minutes."

"On the roof? Why would he want me to meet him up there?"

"I don't know, he didn't say. He just asked us to locate you and give you the message."

She took the elevator to the top floor, and when she walked out onto the roof, she saw Dr. Robbins standing beside a large military helicopter.

"What's up?" Linda asked.

"Get on board, and I'll brief you while we are en route."

They boarded the helicopter and were quickly airborne. They headed due north out of the city, and leveled off at their cruising altitude of four thousand feet.

"Where are we going, and why are we in such a hurry?" Linda asked.

"There has been an attack on Montreal, Canada, and we need to get there as quickly as possible."

It took them almost four hours to reach the command post the Canadian Army had set up outside of Montreal. When they landed, a group of Canadian Special Forces took them to the command tent. Peter Lombard, the senior Canadian scientist still alive, greeted them as they entered.

"William, it's good to see you again. I just wish the circumstances were better. We believe most of the city's population died in the first eighteen hours after the attack. We've managed to retrieve one group who were located in a sealed command and control bunker in the center of the city.

"Unfortunately, two of the eight people were infected, and I don't believe they'll last more than a couple of hours. I've never seen anything kill this quickly. The elapsed time from infection to death seems to be just under twelve hours. The symptoms resemble the reengineered Spanish flu virus you dealt with last year. We tried the vaccine you sent us from the last attack, but it didn't do any good."

"I've brought Linda Bustamante with me," Dr. Robbins said. "She's the young woman who developed the Spanish Flu vaccine. Do you have a lab set up yet?"

"Yes, we do. We finished a few minutes before you landed. Follow me and I'll take you to it."

"Dr. Robbins has told me a lot about you," Linda said. "It sounds like you two have been fighting fires together for a long time."

"Yes, William and I go way back. I do have to say, since he's not prone to exaggeration in any way, you must be exceptional."

"Why, thank you. I hope I can justify some of this flattery."

"It's only flattery if it is not true, and in your case it's definitively true," Dr. Robbins said. "You're the most brilliant doctor I've ever witnessed, but enough of this, let's get to work."

"Is the lab a containment area?" Linda asked.

"Yes, it is, and it should be more than adequate for the task."

They donned their self-contained hazmat suits, and used the airlock to enter the lab. Peter Lombard led them to the victim who was in the worst shape. Linda examined him for almost ten minutes. "I need to draw some blood, and I'll need a centrifuge and an electron microscope."

Peter Lombard handed her a blood kit. "The rest of the equipment you need is on the far side of the room. If you don't mind, William and I are going to examine the other patients, and then we'll go back outside while you work."

"No problem, I'll call you when I'm done, or if I need anything."

"Please don't hesitate to ask for anything. Every resource we still possess is at your disposal."

She started to work while they examined the other patients. When they finished their examinations, they returned to the command tent. They entered the patients' information into the lab computer so she would have access to their findings.

"Do you think we have time to make a pass through the city to survey the damage?" Peter Lombard asked.

"Sure, it's going to take Linda several hours to solve the problem," Dr. Robbins said.

"Several hours to solve the problem?" Peter Lombard said. "I don't believe we could solve it in months."

"I think you're going to be as amazed by her as I am. I don't see why we can't take a few hours. We aren't going to be any help to her waiting out here."

"Let's get going. I have a helicopter waiting outside. It's completely sealed, and should allow us to safely survey the city."

It only took them a few minutes to reach the city. The pilot dropped down to an altitude of a hundred feet, and followed the main highway into the city. Everywhere they looked, there were cars. Many looked as though they were waiting for the one in front of them to move so they could proceed. In other areas, they looked like a child had thrown them. There were cars in the sides of buildings, rammed into telephone poles, overturned, and in some areas, just a jumbled mass of destroyed vehicles.

As they continued down the main thoroughfare, they saw bodies in the streets, on the sidewalks, and even some that were hanging out of the windows. From the positions of the bodies it was evident that most of them had been trying to flee from the horror that was killing them.

While they were surveying the city, Linda had been working feverishly to find a cure for the newest strain of the virus. Peter Lombard had been correct when he said he believed the virus was a variation of the Spanish flu.

It had only taken her two hours to identify the subtle variations the terrorists had made to the disease. She had just finished programming the computer with the modifications needed, when the terrorists struck the outpost.

This group didn't have any weapons other than conventional arms. The Canadian Special Forces had just about wiped out the attackers when a random shot penetrated the containment area, and struck Linda in the upper back.

The bullet missed her vital organs, but the impact drove her face-first into the workbench in front of her. The impact knocked her out and shattered her face mask.

She lay breathing in the infected air for at least ten minutes before the security forces could get suited up so they could safely reach her.

As they rolled her over to see if she was still alive, they saw her face mask was shattered, and there was blood everywhere.

"Close up the hole in the window so we can stop the contamination from escaping," the lead corpsman said.

He placed her on one of the empty beds, removed her suit, and inspected her for wounds. The bullet had gone completely through her, and she had been bleeding profusely. He worked quickly because he knew he didn't have much time to slow the bleeding. It only took him a few seconds to cut her shirt open so he could begin working on her wounds. He rolled her to one side so he could remove her blood-soaked shirt, and found a large amount of blood just above her right breast where the bullet had exited. He wiped the blood off, and had been shocked to see nothing more than a red spot where he expected to find a gaping wound. As he continued to stare, even the spot turned back to a light pink flesh color.

"What happened?" Linda asked. "I remember feeling a jarring impact, and then I lost consciousness."

"You were shot by one of the terrorists. I was going to stop the bleeding, but I can't find the wound. I expected a horrific bullet wound given the amount of blood I see. I don't know what to think, but we have a much bigger problem. The bullet compromised your suit, and you've probably been infected with the virus."

"I just figured out how to modify our existing vaccine to prevent the disease they used," Linda said. "We'll be able to stop the spread as soon as we can produce enough of the vaccine. The only problem is that no one who's already infected is going to live long enough for the first batch to be produced. It'll prove true for me as well. Help me up, and I'll transmit the formula to the other labs so they can begin production."

He helped her up and handed her a lab coat so she could cover up.

"I'm sorry about your shirt, but I believed you were bleeding to death."

"You did fine. I probably was bleeding to death by the looks of it. Luckily, I'm a quick healer. It sure came in handy this time. I'm still weak, but I'm feeling better by the minute. I'm going to run some tests on myself to see how far the virus has progressed. You and your team need to finish securing the hospital, and then you need to get out of here. There's no need to risk infecting anyone else."

"It's only going to take us a few more minutes to repair the breach," the lead corpsman said. "I've already recalled Dr. Lombard's helicopter, and they should be back here within the hour."

"Thank you, and now you need to get going."

She moved to a portion of the hospital that hadn't suffered any damage, and started to work. She drew a vial of her own blood and began to study it.

When she first looked, she saw the now-familiar signs of the infection. As she continued to study the slide, she saw an amazing sight. Her white blood cells had started destroying the virus. In less than a minute, there had been no sign of the infection.

She straightened up from the microscope.

What's wrong? Billy asked. *It felt like you were in extreme pain a few minutes ago. I've been trying to reach you for several minutes and couldn't. What's going on?*

She opened her mind to let him see the events which had just occurred.

You were hurt badly, but you seem fine now. At least I don't sense any pain in you.

I'm fine. It looks as though I have the same regenerative powers you do.

It's a good thing. I would just die if anything were to happen to you. I love you so. I hope you know that.

Of course I do, silly. I know exactly how you feel, just as you know exactly how I feel. I still haven't gotten used to it yet, but it's truly the neatest feeling I've ever had.

I see you've managed to devise a cure for this strain.

Yes, I have. They should be starting production on the new vaccine as we speak. I imagine we'll be heading back to Rochester in a couple of hours. I can't believe how bad the terrorists' attacks are becoming.

The world is almost in flames as it is, Billy said. *If the world finds out what's coming, it's going to fall completely apart. When can I come and get you?*

Dr. Robbins and I were talking about that on the way up here. We're going to need to stay in place as long as possible. We're all that's keeping the terrorists at bay. We have managed to mitigate the damage they're causing, but they're resourceful. If we don't continue our work, I believe they are going to cause what world order there is at the moment to fall into chaos.

I'm going to have to trust your judgment. If anything changes you contact me immediately, and I'll find a way to come and get you no matter what.

I know you will, and we'll leave at the earliest possible moment. I need to get back to work. We have quite a bit to do before we leave.

Me too. I'll talk to you again soon.

22

BILLY WALKED ACROSS the street to where Larry Sheldon was holding a status meeting with the construction teams. There were several hundred people in the smoke-filled auditorium. You could feel the tension in the room as they discussed the progress they were making.

"As you all know, we've been working for ten months so far," Larry Sheldon said. "We've built a hundred and sixty-eight ships, and are almost finished building the flagship. The problem is we only have eight more months left. Do any of you have any ideas on how we can speed up the construction process?"

When Nicholas Stavros stood up to speak you could tell he was agitated. His dark black hair was a mess, and he was chain-smoking as he spoke. "We've held several group discussions on how to speed construction up," Nicholas Stavros said, waving his hands as he spoke. "It isn't a matter of throwing more men at it. We have plenty of men for the job. The issues are the cranes and the scaffolding. The cranes aren't tall enough to build the ships without incrementally raising them on scaffolds as we go. At the rate we're going, we'll not have enough time to build even half of the thousand ships we projected."

They hadn't seen Billy when he entered through a side door. After he listened to the discussions for several minutes, he left without letting them know he had been there.

He returned to his lab to ponder the problem. After an hour or so, he started to envision a solution.

He moved to his CAD terminal to work. After several abortive attempts, he stopped and started to rethink the approach he had been working on. He placed a computer rendition of the ship on the terminal. He decided there would be three large poles on both sides of the ship. The poles would be set deep in the ground, and spaced equally along the side of the ship. A tray would attach to the poles and run the length of the ship. The tray would hold the plates which would make up the outer covering of the ship. He designed the mechanism to allow the construction crews to weld the plates together without leaving ground level.

Once welded, the tray would raise the completed sections to the proper height for installation. Once the tray was at the correct height, the tray would tilt forward to allow the completed section to slide into position.

Once in place, automated plasma welders would run the length of the tray, fusing the newly added section into place. When he finished the plans for the sides of the ship, he added two more poles at the ends of the ship, with the same type of tray. The trays utilized the same form of antigravity which would power the ship to raise and lower the sections of it.

If the trays worked as well as he believed they would, he computed they would be able to get back on schedule, and might even surpass their original projections.

He uploaded the plans to the main server, and left the lab to find Larry Sheldon. He found him in his office talking with Nicholas Stavros and Stewart Hennessey.

"What have you been up to?" Larry Sheldon asked. "We haven't seen or heard from you in over a week."

"I overheard your talk with the construction crew captains, and I believe I have a solution for you."

"A solution? A solution to which problem? We have so many right now. I don't know if I could even prioritize them."

"I overheard you telling everyone we weren't going to be able to assemble the thousand ships we have planned, and I knew I had to try and figure out a way to build the ships faster. I've uploaded the plans for the assembly area modifications. I don't think it'll take more than a week to build the lifts. You already have plenty of plasma welders, and I know we have already received more than enough plates to build the ships. If you can build the lifts in the next week or so, we should be able to build at least one thousand, one hundred fifty ships by the deadline."

"That's great news," Larry Sheldon said. "I'd almost given up hope we'd be able to accelerate the pace of construction. We've been willing to work around the clock, but it hasn't seemed to help much."

"Are your crews going to have enough reactors ready for the ships?" Billy asked.

"We already have more than enough reactors built," Nicholas Stavros said. "We're going to shift those crews over to help with the finish work on the ships. My other crews can assist with the installation of the electronics and flight computers."

"I'm also sending a functional reactor to each of the countries attempting to build their own fleets," Larry Sheldon said. "We sent the plans, but I believe it will help them to be able to see a finished reactor."

It took them almost a week and a half to get the first assembly area up and running, but after the first one, the rest went quickly. As Billy had hoped, the pace of construction had gone up by a factor of three.

It had been over a month since Billy had last seen his parents. He took one of the small shuttles and went to see them. As he walked up to the house, they came out onto the porch to greet him.

"Good morning, stranger," Ben said. "We thought you had forgotten us."

"I'm sorry. I've been so busy, but I know it's no excuse. How have you been?"

"We've been fine, but what have you been so busy with? Does it have anything to do with whatever is being built behind us?"

"It's definitely something to do with the construction, but I can't tell you what exactly."

"Come on, we're your parents," Mary said. "If you can't trust us, who are you going to trust?"

They had asked him to tell them what was happening on several occasions. Larry Sheldon had already told him he could brief his parents anytime he wanted, but he had been trying to put off telling them for as long as possible.

"If you will call Rob and Beth and tell them we are coming by for them, I will brief all of you."

"I will do it right now," Mary said. "I know they're home; I just got off the phone with Beth a few minutes before you arrived."

She finished the call and said, "They'll be ready to go when we get there."

He landed the shuttle in front of their house and opened the shuttle's door.

"Thank you for taking the time to take a ride with us," Billy said. "If you'll get in, I'll brief you as we travel. What I'm about to tell you will be more easily understood if you can see some of what I'm talking about."

When everyone had taken their seats, he took off. He kept the shuttle below seven hundred feet so he wouldn't interfere with any of the aircraft passing by in all directions. Their sleepy corner of New Mexico was now the busiest destination for aircraft in the world.

Even though the activity had been going on all around them, you could only appreciate the scope of it from the air. As far as they could see, there was row after row of gigantic ships. In the front of the storage area was the flagship. It completely dominated their view, since it was twice the size of the other ships. They were all shifting around in their seats to try to take it all in, and couldn't believe what they were seeing.

As they sat in awed silence, Billy started to explain. "About twenty years ago astronomers discovered a gigantic asteroid on a collision course with the Earth. It's roughly the size of the moon, and it's headed directly at us. It'll reach the Earth in just under six months from now."

"How much damage is there going to be?" Ben said.

"There won't be damage. There will be oblivion."

"Oblivion!" Beth said. "You mean like the end of the world?"

"Yes, it will mean the end of the world. There will be nothing left of the Earth and possibly other parts of the solar system."

"How come we haven't heard anything about it?" Ben said. "The government would have warned us if it were true."

"Who do you think is building all of this?" Billy asked. "We aren't going to do a general announcement for another three months, because we're afraid people will panic. Once we make the announcement, we'll have almost three months to gather the rest of the people we can save."

"How many people are you going to be able to save?" Ben asked.

"If we meet our new goals, we should be able to save just over eighty-four million people."

"Eighty-four million people, that's incredible, but how many will be left behind?"

"I believe the current population of the US is around

two hundred ninety-five million people. It had been three hundred million people, but between the wars and the terrorist attacks, it's down to around that number."

"Using those numbers, there will be two hundred eleven million people left behind," Beth said. "What's going to happen to them?"

He didn't say anything for several seconds. "We just don't have any way to help them. I'm afraid they are all going to die."

"There has to be something you can do," Mary said. "Can't we build more ships?"

"The number being built is quite a bit higher than we initially projected, and I'm afraid it's the best we can do. You have no idea how long I've thought about what else we can do. I simply can't figure out how we can do any better."

"I know you've been trying. I'm sorry if I made it seem like I thought you weren't trying. I just can't believe God will allow this to happen," Mary said.

"There are precedents in the Bible of God starting over."

He continued to fly around the area showing them the entire setup. When he finished the tour, he landed at Beth and Rob's house.

"I'm sorry to spring all of this on you, but I felt like it was time you knew what's going on," Billy said.

"It isn't your fault," Rob said. "I can't believe you and your team have managed to build all of this in just over a year. It seems like yesterday when Larry told me he wanted to buy all of my land. I'm truly glad you and Linda have grown as close as you have. It's important in times like these to have someone you can count on."

"Thanks, I think of you and Beth as another set of parents, and I know Linda feels the same way about my parents. I'm sorry to rush you, but I need to be getting back. I'll keep you updated on any changes to the plans. If nothing changes, I'll go and get Linda in five months. She wants to continue working as long as possible. Thirty days after I go after Linda, we'll leave on our journey. I may ask you all to move aboard the ship earlier, depending on what's happening with our security arrangements. We have some concerns there's going to be widespread rioting and attempts to rush the facility."

"Do you think it's going to get that bad?" Ben said.

"Larry Sheldon and I've discussed it at length, and I'm afraid it's going to be much worse."

As he walked into his lab, he saw Larry Sheldon at one of the tables waiting on him.

"What are you up to?" Billy said.

"I'm waiting for you. I have some bad news. We are off by almost five months on our time frame. There's a debris field preceding the main asteroid, and it's going to begin hitting Earth in less than thirty days."

"How could we have missed the date by so large a margin?"

"The leading edges are made up of some sort of dark material which doesn't reflect light very well. The leading edges are also traveling faster than we thought. There will actually be three separate waves of debris. The first is made up of smaller asteroids, but they're still, on an average, over a hundred meters in size."

"How many ships will we have ready?" Billy asked.

"I believe we can have close to seven hundred, but we won't have time to build any more. We'll be back to saving around sixty-five million if we load them all to capacity. I'm also concerned we aren't going to have time to do an orderly evacuation. We need to contact all of the other nations, and let them know the timetable has accelerated. I've already talked with the president, and he's meeting with Congress to try and come up with an approach to take in selecting the rest of the people."

"This is going to lead to almost immediate panic when the news breaks. There's no way we'll be able to keep this quiet much longer."

"You're right," Larry Sheldon said. "I expect it will leak out in the next couple of days. I don't know how we're going to get all of the people here in time. Moving millions of people isn't going to be easy, and we don't have nearly enough transportation to help. We had intended to use buses, trains, and all of the available commercial airliners to get the people here. It would have worked if we had at least five months to move the people. Thirty days or less is just not enough time."

They continued to talk about what they needed to do until well after midnight. Finally, Larry Sheldon said, "I need to get some sleep. I haven't slept in almost two days. I've been on the phone or radio almost constantly since I found out about all of this."

Billy walked across the street to his apartment. He was so tired he decided he would shower in the morning. When he lay down, he felt Linda in his mind.

What's up? Linda said. *I felt a sense of dread a couple of hours ago. Is there anything wrong?*

It's bad.

He let her see what had happened in the last couple of hours.

That's awful, Linda said. *What are we going to do?*

I'm going to come and get you as soon as I can. But it's probably going to be at least two weeks before I can get there.

I'm not sure I can be ready in two weeks, but I'll try.

You have to wrap it up. We simply don't have any more time. I'm going to come in the Imagination. *It'll hold close to two hundred people if we pack them in. You can select up to that number including yourself.*

What about everybody else?

We'll try to get some more of them, but I don't know what sort of plan the president is going to put forth to select the ones who get to come. We intended to hold a national lottery to select the people, but there's simply not enough time. I don't have any idea what he's going to do, but it'll have to be something pretty dramatic to get the millions of people here in time.

I'll contact Dr. Robbins in the morning, and get him to help me select the people to come along. I'm scared.

Don't be scared. I'll make sure you get here. I promise.

I believe you; it's just I've never experienced anything like this before.

No one has. Don't feel bad about it. The whole world is going to be just as scared or worse. Just know I'll be there for you.

I'll see you in two to three weeks. Make sure and give me at least twenty-four hours notice so I can make sure everyone is ready when you get here.

I'll see you then. I love you, and try not to worry too much.

He fell asleep quickly, and didn't wake up until Larry Sheldon called him the next morning. "Are you going to sleep all day?" Larry Sheldon asked.

"What time is it?" Billy asked.

"It's a quarter after six."

"What are you doing up so early? I thought you hadn't gotten any sleep for two days."

"I hadn't, but I don't' have any more time to waste. I've already talked with the president this morning. They have decided not to hold a lottery. They're using existing databases to try to select a good cross section of talents, ethnicities, and complete families where they can.

"The president believes he can deliver the forty-eight million people we need to fill the ships. He also said several countries are going to have at least a few ships ready to go in time. Some of the more underdeveloped areas such as South America and Africa aren't going to have many ships, but they'll each have at least a few ships. I know it may only be six to seven hundred thousand people, but that's more than I thought they would manage. If we hadn't sent them the reactors, I don't think they would have had any ships at all. I just wish we could have sent more. Had we known how short of time we were, we would have sent the remainder of our reactors. I need you to do one more thing for me before we have to leave."

"Sure, what is it?"

"Can you design a ship capable of storing DNA samples for an extended period of time?"

"I don't see why not. What did you have in mind?"

"I want to try and preserve DNA from every form of life on the Earth. If we can, I want to be able to re-create as much of the existing life on Earth as possible."

"I'll get to work on it right away. I'll need a ship or two to store the samples. Can we spare them?"

"We have several we won't have time to finish enough to carry passengers, but they're capable of flight."

As Billy liked to do, he worked straight through. He only took short naps to recharge when he needed to, and it only took him a week to finish the design changes for the ships.

His first thought had been to use liquid oxygen or nitrogen to freeze the samples. He even contacted Linda to get her advice on freezing the samples of animal DNA. After talking with her, he knew freezing in the common sense of the word would not work. Freezing the samples would cause too much damage. He finally decided to place the samples in a vacuum, and hold them in place with magnetic containment chambers. Since they didn't have to construct any physical chambers or walls, they didn't need to rework the ships to enable the storage.

The design called for them to build a series of magnetic projectors to generate millions of honeycombs of magnetic containment areas. Once in place, it would look like the materials were floating in thin air.

While Billy had been working on the ship's design, Larry Sheldon had mobilized scientists from all over the world to gather the samples. By the time Billy handed over the designs, the samples were all in place and ready to be stored aboard the ships.

It took Nicholas Stavros and his crews another week to retrofit the ships with Billy's new designs. As soon as they were finished, Larry Sheldon had some of the soldiers guarding the base store the samples on board the ships.

They were down to their last thirteen days before they had leave.

"I need to get to Rochester," Billy said.

"I know you do," Larry Sheldon said. "But I need you to help us. The president still thinks he can get the millions of people here before we have to leave, but I believe he's being overly optimistic. The last report I got this morning puts the head count at just over a hundred and thirty thousand people. I don't think the current evacuation plans are going to get it done."

"What are you going to need from me? I need to go and get Linda," Billy said.

"I need you to come up with a workable plan to enable us to get the people aboard the ships. I know I'm asking a lot, but you're the only one who seems to be able to think through these types of problems without letting their emotions get in the way."

"Let me go back to my lab and work on this. I'll have something for you as quickly as I can. Please feed me all of the reports you are receiving. I want them worldwide not just from here."

"Will do, but what are you going to do with all of those reports?"

"I don't know, but right now I think I should look at all of the data."

Once again, he retreated to his lab to work through the new set of problems.

He reached out to Linda. *Are you able to talk?*

What's up? I'm up to my ears in patients. There have been large-scale riots all around us, and we're dealing with a huge amount of casualties.

Larry Sheldon has asked me to put off my trip to get you until I can figure out how to get more people to the ships. If we don't solve the issues, we aren't going to save anywhere near the number we should.

No problem, I don't think I could stand to leave right now anyway. There's so much to do, and so few people to do it with.

I will be there for you.

I know you will. I love you, but I need to get back to work.

Me too, I'll contact you as soon as I know when I'm coming for sure.

23

As BILLY STUDIED the situation reports, he saw the president's plans for getting the evacuees to the facility weren't going to succeed.

The widespread panic had caused millions of people to try to reach the facility on their own, and they were using virtually every form of transportation available. The biggest problem they faced was the traffic jams had made the highways and back roads virtually impassable. As a result, a vast number of the vehicles had run out of fuel while they waited for the congestion to clear. With the road conditions the way they were, they were having a difficult time supplying the filling stations with gasoline.

After he studied the available information for an hour or so, he called Larry Sheldon.

"I've just finished studying the data you sent me," Billy said. "I think the first thing you need to do is open up all of the checkpoints. Use your local transportation resources to move the people from the checkpoints to the ships. I think you should start loading them on the ships as they arrive. We don't have enough housing, and it will save valuable time later."

"That makes sense," Larry Sheldon said. "I'll give the order immediately. I don't think there are more than a few hundred thousand people at the checkpoints, but it's a start."

"Next you need to have the Army take every transport

they have and start moving out to the people. Load the transports with gasoline so they can refuel vehicles as they encounter them. Once they have given out all of the fuel, have them load as many of the people as they can and return. You're going to need to turn them around as fast as possible. I'll continue working on a couple of other ideas. Let me know if anything changes."

"I sure will, and I'll get this going as soon as I get off the phone."

"One other thing. Have we got enough pilots trained for the ships we have ready?" Billy asked.

"Yes we do, in fact we have about six hundred more than we have ships."

"Great, I'll get back to you as soon as I can."

Billy used one of his computer terminals to begin researching the latest population census data. He had the most current census data so it was reasonably accurate. He mapped out where the greatest concentrations of people were, and then mapped the ships he had available to the locations.

He had designed the ships for space travel, but they were capable of flight in the atmosphere. Once he had the optimum locations mapped out, he saved the plan to a public folder on the base's mainframe and called Larry Sheldon.

"Have you come up with another plan?" Larry Sheldon asked.

"Yes I have," Billy said. "If you'll look in a folder called evacuation plans on the mainframe, you'll see what I've mapped out. The plan calls for sending every ship that isn't already loaded to the locations I've mapped out. Consolidate all of the people you have here onto a couple of ships. That way we'll be able to use all of the other ships to get evacuees."

"I'm looking at the plans right now, and this looks doable," Larry Sheldon said. "I'll brief the pilots as soon as we finish. We're down to eight days. Do you think we'll be able to fill the ships in time?"

"It's going to be close, but we may be able to if we can maintain control when we get to the locations," Billy said. "To make sure we are as careful as we can be, I believe we should instruct the pilots not to land. When they reach their destinations, they should hover at least twenty feet above the ground. They can lower their gangways to the ground, and put up magnetic fields along the edges to ensure people don't crowd each other off. You'll need to put enough military personnel on board the ships to guard the entrances. They'll need to be seasoned veterans, because I'm afraid they may have to use force in some cases to maintain control."

"No problem," Larry said. "I have three full brigades of Army rangers we just pulled back from the conflict in Africa. They've been in the field for almost three years. So if anything, we'll have to caution the commanders to ensure they don't use too much force."

"I mapped the ships' courses to the largest concentrations of people. That means only the larger metropolitan areas are going to receive ships. If it's all right with you, I'm going to take the *Imagination* to get Linda, and whatever people she has selected to come with us."

"No problem. We're going to have to make some hard choices during this time, but I would never ask you to sacrifice Linda, if there is any chance to save her."

"I want to leave first thing in the morning, if it's all right with you?"

"Yes, of course it is," Larry Sheldon said. "I'll have a squad of Army rangers ready to go with you at oh-six-hundred. If it weren't for you none of us would have a chance of living. Don't waste any time. We'll only have a few days left when you get back."

"I won't take any longer than I have to, and I'll see you

when I get back. Oh, by the way, you're coming on the flagship, aren't you?"

"Yes, I am. I have already put my family on board, and I'll have the rest of the faculty from the university on board by the time you get back. They were late leaving due to the riots, but I think we'll have the road to the pass open by the time they get there."

Billy walked into the hangar where the *Imagination* was stored, but he couldn't see much. He flipped the switch, and a brilliant light illuminated the hangar. Even though it was two hundred meters in length, the *Imagination* looked small sitting in the center of the massive hangar.

After he entered the ship, he walked to the control console and powered up the ship's systems.

He ran through a quick check of the ship's diagnostic programs to verify everything was working properly. When he finished his checklist, he leaned back in the command chair and stretched his arms above his head. As he was trying to relax for a few seconds, he felt Linda's presence.

What's up? I just got off of work, and I'm about to fix myself some dinner, Linda said.

I'll be coming to get you tomorrow, Billy said.

You promised me twenty–four hours' notice.

I can wait, but I can't wait any longer than twenty-four hours. Counting tomorrow, we only have four more days before we have to leave.

I can have everyone ready by then.

I'll call Larry Sheldon and postpone our trip. I'll be at your location by ten A.M. the day after tomorrow. You must be ready to go by then.

I'll be ready. It's bad here. People are being so stupid. Ever since the news leaked out, it's been getting progressively worse. We've been having almost daily riots, and

*the roads are almost impassable in some sections of the
city. How are you going to be able to reach us?*

How tall is your apartment building?

Eighteen floors, but I don't know how tall it is.

*Are there any buildings in your neighborhood taller
than yours?*

*No, it's the tallest building for several blocks. There are
taller buildings downtown, but where I am, we're the
tallest building. Why do you ask?*

*Can you get the people you have selected to gather at
your building by ten A.M.?*

Sure, but why do you want them here?

*I'm going to get you from the top of your building. I'll
bring the ship down to just above the roof and lower a
gangway down to you.*

*I'll have everyone here. I miss you so much. It's going
to be good to see you again. It's been so long.*

*I miss you too. We'll be together again in just a little
while. You be careful, it sounds like it's pretty dangerous
where you are.*

*From what I've been watching on the news, it's not any
worse here than anywhere else, but I'll be careful. I'll see
you soon.*

He opened his eyes and sighed. He hadn't taken the time
to realize how much he missed Linda. The more he thought
about it, the more he couldn't wait to see her again. They
hadn't allowed themselves to fully develop their feelings
for each other, but they had always known they were meant
for each other.

He called Larry Sheldon and informed him of the new
schedule.

"You're cutting it awfully close. You have to make
sure you get right back. I'm not sure we'll even have the
three days we thought we would. We're having a hard

time identifying the leading edge of the first wave. The asteroids are hard to spot. They don't reflect light as well as we thought they would. We still believe we're right on the timing, but there could be some we aren't seeing."

"I won't take any more time than is absolutely necessary."

When Linda finished talking with Billy, she immediately called Dr. Robbins. It took several rings for him to answer, but he finally did. "Hello, Linda, what do you need? Has there been a problem at the hospital?"

"No, we have a different issue. We need to gather our entire group by ten A.M. the day after tomorrow. Billy told me we must leave immediately after he arrives."

"What's the rush, I thought we had some more time?"

"Everyone does. Billy told me they miscalculated the time, and we have to leave no later than two days after he picks us up. We need to make our final decisions on our list, and get everyone to my apartment building."

"We were about to sit down for dinner, but why don't you come over, and we'll work through our list. As soon as we finish I'll begin contacting them."

"I'll be right over."

Linda took the elevator down to the lobby. John Tyler, her doorman, greeted her as she stepped off the elevator. "Good evening, Miss Bustamante."

"John, I asked you to call me Linda."

"Yes you did, Miss, but Zach has threatened to fire me for getting too friendly with the tenants."

"I didn't realize it was a problem. I'm sorry if I've gotten you in trouble."

"Don't be sorry, Miss, but I need this job. My wife Millie is pregnant and is due any time with our first child. Do you need a cab, Miss?"

"Yes I do, if you don't mind?"

"No problem. Most of the cab companies have shut

down, but I have a friend who's still working. He'll be here in just a few minutes."

Linda had never paid much attention to John. He was always very polite, but he never went out of his way to make conversation. As they waited for the cab she was struck by his athletic and self-assured manner. He was six foot and around two hundred pounds, but what stood out the most were his eyes. They were steely gray, and as he looked down the street for the cab, he looked a lot like a hawk seeking its prey.

In just a few minutes, the cab pulled up in front. John Tyler held the door open, and as she started to get in, she stopped and said, "I need to ask you to do something for me."

"I will if I can."

"I need you to listen carefully to me, and to trust what I'm about to tell you. I want you to bring your family to my apartment the day after tomorrow. You must be here before ten A.M. I want you to bring whatever belongings that mean the most to you, but only what you can carry."

"I can do it, but the building owner, and Zach the supervisor, don't want our families around the tenants."

"It won't matter, you aren't ever coming back. You'll be leaving with Billy and me on one of the evacuation ships."

"You can get us on one of the ships? I've heard rumors of the ships, but I didn't think they were true."

"They're true, and yes, you'll be coming with us."

"We'll be here. I can't begin to thank you enough."

"Please don't say anything to anyone else. We'll have a limited amount of space."

"I won't tell a soul."

WHEN SHE KNOCKED, the butler opened the door. "If you'll take a seat in the library, I'll tell Dr. Robbins you're here."

"Sorry, I was on the phone with a couple of people," Dr. Robbins said. "Would you like a drink?"

"I would take a glass of water if you don't mind?"

He poured her a glass of water from the pitcher on his desk, and handed it to her. "You say Billy is coming to rescue us?"

"Yes, he is, and we must be ready by ten A.M. the day after tomorrow. He said we could bring up to two hundred people with us, including ourselves. I've already added two people, so with your family of five, we have a hundred and ninety-two left to select."

"I believe we should bring our doctors and their families."

"I agree, but how many would that be?"

"That's one of the phone calls I just made. They're e-mailing me the list of the doctors and their dependents. The list should be here in just a few minutes."

His computer chimed, letting him know he had an e-mail.

"That should be the list."

He walked to the computer, and printed it out. When it finished printing, he looked at the last page and said, "Counting the ones you just mentioned, we have room for one more."

"One! Who would you suggest filling the last spot?"

"If there is to be only one, it should be Sylvia Goodman. She's the head of the local university's geology department. She is one of the world's preeminent geologists, and a world-class archeologist. I've known her for many years, and she doesn't have any living family. Can we possibly fit one more?"

"We probably could, who else did you have in mind?"

"I can't believe I forgot about him, but I feel like I must bring our butler. He has been almost a member of my family for over twenty years."

"I know we can manage to wedge in one more."

"Well then, our list is complete."

"Are you sure you can get them there in time?"

"Yes, I can, if I'm forceful enough, and you know I can be pretty forceful when I need to."

"I certainly learned that the hard way my first week as a resident."

"I was hard on you, wasn't I?"

"I understand why now, but it didn't make it any easier at the time. I was almost in tears when you started yelling at me. However, I understand now what you were trying to get across to all of us. I learned we must never take a patient for granted. If we have a job to do, we must concentrate to the best of our abilities, and it's always serious when a patient's health is in question. I've never failed to think of that moment whenever I sense my attention to detail slipping."

"I've never seen a better doctor than you, and that includes me and our entire staff," Dr. Robbins said. "You may still be the youngest, but you're by far the most gifted. If I had a life-threatening illness, I would want you to treat me."

"I had no idea you thought so highly of me. I know you have taken a personal interest in me, but those are the nicest things anyone has ever said about me."

"I wasn't saying it to be nice, I truly mean them. You should return home and get your affairs in order. I'll get to work on the people on our list. The rest of the staff can handle what few patients we have left. I would be surprised if we have any left in the morning. They have been leaving steadily since the news broke."

"If you think it's all right, I do have quite a few things to sort through. I'm not going to take much. Billy told me the ships are stocked with everything we'll need."

"I'll call you if I run into any problems, but if not, I'll see you the day after tomorrow at your apartment building."

She returned to her apartment building, and let herself in through the night security door. She wondered how John's conversation was going with his pregnant wife.

When John Tyler got home, Millie had dinner on the table. She had gotten used to his hours, and they had gotten in the habit of not eating dinner until John got home around ten P.M. As they were eating, John asked, "Do you remember me talking about the young lady in 1012?"

"I think so, why do you ask?"

"She wants us to meet her at the apartment building at ten A.M. the day after tomorrow. She has arranged for us to leave with them on one of the evacuation ships."

"Are you serious? I didn't think it was possible. I've heard they don't have nearly enough ships for everyone. You know they are going to take the rich, famous, and powerful people first. There's no way they're going to ask nobodies like us to go. I've been crying myself to sleep at night thinking about how short a life our baby is going to have."

"Me too, but I'm serious. Linda has always been kind to me, and when she heard you were pregnant, she immediately invited us to come along. Honey, we have to take this chance."

"No problem. You know I'd follow you anywhere, and besides, this may well be our only chance to survive."

Neither of them slept very well, and they spent the entire next day sorting through their meager belongings. They ended up with two suitcases with a few clothes, and some family pictures.

The next night they went to bed early so they would be up in plenty of time for their journey. Neither of them got more than an hour's worth of sleep, because they kept waking up every few minutes, fearing they would oversleep and miss their chance to leave.

They were dressed and ready to go by six-thirty. They waited until eight, and then they just couldn't stand it anymore. They placed their bags in their old car, and left for the apartment building. They were within two blocks of the building when they ran into what they thought was a traffic jam.

John Tyler stepped out of the car to see what the holdup was. He quickly recognized it was not just a traffic jam. Rioting had broken out again, and there were people running everywhere.

He heard the sounds of explosions and gunfire. A few seconds later he saw a man and woman running toward them when a burst of gunfire cut them down. There was a mob of young men walking down both sides of the street, and they were shooting at everyone in their path.

The only things John Tyler had kept from his Navy days were the various medals he had won and his sidearm. The pistol was a Beretta 96F, and for whatever reason he had felt the need to load it and bring it along with them. As an afterthought, he had also strapped on an ammo belt. He hadn't thought of carrying a gun in the three years he had been out of the service, but today, for some reason, he felt the need.

He grabbed their suitcases, ran around the car, and helped Millie out. "Honey, move behind me, and stay there. No matter what happens, you try to keep me between you and the gang coming toward us."

He knew the stores on either side of the street normally had back exits, so he moved toward a small deli to the right of their car. As they moved through the door, two of the young men spotted them, and started across the street toward them.

"Honey, move toward the back of the store. There should be an exit there. Wait for me by the door. Don't go out until I get there, and don't come back out no matter what you hear."

"Please be careful. Those boys are killing everyone in their path."

"I don't kill that easy. Just wait by the door; I'll be there in a few minutes."

He moved back from the front door as far as he could. As he looked around for the owner or customers, he saw they had long since left. He moved behind one of the display cases so he would have some cover and waited. It only took a few seconds for the two boys to come rushing through the door.

The one in the lead was screaming obscenities. John didn't have any idea why he was so agitated. Maybe he was on drugs, or maybe he had gone insane. It didn't matter.

He had made this same decision many times, and he didn't hesitate. He felt a twinge of regret, but he realized he had to protect his wife from the thugs. He sighted in on the first young man, and put two bullets into his chest.

The hollow point .40 SW slugs dropped him in his tracks. He hadn't even hit the floor when John shifted to the second young man, and put two rounds into him. He tried to duck John's fire, and took the second round in the throat.

Satisfied the immediate threat was over, he moved to the back of the store to find Millie. It just took him a few seconds to locate her. "Let's get going before the rest of them come to check on those two," John Tyler said.

"I heard shooting. Are you all right?"

"Yes, I am. Let's get going."

As they moved into the alley, he glanced in both directions, and when he didn't see any immediate threat, they started moving down the alley. The rioters had continued down the block away from where they were going. They continued to hear gunfire on the way, but they were able to reach Linda's apartment building without further problems.

When they reached the building, the day doorman greeted them. "What are you doing here?" Frank asked. "Your shift doesn't start until two. You know Zach doesn't like us to hang around when we're not on duty. I can't believe you brought Millie here. You know he'll throw a fit if he sees her here."

"You don't need to worry about it," John Tyler said. "We're here to see Linda Bustamante, not to come to work."

"You know you aren't supposed to get friendly with the tenants. You're definitely going to get fired, because you know I'm going to have to turn you in."

"You do whatever you need to do; now get out of our way."

They took the elevator up to Linda's apartment on the tenth floor.

"Hi, John, and this must be Millie," Linda said. "I'm Linda Bustamante, and I'm glad you made it. I just heard there are riots breaking out all over town. The police have all left, and the entire city is going nuts."

"I'm so glad to meet you, and I want to thank you for allowing us to accompany you," Millie Tyler said. "We ran into some trouble ourselves. We had to abandon our car, and we walked the last two blocks."

"That sounds scary. Were you in any danger?"

"There was quite a bit of gunfire, and then we had to cut through a store to the alley to get away. I was so scared; I thought they were going to hurt John."

"What happened?" Linda said.

"I don't want to talk about it, but I took care of the situation," John Tyler said.

Just then, she noticed the ammo belt and the bulge under John's jacket. "Are you armed?"

"I am. Does it concern you?"

"Not at all, I'm actually glad we have someone who is. I grew up around all sorts of guns, so they don't worry me as long as they are in the hands of someone I trust."

"Why thank you. I'll never break your trust."

"I don't know why, but I immediately sensed that in you, and I'm a good judge of character. Please sit down. We still have an hour or so until Billy is supposed to be here."

Over the next thirty minutes, the other members of their group began to arrive. Frank the doorman was starting to get agitated. He called up to Linda's apartment to talk to John. "What's going on? You know we're not supposed to allow this many visitors for one tenant. I must have checked in over a hundred so far. What kind of a party are you guys throwing up there?"

"We're having a going away party for Linda."

"I didn't know she was leaving the building. Has she given her notice already?"

"No, I think she's going to give her notice today."

"Well, you tell her she had better give us at least a month's notice, or she'll lose her security deposit."

"Like I told you before, don't worry about it."

Over the next fifteen minutes, all of the remaining people, except Tom Billings and his family had arrived. Dr. Robbins and his family were in the last group that made it to the building.

Linda had been sending everyone directly to the roof as they arrived, so the only people still in her apartment were John and Millie. When Dr. Robbins knocked on the door, she opened it and said, "Good, you're here. I was starting to get worried; you're almost the last to arrive. The only other ones not here are Tom Billings and his family. We can't wait any longer. I'll leave a note on the door telling them to come to the roof when they arrive. Let's go on up to the roof. Billy should be arriving in a few minutes."

They took the elevator up to the roof, and when they arrived, Dr. Robbins held up his hands and said, "Quiet everyone, quiet. If you'll give me your attention I'll explain what's happening. I've asked all of you to meet me here because Linda Bustamante has arranged for all of us to be transported to one of the evacuation ships. Her friend Billy West should be here in less than ten minutes. Please hold your questions until we are on board Billy's ship."

While they stood and waited for the ship to arrive, the sounds of explosions and gunfire echoed throughout the neighborhood. They could see plumes of smoke rising from several areas of the city.

John Tyler leaned over the side of the building to see what was going on. All around the building there were gangs running through the streets firing as they went.

He saw a large group of rioters rush the front of the apartment building. Frank was standing out front, and yelled at them to stop. They didn't even slow down. They cut him down with a volley of bullets and rushed through the front of the building.

The rioters that John and Millie Tyler had barely escaped caught Tom Billings and his family. They slaughtered his family, and then they tortured him until he told them where he was going and why he was going there. The leader of the gang rallied the rioters to storm Linda's building so they could try to seize control of the ship.

The rioters had to take the stairs to the tenth floor, because the electricity had just failed due to the destruction caused by the rioting. When they reached the tenth floor and Linda's apartment, they saw the note she had left for the Billings family. The leader read the instructions and called out to the mob, "Let's go to the roof! They're all up there. The ship will be here in less than five minutes, and we need to hurry if we want to take control of it."

They rushed to the stairwell, and began the climb to the roof. Two of them were quicker than the rest, and reached the roof well ahead of the main group. When they burst through the door to the roof, John Tyler spotted them.

He had watched them gun down Frank as they rushed the building, so he knew they weren't there for a good purpose. He drew his pistol, and shot both of them in the chest.

As they fell mortally wounded, John called to the group.

"Some of you men grab their weapons. There'll be more of them coming any minute."

Several of the men rushed over to where the two men lay dead, and picked up their rifles and handguns. They now had five weapons counting John's pistol.

He told them, "Get over here behind the air vents for some cover. The rest of you move to the far end of the roof away from the door. There's going to be more shooting, so hide behind whatever you can find."

They had gotten into position by the time the main group of men started to come through the door. John Tyler was in front, and he shot the men when they stepped onto the rooftop. He had killed eight of them when he called to the men behind him. "You men start shooting while I reload. Shoot for the body, and keep shooting until they fall down."

It only took him a couple of seconds to reload, and the other men had been firing steadily. They had missed more times than they had hit, but they had managed to kill the next two rioters through the door. The rest of them were starting to hang back now that they knew there was armed resistance on the roof.

The leader arrived and attempted to rally the remainder of the rioters. "You men listen up. I want you all to go through the door as quickly as possible. Number off in even and odd. I want the even numbers to go right, and odd left. I'll follow in the center. I don't think there are too many of them out there, so I think we can easily overwhelm them. Okay, let's go."

There were eleven of them left, and as they rushed through the door, John Tyler was shooting as fast as he could. He was down to just putting one bullet in each attacker, and he managed to hit all but one on the right and two on the left.

He paused to eject his empty clip, and pulled another from his ammo belt to reload. As he did the group behind him resumed firing. They were getting the hang of the weapons, because they managed to kill all three of the remaining rioters. The only one left was the leader, and he was firing steadily as he came through the door. He hit two of the men behind John with his first shots. As he turned his weapon toward John Tyler, John fired four quick shots at him. The first missed cleanly when the riot leader dived to the side. The second caught him in his left shoulder and caused him to go sprawling across the roof. As he came to a stop, the next two shots struck him in the top of the head and killed him instantly.

John Tyler continued to stare at the doorway for at least a minute before he turned to the men with him. "Is everyone all right?"

As he asked the question, he saw the two wounded men. He called to the group gathered at the end of the roof. "We need some help down here. We have a couple of wounded men."

One of them had a light flesh wound in the leg, but the other one had a bullet in his chest. Dr. Robbins and Linda rushed back to where his group was located. "We'll move these two to the far end of the roof and away from the door. Are you all right?"

"Yes, I am, Miss Bustamante," John said.

"John, please call me Linda. There's no one going to fire you anymore."

"I suppose you're right. The man on the right sounds like the bullet punctured a lung."

"How do you know that?"

"Unfortunately I've seen many wounded men in my life, and I recognize the sound."

"I suspect you're right. We'll take care of him. We have the entire surgical staff from the hospital here with us."

"I'm going to check out the stairwell, and see if there are any more of them coming. I don't believe there are, but I want to check and make sure."

"Okay, we'll take care of the wounded while you check. Don't go too far, Billy will be here at any moment."

He had barely gotten inside the door when he heard the people yell, "The ship is here! The ship is here!"

He continued through the door and went down two flights of stairs. He didn't encounter any more rioters, and as he stopped to listen, he didn't hear anyone else coming up the stairs. After he listened for a minute or so, he returned to the roof and stepped over the bodies of the rioters to reach the others.

The men who stood with him were all doctors or nurses, but they had all been ex-military of one form or another. They were all talking about what just happened. They couldn't believe what they had just witnessed. They had managed to kill three or four of the rioters, but John Tyler killed all of the rest.

They were amazed at how he had stood and coolly fired

as the men rushed them. He only missed one shot out of all the ones he fired, and the rest were deadly accurate.

What they didn't know was John Tyler was an ex-Navy SEAL, and he was once a part of an even more elite group of specialists. They had gone all over the world to engage with the worst of the world's terrorist organizations on their own turf. He wasn't an imposing physical specimen at six foot and two hundred pounds, but he was a highly trained killer. One look in his steely gray eyes and you just knew you wouldn't want to cross him.

As John Tyler walked across the roof, he looked up and saw a sight he couldn't believe. The *Imagination* seemed to be floating above them. He didn't know what he had expected, but it was much larger than he'd thought it would be. It was easily as large as one of the Navy ships he had used for transportation to hotspots around the world.

It came to a stop over the roof and deployed its front gangway to the roof. As Billy hurried down the gangway, Linda spotted him and rushed to meet him.

She grabbed him and they kissed. He picked her up off the ground, and she wrapped her legs around his waist as they kissed.

To everyone on the roof it looked as though two young lovers were kissing. While they were kissing, they were talking to each other's minds.

I've missed you so, and it has just been horrible, Linda said. *During the last few minutes there have been rioters rushing the roof trying to kill us. I guess they wanted to take over your ship.*

I know. I saw the last part. I wanted to do something, but I couldn't use any of our weapons without killing all of you. Who was the guy who saved all of you? He was amazing. I've never heard of anyone who was so cool under fire, or could shoot like he did.

His name is John Tyler, and he's the doorman to my building. I invited him and his pregnant wife along.

It looks like he has already earned his way. A doorman, I don't believe he has always been a doorman.

Probably not, but I've never thought to ask him what he did before.

24

THEY CONTINUED KISSING for another ten seconds, and then Billy lowered her to the rooftop. "How many people do you have?" Billy said.

"I believe we have a hundred and ninety-seven." Linda said. "We had two hundred and one on the list, but one family hasn't made it yet. They probably aren't going to if they haven't made it by now. With everything that's happened today, they must have run into some of the same people who tried to overpower us."

"You wouldn't believe the amount of destruction we saw as we came in over the city. Almost every section of the city has some sort of riot and/or fires going on. There were people shooting at us the entire time. We need to begin getting your people on board. I don't know how long it's going to be before someone else spots us."

"I'll get them started right away. I need to get the two wounded men on board first. Do you have any sort of medical supplies?"

"We sure do. We even have a small hospital, and it's completely equipped. You can even operate if you need to."

"Great, I'll get Dr. Robbins and his main surgical team on board first to start treating the wounded men. Why don't you ask John Tyler to organize the rest of our group for you? I'll introduce you before we go on board."

"John, Millie, it's my pleasure to meet you," Billy said.

"I saw what you just did, and I'd like to thank you for saving everyone's life."

"No thanks needed," John Tyler said. "It's our pleasure to meet you. We had all but given up hope of surviving the upcoming events, until Linda was kind enough to invite us along."

"We'll talk more after we're on our way, but right now we need to get off of this roof before they try again. Would you mind organizing the rest of the group to begin boarding? We're going to let Dr. Robbins and Linda load the two wounded men first, so they can begin treatment. Millie, why don't you go on board with them and get settled in."

"No problem. I'll get them going," John Tyler said. "Honey, I'll be on board as soon as we get everyone off the roof. Linda, would you mind taking Millie to the hospital as well? She has had a difficult day so far."

"We sure will, and as soon as we have the two wounded men fixed up, I'll give her a complete physical."

"Where do you have Klaus?" Billy asked. "I would like to talk to him before we get everyone on board."

He saw the look on her face and reached out to touch her mind.

He died last night, Linda said. *He was doing so well with his new heart, but somehow he caught an infection from one of the terrorist victims we were treating. I don't know how the infection got out of the quarantine area, but it did, and he wasn't strong enough yet to recover. I'm so sorry, I know how good a friend he was to you.*

Klaus and I talked about what could happen before he left. I know he felt like he had lived a full life, and that he appreciated everything you tried to do for him. I'll miss him a lot, but I'll always remember what a great man and a friend he was.

Linda left the group to gather Dr. Robbins and the team.

In just a few minutes, they were carrying the two wounded men on board. Once on board, it took them less than ten minutes to get the most seriously wounded man onto the operating table.

While they were attending to the wounded, John Tyler had been organizing the rest of their group so they could begin boarding. Billy had a squad of Marines take over rooftop security. They stationed snipers at all four corners of the building, and had three more men in the stairway to ensure there would be no interruption to the evacuation.

It took them less than twenty minutes to get the rest of the group on board. When the last one disappeared through the hatch, John Tyler called to the Marines guarding the roof.

"That's the last of the passengers, let's get on board."

John Tyler was the last one up the ramp. When he reached the top, he stopped and turned to look at the city one last time. As far as he could see there were fires raging out of control. Smoke covered the entire city, and the sound of gunfire continued to ring out in the distance.

"Is that the last of your group?" Billy asked.

"Yes, sir, it is."

"John, please call me Billy."

"No problem, Billy. It's just I'm used to calling the one in charge 'sir.' "

"I understand, but it's not necessary. I want to learn a lot more about your background, but right now we need to get out of the city and back to base."

"Where's your home base?"

"Our base of operations is in Clayton, New Mexico. I don't imagine you would have heard of it, but it's about a hundred miles northwest of Amarillo, Texas."

"I spent some time at the Pantex facility outside of Amarillo, so I know the general area."

"We'd better get started. If you'll take a seat at one of the consoles along the wall, we'll leave."

Billy took his place at the pilot's console and tapped the screen to retract the gangway.

When the ship began its ascent, he extended the magnetic protection fields even farther from the hull. He had lowered the power to the shields to its lowest level so they could load their passengers.

As the ship was climbing away from the city, an alarm sounded, and his console lit up with a missile warning. He glanced at the screen and saw it approaching from the front of the ship.

He quickly raised the power level on the forward shields. The missile continued to track directly to the front of the ship, and when it got within about a hundred yards, it exploded with a brilliant flash. The ship didn't even shudder when the missile exploded.

"What happened to the missile?" John Tyler asked. "We didn't even feel the explosion."

"I'll give you a full briefing when we have more time, but for the moment I'll explain it this way," Billy said. "The ship has a magnetic barrier that protects it from virtually any form of matter or energy. It's also the same force the ship uses for propulsion."

"How long is it going to take us to reach New Mexico?" John asked.

"I'm going to take it easy on the way back, but it won't take more than ninety minutes."

"Isn't it over a thousand miles to New Mexico from here?"

"Yes, it is, but the ship is actually capable of even greater speed. I just don't want to unduly alarm anyone on the ground by going any faster."

They had been traveling for about twenty minutes when the front camera picked up a gigantic supercell thunderstorm. The storm clouds towered at least forty thousand feet above their altitude.

"Shouldn't we go around or over the thunderstorm?" John Tyler asked. "It looks pretty vicious."

"It'll be all right, the *Imagination* shouldn't have any problem with it."

"You're kidding, right? That's a supercell thunderstorm. It'll rip the ship to pieces."

Billy didn't respond. Instead, he verified the shields' power settings and enabled the virtual reality system.

The nose of the ship seemed to disappear, giving the illusion that the front of the ship was no longer there. They now had an incredible view of the thunderstorm as the ship approached it.

The view startled John Tyler, but he managed to hide his discomfort. The clouds were billowing ever higher as they watched. The thunderheads were growing by hundreds of feet every minute. The view was so detailed that John Tyler thought he could see the grapefruit-size hailstones being tossed around by the storm's updraft. The storm would have ripped their ship to pieces if they had been in a normal aircraft.

As John Tyler watched in awe, it looked like they had flown into a cauldron of destruction. There was almost constant lightning, and the wind and hail continued to grow in ferocity. They continued to watch the storm, but they felt no effect from the storm's violence.

John Tyler had been in many hazardous situations, and had suffered through many trips in violent weather, but he had never seen a storm like this one. He couldn't believe they were still alive, and hadn't felt any effect from the storm.

"How fast is the wind in this storm?" John Tyler asked.

Billy checked his console. "The updrafts are in excess of three hundred and fifty miles per hour, and the straight winds are about the same. I believe we've just flown into an F5 tornado. That's the only thing I've ever read about with this much wind velocity."

They continued to watch the unbelievable spectacle as the *Imagination* rushed through the storm. When they exited the storm, Billy turned to John. "Now that we're clear of the storm, why don't you tell me about you and your family?"

"There's not much to tell," John Tyler said. "We aren't anyone special. We're just plain people trying to make our way in these difficult times. I've been out of the service for thirty-six months. I served in the Navy for almost ten years. I was a commander in the Navy, but the only work I could find when I got out was working as a doorman at Linda's apartment building. My wife Millie is eight and a half months pregnant, and the doctor, at the free clinic, told us she could deliver anytime now. The clinic didn't have any real diagnostic equipment, so that was as close as he could call it."

"I think you're being too modest," Billy said. "From what I could see of the fight on the roof, it looked like you can take care of yourself. I'm sure if you hadn't been there, at least some of the group would have been killed by those rioters."

"I'm afraid you're right. I had a run-in with some of them on the way to the apartment building, and I had to kill two of them before we could escape."

"These are terrible times we are in, and I'm afraid there are many horrible events taking place right now. I'm just glad we could help you and your wife. I'd like to spend some more time talking with you, but right now I'd better concentrate on getting us back to base. Why don't you go and find Millie, and make sure she's all right. You might try the infirmary first. It's on the deck right below this one, and about halfway aft."

Billy turned back to the command console and called Larry Sheldon on the radio. "This is the *Imagination* calling Larry Sheldon. This is the *Imagination* calling, please come in."

"This is Larry Sheldon."

"I need to talk with you."

"Switch to secure channel two."

"Okay, I'm on channel."

"What's up?" Larry Sheldon asked. "I thought you might stay in Rochester for the day before you started back."

"I was thinking about it, but we ran into some trouble," Billy said.

"Is everyone all right?"

"We have a couple of wounded, but they're going to be all right. There were several rioters killed during the pickup."

"The Marines had to kill some rioters?"

"No, not the Marines. Actually, a young man named John Tyler saved Linda and the group. I couldn't land quickly enough to let the Marines help. I couldn't believe it. He killed at least a dozen of the rioters as they rushed the group. He was incredibly cool under fire. Would you mind looking him up in the DOD databases for me?"

"Sure, do you know his full name?"

"His name is John William Tyler. He said he was in the Navy for ten years, and was a commander when he got out thirty-six months ago. I think we should add him to our ship's roster. He has his pregnant wife with him, and I'm sure Linda is going to want to take care of her."

"The name sounds familiar, and it sounds like your benefactor has some specialized training. I'll look him up for you. If his record looks all right, I'll add him and his wife to the ship's roster. We have plenty of room so it won't be a problem."

"One other thing," Billy said. "Have we gotten the other ships ready to pick up people?"

"The first ones will be leaving in an hour or so. I'm afraid things are deteriorating faster than we thought. We have had several reports of the same kind of rioting you ran into in Rochester. I just talked to the chief of police in LA, and he told me he isn't sure he can maintain order well enough for us to land and pick up people."

"I think you can still send the ships. A shoulder-fired surface-to-air missile was launched at our ship as we were leaving, and the shields held up just fine."

"A missile! Where did it come from?"

"I'm not sure, but we passed over a National Guard armory on the way into the city. It's quite possible it was overrun during the rioting. If the ships will stay at least twenty feet off the ground and just lower the gangplanks, I think they should be all right. Make sure they keep their shields at no less than twenty-five percent power. They'll need to turn off the shields by the gangplanks, so the people can board. If they notice any problems, they can simply turn their shields back on. They can also use the ship's lasers and pulse cannons for protection if they have to. But they're going to cause a lot of damage, even on their lowest settings."

"I've already dispatched most of the ships, but I'll pass your strategy along to them. Are you sure these tactics will be effective?"

"I believe so, but there's no way to know for sure what they're going to encounter. After what happened to us in Rochester, I do know the crews are going to have to be strong. They are going to see things no one should have to see, and they may have to do some things which may bother some of them."

"I've made sure there is a military officer on board each ship to make those kinds of calls. I don't want to count on finding any more civilians like your John Tyler."

"Okay, thanks. We'll be there in about an hour. I'll

come by and talk with you when I get everyone settled in on the flagship."

"There's no need to hurry. I'm going to LA with the first ship so I can see for myself what's going on. I'll find you when I get back."

"Okay, you be careful."

"I can take care of myself, my young friend."

Forty minutes later, Billy brought the *Imagination* to a hover next to the flagship.

He went to find Linda, and as he suspected, she was in the infirmary treating patients. "We're at the base," Billy said. "How many patients do you have in here?"

"I have the two men who were wounded while they were helping John Tyler, and Millie Tyler, John's wife."

"Can we begin moving them?"

"Yes, they're all stable. How long do we have until we leave to escape the asteroid?"

"The last status report said we had about three days."

"When are our parents going to board?" Linda asked.

"They should have come aboard this morning. I asked Larry Sheldon to make sure they would be on board before we got back. I'm sure he would have said something if there had been any problems. I'll look up what deck they're on when we board."

After they made sure the patients were comfortable in the hospital, they located their parents on deck 50. Their parents had their pick of quarters, and they decided to make sure their quarters were directly below one of the agricultural areas.

Rob and Ben had spent their entire lives working the land, and they wanted to be as close as possible to what little was going to survive.

After they made one last check on the patients, Billy and Linda called their parents and had them meet them in the main galley area.

Linda's parents hadn't seen her in almost two years. They had only been able to visit her once while she had been at the Mayo. When they had all said their hellos, they sat down to talk.

They had only been talking for a few minutes when Richard and Shirley Patterson came over to say hi. "It's great to see you together again. Linda, we haven't seen you in years."

"I've been doing my residency at the Mayo Clinic in Rochester, Minnesota."

"What have you two been doing since you came on board?" Billy asked.

"Larry Sheldon let us take over the operation of the main galley," Richard Patterson said. "We've been running the café in Clayton for twelve years, and it's all we know how to do."

"It's great to have you on board. We'll need everyone to pitch in, and this is a perfect way for you to contribute."

"Thanks. Would you guys like something to eat?"

"I know its lunchtime, but could we get some pancakes and eggs?"

"You can have anything you want. If it wasn't for you we would have never gotten on one of the ships, and we would have been left to die. Would the rest of you like something different, or will breakfast work for you?"

"We all love to eat breakfast," Mary said, "so just bring enough for all of us."

"Can we get some maple syrup with our pancakes?" Billy asked.

"Of course you can," Shirley Patterson said. "Pancakes shouldn't be eaten without hot maple syrup."

They ate and visited for almost an hour before Billy said, "I hate to eat and run, but I need to go to the bridge and check on a few things. You guys take your time. I'll catch back up with all of you in the morning."

25

WHEN BILLY REACHED the bridge, he used one of the consoles to log on to the computer in his lab. He saw they were still working on over a hundred ships. When he checked the construction status of the ships, he saw they had ceased construction on all but two ships. In an attempt to save as many people as possible, they had every construction worker they had left working feverishly to try to finish them.

Next, he checked the flight status of the ships that had already left. The ships were trying to pick up people from all of the major metropolitan areas, so they could maximize the number of people they could save.

All of them were still en route except for the one carrying Larry Sheldon. His ship had just arrived at the Los Angeles Coliseum.

He tuned to secure channel 2 and called, "Larry Sheldon, please come in."

He was about to call again, when Larry answered. "I'm here. What do you need?"

"I see you have just arrived," Billy said. "How are the conditions there?"

"Most of the city is in shambles. There are an incredible number of fires, and there are rioters running everywhere. I saw what looked like dead bodies in many of the areas where I could see the ground through the smoke."

"You be careful. Did you set the shields like I told you?"

"Everything is set as you instructed, and we seem to be doing fine so far. I'll let you know if we have any trouble. We brought plenty of help with us, and they're combat-hardened troops. So I don't foresee running into a situation they can't handle."

"Okay, give me a call before you leave."

"Will do, and if you need anything give me a call. I'm connected to everything I need from here, so don't hesitate to call on me."

Billy spent the rest of the day monitoring the rest of the ships. Satisfied the rescue missions were proceeding as planned, he decided to find Linda and see if she would eat dinner with him.

He found her in the hospital, where she had just finished a second surgery on the wounded doctor from the roof. When she saw him she ran over, gave him a big hug, and then they kissed. As they kissed, Linda entered his mind.

I'm so glad you came to find me, Linda said. *This has been an awful week, and I needed something to pick my spirits up. I just finished working on Matthew Goldberg, the doctor who was shot helping John Tyler.*

How's he doing?

He's going to be fine. He fell in the shower, and re-opened his wounds. We had to go back in and stop the bleeding. He's going to be laid up for an extra week or so, but he'll make a complete recovery.

That's great news, and you're right, it's been a horrible day. But we did manage to recover you and your whole team, so it hasn't been a complete waste. I've missed you so much. It's been such a long time since I've been able to hold you.

Three years, ten months, and eleven days, to be exact.

Wow, you kept good count.

You know very well you knew it to the second, just as I did.

Yes, I did, but let's enjoy this moment.

As they continued to kiss, they had completely bonded their minds. This time they weren't actually talking, it was more like a bonding of emotions.

After a couple of minutes, they parted. "Wow, that was even better than I remembered," Linda said. "We had better cool it for a while longer. We still have far too much to do right now. It won't be too much longer before we can take some time for ourselves, will it?"

"It won't be much longer. We have to leave no later than the day after tomorrow."

"What do we do next?"

"Right now you and I are going to go and get a bite to eat in the galley. Then you need to get some rest while I prepare the ship for departure. We still don't have a full load of passengers, so I'm going to try to identify a likely location for us to try and save some more people."

"You need to get some rest too. I know you don't need much sleep, but when was the last time you slept an entire night?"

"I'm fine, and there's still too much to do."

While they were eating, there had been an immense amount of activity going on outside. There were still people streaming into the facility from as far as you could see. All of the roads leading into the facility were jammed with the last groups of people who had been able to reach New Mexico.

The flagship had a capacity of over 120,000 people and so far, they only had just over 40,000 people. They had initially believed they would be able to get many more people to the facility, but the nationwide riots had caused most people to give up trying to reach them.

Billy finished his snack. "I'm going to my lab and work. Why don't you try to get some sleep, and I'll see you in the morning."

"All right I will," Linda said. "I'm tired, but I worry you're going to burn out."

"Don't worry about me. I know it seems like I never get any rest, but I rest when I need to. I don't seem to need much downtime. I'm going to try to get a few hours of sleep after I check in with Larry Sheldon. Then I'll identify a location where we can safely pick up another eighty thousand people."

He used the lab terminal to log in to the server in his lab and initiated a utility to download the contents of his server to the ship's main computer system.

While the lab files were downloading, he logged in to the base's main system and began to download its contents. The base system was one of the largest in the world, but the ship's capacity dwarfed it.

When he designed the ship's computer system, he gave it over ten times the total capacity of all of the systems currently in use in the United States. Unlike the base's systems, the storage on the ship was all solid state. He had used a form of nonvolatile flash memory, only immensely faster, instead of the traditional hard drives.

He spent most of the night monitoring the other ships' progress, and searching for a location where they would be able to rescue some more people. Around four o'clock, he began feeling tired. He checked the status of his downloads, and then he lay down on a cot in the lab for a short nap.

He woke up at eight the next morning. He turned on the communication systems and called Larry Sheldon.

"Larry Sheldon, please come in. Larry, please answer if you are listening."

"What's up, Billy?"

"Nothing, I was just worried about you."

"It's pretty bad here. We couldn't land when we got here, and we've been awfully slow in getting started. The sun is just coming up so we can see to work again. I have our ship hovering just above the upper deck on one side of the Coliseum. I put down three gangways to the uppermost level and we've just started loading passengers. We have Marines on the field controlling the crowd to ensure we have an orderly flow of people.

"There's quite a bit of gang activity going on outside the Coliseum. I'm picking up an incredible amount of gunfire on the sensors, and it sounds like it's moving this way. One of the local radio stations is reporting several of the gangs, acting together, have overrun the main National Guard armory. They were dangerous enough when they were acting alone, but now that they are working together, they are much more dangerous."

As Billy was about to respond, he heard Larry cry out.

"What was that?"

There was lots of yelling and screaming in the background. "What's going on? Are you all right?" Billy said.

There was no answer and a few seconds later the radio had gone off the air. Billy continued to call for almost ten minutes before he gave up. He didn't know what happened, but he knew it couldn't be good.

When the gangs had overrun the armory, they captured several surface-to-air missile launchers, and they had used them to attack Larry's ship.

They fired twelve missiles in all, but only four of them struck home. They came through the open hatches in the front and the middle of the ship. Due to its size, the missiles didn't completely destroy the ship, but there was enough damage to cause it to lose its main power. Without main power, it was unable to stay aloft and it crashed on top of the Coliseum, crushing thousands of people.

Billy moved quickly to take control of an NSA spy satellite Larry Sheldon had shown him how to access. He repositioned it to have a view of LA, and zoomed in until he had a good view of Larry's ship.

He could see it had crashed on top of the Coliseum, and there were hundreds, if not thousands, of gang members converging on the ship. He could even see the Marines stationed in the rear of the ship starting to fight back.

He watched as they set up several heavy machine guns, and started to drive the gang members back from the ship. They started with almost four hundred battle-hardened Marines on board, and now there were less than 140 left alive.

Even though they were vastly outnumbered, the Marines had started to make progress until the gangs brought up several armored Humvees. The Humvees had heavy machine guns mounted on the top, and they quickly decimated the Marines' perimeter.

There were still twenty Marines left alive inside the ship, and they managed to close the hatch on the far end of the ship. Once they had secured the hatch, they started to move toward the control room at the front of the ship.

Larry Sheldon survived the initial missile explosions, and the ship had automatically sealed him inside the control room. The ship still had enough power to maintain the internal shields around the control room, but not much else.

They had only managed to load around 3,500 people before the ship went down, and the initial attack killed most of them. The rest died shortly afterward, when the gangs started to board the ship. They killed everyone they met as they moved through the ship.

The surviving Marines were still attempting to fight their way toward the bow of the ship. They were badly outnumbered, but their training was allowing them to fight their way forward.

Larry Sheldon was safe for the moment. The blasts that downed the ship had destroyed or disabled many of the ship's systems, but the control room was intact. He scrambled to make sense of what had happened. The ship's reserve power would only last a few hours at most.

He tried the main radio, but it wasn't working. He switched to one of the emergency transmitters and tried again. With the ship resting on the ground, the emergency transmitter was not strong enough to reach Billy directly. He scanned for any available satellites and discovered the NSA satellite Billy had brought over his position.

He established an uplink to the satellite, and called to him.

"I'm transmitting through an NSA satellite I suspect you have moved over us. I don't know how long the transmitter I'm using is going to last, so I'm going to give you a situation report. We've been brought down by what looked like surface-to-air missile batteries. The explosions have me trapped in the forward control room, and I have ten survivors with me. There's a small contingent of Marines still alive and they're fighting their way to us, but I don't think they're going to make it to our position," Larry Sheldon said.

"I'll recruit a crew for the *Imagination,* and I'll be there as soon as possible," Billy said. "Can you hold out until I get there?"

"We don't have much choice. I think we'll have enough power to keep them at bay until you can get here, but don't take any longer than you have to."

"We'll be there as soon as possible."

Billy contacted the base commander to see how many men he could get. "I can't spare any men. I'm barely able to keep our perimeter around the base secure. My men have been in almost constant combat for over a week."

"I understand. Isn't there anyone you can spare?" Billy asked.

There was a short pause while the base commander considered his options. "The best I can do is thirty reserves from our support staff. They aren't combat soldiers, but they are at least trained. But I don't have any officers I can spare. Sorry, that's the best I can do. I wish I could do more. I've known Larry Sheldon for a long time, and I would do anything I could for him."

"That's all right, General, we'll make do."

They had known the news of the imminent disaster was going to cause problems, but even their worst scenarios hadn't allowed for what was happening. Not only had the normal systems of law enforcement broken down, but there had been a steady stream of rebels coming up from South America.

The Venezuelan president had been picking fights with the United States for years, and he had taken this opportunity to try to overthrow the US government. He had almost unlimited funds at his disposal from years of oil profits, and he used the vast amounts of money to build a large well-armed force of mercenaries.

He had them in place in Central America just waiting for an opportunity like this. Larry Sheldon had tried to get them to use their vast resources to build ships to save their people, but the Venezuelan president had chosen to use the confusion brought on by the riots to try to destroy the US.

While he had doomed his people with his obsession, he had managed to overrun South Texas, parts of New Mexico, and Arizona. The Army had halted their advances, but they had taken severe casualities, and hadn't been able to disengage from the remaining rebel forces.

Billy knew he needed someone to lead the reserves so he decided to see if he could get John Tyler to come along.

"I have a huge favor to ask of you, and I want to start by saying it's all right if you don't want to do what I'm about to ask," Billy said.

"Ask away," John Tyler said.

"Larry Sheldon's ship has been shot down by the gangs in LA. I've managed to get thirty soldiers from the base commander, but he doesn't have an officer he can spare. There's one other thing. The soldiers are all rear echelon types. None of them has ever seen any sort of combat."

"When do we leave?"

"Are you sure?"

"You and Linda saved my wife and unborn child. Of course I'm going to go. When do we leave?"

"We need to leave as soon as possible. I'll meet you in the command center in ten minutes. If that will give you enough time to get ready?"

"I'll be there. I'm going to write Millie a note to tell her where I've gone, and then I'll be right up."

Billy had been in the command center for less than a minute when John Tyler came walking in.

"Thanks again for coming. I'm afraid it has gotten even worse in the last hour. The gangs have over two thousand men surrounding what's left of Larry's ship. They're attacking with everything they have, but Larry and his group are still all right."

They walked down the gangway of the flagship, and across the runway to where the *Imagination* was hovering. The thirty men the base commander had sent him were waiting beside the front gangway of the *Imagination*.

"Men, I'm Billy West, and this gentleman on my right is Commander John Tyler. John is going to be in command of the military portion of this mission."

John barked, "Follow me, men. We need to get going."

He led the men to the second level where the ship's armory was located. Billy went directly to the flight console, sat down, retracted the gangway, and sealed the hatchway.

Once he had the ship prepared, he took it straight up to an altitude of fifty thousand feet. He leveled off and accelerated to 7,500 miles per hour. In less than twenty minutes, he slowed the ship to a stop directly over the Coliseum.

He focused the cameras so he had a clear view of the carnage below him. The scene below made his blood run cold. Larry's ship was surrounded, and under constant attack.

The gangs had brought up several M175 battle tanks from the reserve center, and were shelling Larry's ship. The ship's shields had failed in all areas except for the command center.

The *Imagination*'s shields could easily stand up to the weapons they were using. However, like Larry's ship, if he opened a hatch to allow the survivors to board, they would be vulnerable. He considered his options for a minute or so and then he decided on a course of action.

"How's it going down there?" Billy said. "I'm directly above your position."

"We aren't doing very well," Larry Sheldon said. "I believe they have wiped out the rest of the Marines. They fought their way most of the way here before they were killed. They were some of the bravest men I've ever worked with, but they're gone. I don't think there's much hope for us either. We lost the last of our reserve power about ten minutes ago, and we only have about twenty minutes of emergency backup power left. When it's exhausted the shields are going to drop, and we won't last long after that.

"Don't waste your lives trying to save us. If you open up the hatch, they'll hit you just as they did us. Besides, they have way too many men surrounding our ship for us to have any chance of making it to your ship."

"The command center is sealed inside an energy field. I'm going to descend to eight thousand feet, and then I'm going to cut the command center out of the ship. Once I have it free, I'm going to use the magnetic hull plates to raise you up to our altitude. Once I have you at our level I'll use a magnetic containment tube to transfer you to the *Imagination*."

"I can't believe it'll work, but we don't have any other choices, so let's try it."

He lowered the *Imagination* to eight thousand feet and placed it in hover mode. Once the ship stopped, he trained one of the lasers on the ship below. He triggered the laser, and it started to cut the forward section off Larry's ship.

As the laser was moving across the milewide ship, the gangs spotted the *Imagination*, and began to fire their missile batteries at the ship. Unlike Larry's ship, the *Imagination*'s shields were in place, and easily stopped the incoming missiles. The gangs continued firing until they had exhausted their supply of missiles.

Once they ran out of missiles, they switched to shoulder-fired missiles, and then antiaircraft guns. They kept up a steady barrage while Billy continued to cut through the hull of the fallen ship.

It took him almost ten minutes to finish cutting through the hull. When the laser finished, Billy turned it off, and focused several of the *Imagination*'s hull plates to attract the nose of Larry's ship.

The gangs ceased firing as they watched in amazement. The nose section of the milewide ship seemed to float free of the collapsed wreckage of the Coliseum.

Frustrated because they had expended most of their heavy ordnance in the vain attempt to shoot down the

Imagination, the leader told them, "All right men, we aren't going to get that one. Let's search the rest of the ship and see what we can salvage. They'll be back to try and save some more people, and we'll try again when they do."

It took Billy a couple of minutes to bring the wreckage of the ship to his altitude. Once it was directly below, he called.

"Turn off the center two plates on the top of your ship. Once they're off, move away from the center of the bridge. I'm going to cut a hole in the roof, and then I'll lower a gangway down into the opening."

"I still can't believe you managed to do this. I don't need to power anything off, because we just lost the last of our reserve power."

It only took him a few seconds to cut a hole in the top of Larry's ship, and insert a gangway through the opening. John Tyler led his group down the ramp to help Larry and the rest of the survivors up the ramp and into the *Imagination.*

Billy met Larry Sheldon as he came up the ramp. "I was afraid we had lost you," Billy said.

"I was afraid you had lost me as well. It was looking grim for a while. We lost a lot of good men. I served with some of them for over a decade. I still can't believe those gangs managed to bring our ship down. I think they just got lucky, but it seemed like they knew where we were most vulnerable."

"How many men did you have in the control center with you?"

"I only had ten."

"That's all? How many did you have in your original crew?"

"We originally had just over six hundred, but most of them died in the initial attacks."

After the last of the survivors were on board, Billy retracted the ramp and closed the hatch. Once the ship was sealed, he released what was left of Larry's ship, and allowed it to drop back to Earth.

They were still directly over what was left of the Coliseum, so when the milewide remnant of the ship hit the ground there was an immense cloud of smoke and dust. The impact killed a thousand or more of the gang members gathered around the remains of the ship.

"Let's get back to base," Billy said. "We still have room for over eighty thousand people on the flagship, and we need to see if we can save at least a few more people before we have to leave."

"I'm going to use one of the other radios, and see if I can find out how the rest of the rescues are going," Larry Sheldon said. "I certainly hope they're faring better than we did."

It only took a few minutes for them to get back to the base. "How are the other teams doing?" Billy asked.

"Several of them have run into resistance and riots, but none of them have had catastrophic problems," Larry Sheldon said. "Not counting the losses in LA, we have sustained another two hundred casualties. Considering the number of people we have in play, it's not as bad as it could have been. We don't have more than twenty-four hours left. How many more stops do you realistically think we can make?"

"Let's get everyone on board that's left at the base and then we'll see what else we have time for."

They walked down the ramp of the *Imagination* and started across the runway to the flagship.

26

WHEN THEY REACHED the flagship's gangway, Larry said, "I'm going to visit the base commander. I'm going to instruct him to bring in all of his men and any other people who have managed to make it this far."

"Okay, I'm going to call Nicholas Stavros and get him to move the *Imagination* into landing bay two," Billy said.

"I'll come back and help you get organized as soon as I get him started," Larry Sheldon said.

"Okay. After I call Nicholas, I'm going to find Linda and see how she's doing. Then I'm going to do the final plots for the initial leg of our trip. I also need to check and make sure the timeline hasn't changed for the first wave of the asteroids."

He found Linda talking with their parents in Rob and Beth's quarters. "Hi everyone, it's good to see you all together again," Billy said. "I needed some normalcy in my day; it's been a rough day so far. How are your patients doing?"

"The two wounded men are doing fine, but I'm worried about Lucy Wilson," Linda said. "I'm running some more tests to confirm what I think is wrong, but she's very sick."

"How's Millie Tyler?"

"She's doing fine, but I don't think it's going to be

many more days before she goes into labor. I hope she waits until we're on our way so I'll be able to focus my full attention on her. There's been quite a bit of trouble around the base in the last couple of days, and I have thirty wounded soldiers who have come in from the skirmishes around the base."

"Nothing like what happened to Larry in LA."

"What happened in LA?"

"They lost the ship, and all but eleven of the crew."

"That's terrible. All of those people gone and think of the thousands who are going to die now that we have one less ship."

"I know, but there was nothing I could do. By the time I got there, it was over."

"How much longer do we have before we need to leave?" Ben asked.

"I think we have at least another twenty-four hours," Billy said. "As soon as I finish here I'm going back to my lab so I can confirm how much time is left."

"I'm scared. Are we going to be all right?" Beth said.

"We're going to be fine, and please try not to worry," Billy said. "Now that you have settled into your quarters, what do you all think?"

"Our quarters are unbelievable," Mary said. "We must have three thousand square feet or more, and it's so nice. I've never lived in anything this nice."

"We tried to make all of the quarters as comfortable as we could. They are going to be our home for a long time."

"How are we going to live cooped up inside all of the time?" Rob asked.

"Billy designed several of the areas on the ship to be able to simulate the Earth's surface," Linda said.

"Yes, I did. There are parks, fields, lakes, and even areas where we can still experience the four seasons."

"Impossible," Rob said. "We're on board a ship."

"It'll be easier for you to see and experience than it will be for me to try and explain," Billy said. "After lunch, will you take our parents up to some of the upper decks and let them see for themselves?"

"Sure," Linda said. "But can't you come with us? I would love to spend some time with you. We've only gotten to spend a few minutes together since I've been back."

"I would love to spend time with you, but I have to take care of the last-minute details so we can leave on time. Our ship is in charge of the navigation for all of the ships in the fleet. I promise, as soon as I can, I'll spend time with you."

After a few more minutes, Billy said, "I'm sorry, that's all the time I can spare. I have to get back to work. I'll see all of you as soon as I can."

As he got up to leave, Linda stood and gave him a long kiss. As they kissed, she told him, *All right, you, don't you forget about me. I miss you so much.*

If you weren't seeing what I'm thinking, I would tell you that you have no idea how much I miss you. Since you can see it in my mind, you know it's true.

Yes, sweetie, I do. I can hardly wait until we can be together.

While Billy was making his final preparations, the Logos leaders were making their final plans. Clayton Edwards had just died from a massive heart attack, and their new leader, Luther Warburg, was hosting their final assembly before they were to leave.

They were holding their final meeting on Earth at Glen Eyrie, the site of Billy's birth and transformation.

"Ladies and gentlemen, the time grows short," Luther Warburg said. "I've just talked with President McAllister, and he tells me they are going to divert one of the Denver rescue ships to our location so they can pick us up. The original texts, which form the basis of our sect, prophesied the events we are experiencing. It's our belief God placed Adamartoni and Evevette on the Earth to advance the race of man. We also believe much of the information contained in the gospels was misinterpreted as it was rewritten and translated over the years. Dr. Evans's accidental actions may or may not have been caused by God, but they have provided the mechanism of our salvation."

"As you all know, we had been working to unlock the mystery of Adamartoni and his family, but the accident destroyed all of the artifacts. What we do know is that Dr. Evans's inadvertent injection of Billy West has provided the mechanism of our salvation. The ship will be here in less than two hours, and we must be ready, because they can't afford to stop for long."

Billy started to verify that his calculations for their departure were up-to-date. He used all of the available satellites to verify the asteroids were still twenty-something hours out. As he scanned the images and data, he saw the main body of asteroids was still twenty-three hours out. As he continued his scan, he was horrified to see there were considerable amounts of smaller ones that were less than twenty minutes from the Earth's atmosphere. He quickly verified his findings, and then he turned to call Larry Sheldon.

"Get back here right now," Billy said. "The first asteroids are going to hit in less than twenty minutes. Tell everyone to drop whatever they are doing and run this way."

"That's not enough time for most of them to reach the ship," Larry Sheldon said.

"I know, but there's no more time. I'm going to try and contact the other ships, so I can warn them."

He recorded a warning message detailing the threat, programmed the transmitters to loop continuously, and started the broadcast on all the frequencies used by the fleet.

Once he had the message transmitting, he checked the satellite images for the status of the incoming asteroids. As he scanned the images, he saw the first ones were already beginning to hit the East Coast.

He managed to capture several images of the asteroids as they approached the Earth. He got two images of the one that struck New York City. The asteroid split in two as it hit the dense portion of the atmosphere. One piece hit just offshore, and the second hit on the outskirts of the city on the west side.

Immediately after he captured the two frames of video, the satellite he was using went dead. Another one of the asteroids had destroyed the satellite he was using.

He switched to one farther to the west, and as he did, he saw an immense tidal wave come ashore on the city's east side. From the other direction, there was a fireball from the blast generated by the second piece of the asteroid. The two forces met somewhere near the center of the city.

One minute he had a clear image of the most populous city in the United States, and the next it was gone. Four of their ships were in and around New York attempting to pick up passengers.

They disappeared from sight as the two waves of destruction met. As he continued to watch, it took a couple of minutes for the picture to clear enough for him to be able to see the ships.

The ships received Billy's warning less than thirty seconds before the asteroid struck. Three of them immediately retracted their gangways, sealed the hatches, and increased their shield power as Billy had instructed.

Due to their quick reactions, the ships were intact, and still on station around what had been New York City. The fourth had been slow to respond and was incinerated by the fireball. Shortly after he verified the three ships were intact, the second satellite went offline.

He turned to the flagship's cameras to see whether Larry Sheldon was approaching yet. To his relief, he saw him coming up the gangway. As he watched Larry enter the hatch, he saw there were hundreds of people on their way. He glanced at the satellite image of their position and saw there was an asteroid closing in on them.

He retracted the gangway, sealed the hatch, and immediately increased the shields' strength. He had previously programmed the ship's navigation computer on a course to San Francisco so they could pick up more people.

When the hatches closed, he hit run on the computer, and the ship started to ascend for its journey to the West Coast. The flagship was only a hundred feet or so from the main hangar, and as it left, it ripped one side of the hangar to shreds. The ship had only reached an altitude of fifteen hundred feet when the asteroid struck the ship on the side nearest the hangar.

The asteroid was only about a hundred meters across, but it hit with immense force. The ship's shields disintegrated a portion of the asteroid, and the rest of it hit the ground causing a tremendous explosion.

The impact was roughly equivalent to a fifty-megaton bomb. The blast vaporized the base, and everyone who was still trying to reach the flagship.

There wasn't even a shudder from the massive ship as the asteroid hit. Even though he had designed it, Billy marveled at the power of the ship. He turned to Larry Sheldon and said, "I hate that we lost all of those people, but we might as well move to the West Coast, and see if we can save a few more people. There's nothing left for us here. The base and most of Union County is gone."

Larry Sheldon got a tremendously sad look on his face as he remembered the friends he had just lost. He had worked with the commanding general for most of his adult life, and in a heartbeat, he and all of his men were gone.

He didn't say anything for a few seconds, as he said a quick prayer for them. When he finished he raised his eyes from the floor. "Yes, we should. Do you think there's any chance we can save anyone?"

"I don't know for sure, but it won't take more than twenty minutes to get to San Francisco, so we can at least try."

He scanned the various satellites still available to him as they raced toward the West Coast. When the console beeped to tell him the ship had stopped over San Francisco, he already suspected what he would see.

He turned to look where the city should have been, but all he saw was water where San Francisco and Oakland used to be, and it extended inland for at least twenty miles.

The debris from the blast had already clouded the sky to the point where most of the sunlight couldn't get through.

"I don't think there's any use in continuing to look for survivors, at least not in the US," Billy said.

"I've been in contact with several of the other ships, and they are all reporting the same conditions," Larry Sheldon said. "If this is just the minor debris in front of the asteroids, we need to go ahead and get out of here."

"How many ships do you think we have left?"

"We won't know for sure until we meet them at the rally point. But I know for sure we have over a hundred."

"We had over five hundred when we sent them all out."

"I know, but I haven't been able to contact the rest. I only had a few minutes to make contact, so I'm sure there are more. I just don't know how many."

"I'm going to put us in orbit to see if we can get a better look at what's happening. Then we can decide what we're going to do next."

He piloted the flagship to an orbit 19,323 nautical miles above the Earth. As they orbited the Earth, they anxiously searched for some signs of life so they could attempt a rescue.

As they orbited, Larry Sheldon was transmitting a call for all ships to rendezvous with them at the rally point. The initial rally point was halfway to the moon. Growing more desperate, Billy increased their speed, so they could make a complete orbit quicker.

He continued to scan the surface of the Earth for signs of survivors, but he hadn't been able to identify any. The dust in the atmosphere made it almost impossible to see anything, so they were focusing on electronic emissions.

As they completed their orbit Billy said, "This isn't going to do any good. I haven't been able to pick anything up on our sensors. I hate it, but I think we need to get going. There's a steady stream of debris approaching the Earth, and we need to get out of the way."

"I agree," Larry Sheldon said. "I've instructed all ships to leave immediately for the rally point. I've told them we'll wait for three hours, and then we're leaving."

"Do you think anyone is still alive down there?" Billy asked.

"I'm sure there are some, but I'm also sure we would get more people killed trying to save them."

"All right, we're leaving."

He selected the proper flight plan from his preprogrammed lists, and hit enter. The ship immediately accelerated, and left orbit for its next stop.

Since the ship was well outside of the atmosphere, it moved much more rapidly than before. It only took them forty-five minutes to reach the halfway point to the moon.

As the ship slowed to a stop Billy said, "We've arrived. I'm going down to talk with Linda and our parents about what has happened."

"No problem," Larry Sheldon said. "I'll keep an eye on things. I'll call you if I need you. The other ships should begin arriving shortly, so I'll be traffic cop while you're gone."

"I'll be back well before it's time to leave."

Larry Sheldon stopped to wonder whether the Logos managed to get out of Glen Eyrie. The Logos had instructed all of their members to come to Glen Eyrie so they would all be on the same ship. The ship which was coming for them was still en route when the first small asteroids began to hit.

Around the same time as the asteroid hit Clayton, a cluster of asteroids struck the Colorado Springs area. The result of the impact was the complete annihilation of the area, including Glen Eyrie. The loss of virtually all of the Logos leadership made Larry Sheldon the highest-ranking Logos still alive.

Billy found them in Rob and Beth's quarters, where they were sitting in front of a large fireplace talking. He joined Linda on a love seat, and put his arm around her.

"I'm taking a few moments to let all of you know what's going on," Billy said. "We left the Earth about an hour ago. We have stopped at the halfway point to the moon, and are waiting for the rest of the ships to catch up to us. We thought we had more time, but a leading group of asteroids took us by surprise. We ended up having almost eighteen hours less than we had planned. We have lost a number of ships and people, but we won't know for sure how bad it is until all of the ships are accounted for."

"Is anyone still on Earth going to survive?" Ben asked.

"No, I don't think they will. I believe when it's all over, the Earth itself isn't going to survive. As I attempted to map the path of the asteroid swarm, I found it sweeps away everything in its path. It continues to gather a bigger debris field as it sweeps away more objects. The leading edge of the debris field is all that has hit the earth so far, but that's been bad enough. We're going to hold here for another two hours, and then we are going to leave. I hope the rest of the ships are able to join up with us, but we have already transmitted the complete flight plan to the other ships in case they have to proceed on their own."

"I can't believe this is happening," Mary said. "What are we going to do?"

"As I said before, we're doing everything we can. I believe we'll be successful in eluding the asteroid swarm. After that, we're going to have to improvise. I have no idea what we're going to do next, but I do know we'll at least have a chance. Rob, what's the matter, you look like you lost your best friend."

"Clayton was the only home Beth and I have ever known. We haven't ever been farther away than Denver. Now everything we've known is gone forever. It's just too much for me to comprehend. I'm not sure we shouldn't have stayed and taken our chances."

"I can't even imagine what you are going through, and Clayton is the only home I've ever known as well. But, if we had stayed, we would all be dead. The asteroid that hit the base vaporized Clayton. I've asked Richard and Shirley Patterson to fix a nice picnic lunch, and bring it to you on the park deck. Why don't all of you go and have a nice lunch? I'm going to be busy for several hours, but I'll try to join all of you for dinner."

"We can't have a picnic while the world is being destroyed," Mary said.

"Yes, you can, and I want all of you to try and forget about what's happening for a few hours. I know it'll be difficult, but you can do it. I have to go. Larry Sheldon is watching the bridge while I take a few moments with you."

"I've been busy while you were gone," Larry Sheldon said. "Several more ships have shown up."

"How many do we have?"

"Let's see, we have a hundred and thirty-three ships accounted for. The last ship that came in was from Europe.

It only had a few thousand people on board. They had just started to load when the asteroids started to hit. Their ship took some damage in its aft hatch, but they managed to get it sealed."

"Where are the rest of the ships?" Billy said. "We're hundreds of ships short."

"I've asked that question to all of the ships as they come in. A few of them had reports which would explain why some of the ships are missing, but certainly not enough to account for the shortfall we have."

As they were talking about where the rest of the ships were, another group of ships arrived.

"This is General Songkainu. I'm on board the *Genghis Khan* from the Peoples Republic of China. Who's in charge here?"

"I'm Larry Sheldon, and I'm on board the flagship from the United States' fleet. I'm glad you made it. How many ships do you have in your group?

"There are ten ships in our group."

"Do you have any idea where the rest of the ships are?"

"If it's anything like what happened with the rest of our ships, they aren't coming. We had several of our ships disabled by terrorist attacks. The terrorists were mingling with the passengers, and were coming on board with either small nuclear weapons or biologic weapons. We believe they were using a superstrain of the Ebola virus. It infected the ships in a matter of hours, and the death rate, as far as we can tell, was one hundred percent. Our doctors have never seen anything like it. We have been unable to control the virus. We have two cases on board now, but we believe we have them isolated in one of the bottom landing bays. We have put two doctors in hazmat suits in with them to try and treat them, but I don't hold out much hope."

"My name is Billy West. We have one of the premier germ warfare teams in the world on board. Dr. William

Robbins and Dr. Linda Bustamante have had great success in constructing cures for engineered viruses. If you can get a blood sample drawn and placed in a hazmat container, I'm sure they will work with your doctors to find a cure."

"We're grateful for the offer of assistance, but I'm sure we can handle it on our own. If we can't, we'll call you back for assistance."

"Are there any more of your ships coming?" Larry Sheldon asked.

"We won't have any more, and we didn't see any other ships on our way. We had twenty-three ships ready, but we lost all but the *Genghis Khan* and nine others. We weren't even able to fully load the ships we have. There are only twenty thousand people on board the *Genghis Khan*. We stopped boarding when we realized what was happening."

"We'll call you when we have the fleet ready to leave," Larry Sheldon said. "The current plan calls for us to leave in one hour and nineteen minutes from now. Do you have the next course plot loaded in your navigation computers?"

"Yes, we do. We finished loading it on the way. We'll await your signal."

Billy turned to a bank of cameras showing the *Genghis Khan* so he could check for any visible damage. He had just zoomed in to get a better look, when he and Larry saw a burst of what looked like high-pressure gas expelled from the lower side of the ship.

The gas cloud contained several dark objects. He zoomed in. As the image came into focus, they saw the Chinese had jettisoned their two patients, and the doctors who were treating them.

As they continued to watch, they saw a burst of high-intensity light emitted from the landing bay door.

"They've jettisoned the doctors and patients, and I believe they have superheated the landing bay to sterilize it," Billy said.

"I thought it was strange when he turned down your offer of assistance," Larry Sheldon said. "It makes sense now. They had already decided to dump their problem into space. It's not hard to believe coming from the Chinese. They've always been pragmatic about losses. I would guess what they experienced is what happened to the rest of our ships. As long as I have been around the terrorist mind-set, I still can't believe how they will sacrifice everything to inflict damage on us. I guess we are lucky to have as many ships as we do."

"Did you manage to get a head count from the ships as they came in?" Billy said. "With a hundred and forty-three ships we should have almost ten million people."

"When I add the *Genghis Khan* and their ships, we have one million, two hundred and forty-six thousand people."

"That's less than eleven percent of what we should have with that many ships."

"I know, but none of the ships are fully loaded, and we have a couple of ships with just a few thousand passengers. We have one of the largest contingents with fifty-six thousand people, but we aren't nearly full either. The situation deteriorated more quickly than we anticipated, and we failed to take into account the level of desperation from the terrorists. I had hoped my experience in Los Angeles was an isolated incident, and the rest of the ships would succeed."

"Are all of the ships sound enough for the trip?"

"We might want to check on Jeremy Kilgore's ship. He told me they took some damage to their forward hatch. One of the European ships had some damage as well, but it has already verified they are ready to go."

It took Larry another ten minutes to verify Jeremy's ship was sound enough to make the trip. "Everyone is ready to go. I don't think we need to wait any longer, because I don't believe there are any more ships coming."

Billy checked the ship's status. "All right, I think I'm ready to go," he said. "Send the message, and we'll leave. The sooner we get out of the asteroid's path the better."

Larry waited until they had received confirmation that everyone had heard the message, and was ready to go. Then he gave the command. "Everyone execute on a countdown from three. Three, two, one, execute."

Billy hit execute along with the rest of the fleet, and what was left of the human race began the search for a new life.

27

THE SIGHT OF the one hundred and forty-three ships moving as one was quite a sight. Most of the ships were exactly the same size and design, except for the Chinese ships and the flagship Billy was piloting.

Each of the one hundred and thirty-two ships was exactly two hundred and seventy feet tall, one mile wide, and two miles long. There had never been larger vehicles in the history of man, and the sight of all of them traveling as one was a truly impressive sight.

The Chinese ships were different from all of the rest of the fleet. They had modified Billy's plans in several areas. Their ships were one-point-two miles wide, two and a half miles long, and were only two hundred feet tall.

They hadn't utilized Billy's technology to assist them in the construction of their ships, so they had a difficult time even getting to two hundred feet in height. They had also modified his fusion reactor plans to their own specifications.

The other oddball ship was the US flagship. It was truly immense. It was five hundred and forty feet tall, two miles wide, and four miles long. Billy had installed multiple fusion reactors in the ship. When they had all of the reactors online, it had several times the amount of power available on the entire Earth.

The ships accelerated much quicker than before. In

less than twelve hours, they had achieved a speed of 175,000 miles per hour. If the inertial dampening effect hadn't been in place, they would have been extremely uncomfortable due to the G-forces. The ships' magnetic fields were causing immense eddies of magnetic energy to flow outward from the fleet.

Billy had plotted a course which would take them within a few miles of the moon, and was at a ninety-degree angle from the path of the oncoming asteroid.

The ships' designs called for them to operate at constant thrust. Billy had computed that using all available power; they would max out at just under 56 percent of the speed of light.

Even though the ships had enormous amounts of power, the faster they went the more power they needed to continue accelerating. He had a plan to allow them to go faster, but he hadn't had a chance to complete it.

He had computed the flagship's top speed to be 75 to 80 percent of the speed of light, due to its considerable advantage in available power. Even at that speed, the distances they needed to cover to reach any other habitable planet would take far too long.

Billy and Linda made plans for a nice dinner with their parents. They took them to the deck that had been outfitted to look like a normal American small town.

The small pizza shop where they were eating could have been mistaken for Main Street in many towns in America. They all managed to act as if it was a normal dinner, but each of them was almost completely overwhelmed by the events of the day.

"What's going to become of us?" Ben asked.

"I don't know how to answer your question," Billy said. "Other than to tell you I believe we're going to have good lives. I'm sure God has something else in mind for us. Why else would He put everyone through this much trauma? I just wish He would let us know what it might be. I'll keep you all updated as our plans change, but right now let's just enjoy this opportunity to be together."

The next day Billy was in the command center monitoring their progress. He saw they were going to miss the main asteroid, but they weren't going to escape the smaller asteroids on the outer edges of the debris field.

Their ship was in the lead, so he decided to see if he could buy them enough time to get out of the way of the asteroids' debris field.

He changed course to position the ship on the side closest to the oncoming asteroids. He powered up the lasers on the side facing the debris field. As he ran through his final computations, he determined he was going to need more firepower, so he powered up the pulse cannons. The pulse cannons had been a late addition to the ship's plans. They were capable of delivering an energy pulse equal to fifty megatons of energy.

He programmed the weapons' fire control computers to be able to recognize the profiles of the asteroids. Once he was satisfied the computers could identify them, he enabled the system to auto fire, and leaned back to see what was going to happen.

He had programmed the weapons systems to work in clusters. There were ten Petawatt lasers per set, and five pulse cannons programmed to work in conjunction with the lasers. The system was set to only fire on the asteroids in their path, and as the fire control computers locked onto the closest asteroids it began to fire. The lasers fired for ten seconds, and then the pulse cannons fired continuously for five seconds. He marveled at their power as he watched the concentrated fire virtually vaporize the first asteroid.

Over the next hour the ship's weapons continued to clear away the asteroids from their path. As they neared the edge of the debris field, he saw there were going to be too many for the weapons to clear.

He left the fire control computers online, and changed course to bring the flagship between the asteroids he couldn't destroy and the rest of the fleet.

He knew the timing for the maneuver was going to be critical. He transferred all the ship's surplus power to the shields facing the oncoming asteroids. He was going to allow the weapons to continue destroying the asteroids until the last second before he transferred the weapons power to the shields.

He already had enough power flowing to the shields to handle most threats. But the last two asteroids were over a quarter of a mile wide. Once he had the timing calculated, he entered the data into the main fire control computer and waited. The ship moved ever closer to the asteroids, and when they completely filled his screen, the computer made the power shift.

The weapons ceased firing, and the shields went to maximum power. He watched the asteroids hit the ship's shield. There was a tremendous burst of light that continued for almost thirty seconds. The light was so intense the cameras went off-line.

When they came back online, there was nothing visible, except the black of space. A shudder passed through his body as he thought of the destructive power he just witnessed.

He checked the screens, and saw they had moved out of the asteroids' debris field. Satisfied the danger was past, he returned the flagship to the front of the fleet, and they resumed their preprogrammed course.

He hadn't gotten a complete night's sleep since he found out about the asteroid, so he decided to try to take a short nap. A couple of hours later he was jolted awake by the sound of an alarm.

He ran across the room to the console to see what was happening. He had programmed the computers to alert him to any danger, so the alert could be from any number of possible threats.

He silenced the alarm, and looked to see what triggered it. He scanned through the list of issues on the screen and saw a collision alert–triggered alarm.

He checked the screens to see where the danger was coming from and saw it wasn't threatening them. The threat was to Earth.

Even though they were already millions of miles from Earth, the ship had sensed an imminent danger to the Earth and sounded the alarm.

He adjusted the long-range sensors and cameras to focus on the Earth. The main asteroid field had reached the Earth. As he surveyed the scene, he saw the moon was already gone, undoubtedly destroyed by the massive asteroid. Even the sun was no longer in its normal position.

The main asteroid was slightly larger than the moon, and it was not a normal asteroid. It was a remnant of a neutron star that was about to collapse into a black hole. The collision with the comet altered its path, and put it on a collision course with Earth. It was extremely dense, and when it struck the Earth at the North Pole, the resulting explosion shattered the Earth into billions of fragments. He watched the asteroid sweep the remnants of the Earth into its debris field.

He lowered his head, and asked God to receive the souls of the billions of people who had just perished. As he finished his prayer, he felt a tremendous outpouring of terror and hate from the nonbelievers.

A feeling of euphoria, more powerful than anything he had ever experienced replaced the terror and hate, and he knew God had received the believers' souls.

Shaken by the intense feelings, it took him several

minutes to gather his thoughts. When he had finished
absorbing the experience, he reset the alarms and sensors.

He took a few minutes to delete the programming monitoring the Earth. Next, he archived the video of the destruction to an encrypted, classified folder, and then deleted it
from the areas the rest of the ship could access.

He had just finished removing the files, when he felt
Linda's mind touch his. *I felt a huge rush of terror and
hate a few minutes ago, and then the most incredible feeling of peace and joy. What's going on?*

He opened his mind to let her experience the events he
had just witnessed. It took several seconds for her to ab-
sorb the experiences, and when she finished, she told him,
*That was just awful. I know we abandoned the Earth, and
we all knew it was doomed, but to see it end isn't something I ever expected to experience.*

*What were the feelings we experienced after you prayed
for God to take their souls? I don't believe I've ever felt a
more intense feeling of joy. Were those feelings from God?*

Yes, I believe they were. Wasn't it the best feeling ever?

Yes, it was.

Was the terror and hate what I think it was?

*Yes, I'm afraid it was. I don't think it will serve any
purpose to tell anyone what we just experienced. It's going to be hard enough keeping everyone positive about
what is going on.*

*No problem, I won't let anyone know. I won't even
share it with our parents. I'm not sure Daddy would take
the news very well. He seems to be struggling with accept-
ing the fact we'll never return.*

*Your dad did seem to be kind of down the last time I
saw him. We need to get him and my dad some projects to
take their minds off what has happened.*

When the government started paying them all of the

money for use of their land, I think in a way it ended up depressing them.

I'll think of a meaningful set of tasks for them.

What did you have in mind?

You know I built several levels on the ship to function as agricultural areas, don't you?

I'm sorry, but I'm not that familiar with the ship yet. I've been so busy with patients since we came on board. I just haven't paid any attention to much else.

He opened his mind again to show her the areas he had in mind for their dads. She saw the images of the forested level, the parks, and finally the fields of grains and vegetables.

I can't believe you have all of that on board a spaceship. How in the world can they grow indoors?

All of the areas, except for the actual living quarters, can simulate night and day. There are even several which are able to simulate the four seasons.

That's so cool. I've known you my whole life, and you never cease to amaze me. In the middle of trying to save the human race, you have time to think about our longterm comfort and mental health.

Why, thank you. But it all has to work together, or we'll never be able to survive long term. Would you like to have dinner with me tonight? Billy asked.

Let me check my busy social calendar. Yes, I believe I can work you in.

I'll come by your quarters at eight tonight.

Okay, but why the mystery? We usually just meet in the galley.

No mystery, I'll explain when I come by for you.

He spent the rest of the day finishing his preparations for dinner. On one of the upper levels of the ship, which would have been the fifty-fourth floor if it had been a building, he had outfitted several of the rooms as observatories. Similar to the virtual reality in the command center, the technology could make the room seem like it was actually open to space.

He remembered the first time he used the virtual reality during *Imagination*'s test flight around the moon. Even though he knew what to expect, the experience was almost overwhelming.

He was using one of the smaller areas, and it was finished out as a formal dining room. Larry Sheldon had made a point to outfit the ships with nothing but first-class furnishings. When Billy asked about it, he told him the ships were going to be all they would know for many years, and there was no reason not to be comfortable.

When he finished preparing the room, he went to find Larry Sheldon. He found him in the control room talking with John Tyler.

"I'm glad you two are getting acquainted," Billy said.

"Actually, I've worked with John before," Larry Sheldon said. "I first met him when he was leading an operation in Prague."

"Now I see why he seemed to handle himself so well," Billy said. "If you've worked with Larry, you're used to taking care of yourself."

"That's a bit of an understatement," Larry Sheldon said. "Our friend here is one of the most skilled operatives I've ever seen. When we had the tough assignments, John Tyler is the one we would call for."

"How is it you were working as a doorman in Linda's apartment building?" Billy asked.

"I was forced to leave the military for medical reasons."

"Were you wounded?"

"No, I have a bad heart. The doctors at Bethesda said it was a birth defect, and that I've always had it. It wasn't until I got older that it started to cause me problems."

"Why didn't they just fix it for you?" Billy asked. "I assume the doctors at Bethesda offered to, didn't they?"

"They told me that due to where the problem is located, they didn't think they could do anything for me. It had progressed so far that they felt the only thing that would help would be a transplant."

"I'll talk with Linda tonight, and see what she can do for you," Billy said.

"I appreciate it. But I'm sure if there was anything that could be done, the doctors would have."

"I'm sure they would have done everything they could, but Linda is pretty inventive. Let's give her a chance to look at you, if you don't mind."

"I don't have much to lose, so why not?"

"Were you looking for me?" Larry Sheldon asked.

"I was. Did you by any chance have time to do the favor I asked of you?"

"Yes, I did. I sent a special flight to Amsterdam to pick it up."

"What are you two talking about?" John Tyler asked.

"Billy asked me to pick out a wedding ring for him. I called a good friend at the diamond exchange, and arranged for him to put together the best set he could. I haven't had time to open the package he sent. But I would be surprised if it wasn't truly special. I told him there was no spending limit, and it needed to be the best he had ever put together."

"Thank you. You didn't have to go to that much trouble. You know I don't know much about that sort of thing, and I knew you would know somebody who did."

"My young friend, there's nothing I wouldn't do for you. I still can't believe the luck mankind had for you to come along at this point in our history. If you hadn't been born, there wouldn't be even a remnant of the human race right now. Besides, you and Linda are two of the nicest young people I've ever met.

"Both of you have put your lives on hold to try to do as much as you possibly can for other people. Neither one of you ever questioned whether to do it; you just step up and do it. John and I are used to working with truly exceptional people, but I think I can speak for both of us when I say, you two are truly special."

"Coming from you that means the world to me. You know how much I respect you and your opinions."

Larry ripped the paper off the package, opened the cardboard box. "Let's take a look at what we have."

He pulled out a black quartz ring box. He opened it, and turned it to Billy and John.

"That's the most gorgeous ring I've ever seen. Your guy did great," Billy said.

He took it from Larry's hand so he could get a better look. The stone in the engagement ring was a flawless, colorless, four-carat diamond. The wedding band had four one-carat flawless diamonds. If Billy had purchased it, the bill would have been tens of thousands of dollars.

"This is a truly impressive wedding set. I don't know what it cost, but you know I don't have much money to work with."

"It was never a question of money," Larry Sheldon said. "The world owes you more than it could ever repay, and now money has no value whatsoever. If it had turned out money was needed, the government would have picked up the cost. You just take it, and ask your young lady to be your wife."

"I'm going to do that very thing, tonight at dinner."

"Congratulations," John Tyler said. "I don't know Linda

very well, but if it weren't for her, Millie and I would be among the casualties. I hope you two are as happy as Millie and I have been."

"Thanks, John."

"Let me add my best wishes," Larry Sheldon said. "Once you have asked her, I'll congratulate both of you."

They spent a couple of hours talking about what comes next, and Billy briefed them on the fleet's status.

"We have a hundred and forty-three ships in the fleet, and within the month we will be moving at fifty percent of the speed of light. No human has ever gone anywhere close to this fast before, but even at that speed it will take us many years to reach another habitable planet."

"Do you think we can find another place for us to live?" John Tyler asked.

"Yes, I do. But none of the research I've read has allowed me to form an opinion on where to look first. The technology the researchers had to use just didn't allow any real quality to the research. If I can get time to use the observation points on the upper deck, I think I can identify a direction to begin looking."

"Do you think we'll ever be able to return to the Earth?" John Tyler asked. "Is it possible it will stabilize after a few years?"

Billy hadn't intended to share what he had just experienced with anyone other than Linda. As he considered how to answer John's question, he thought of what Larry Sheldon and John Tyler had already experienced, and decided they would be able to handle the news.

"The Earth is gone," Billy said. "When the asteroid struck the North Pole, the impact and resulting explosion was so massive, it literally shattered the Earth into billions of pieces."

"It may have been a blessing in a way," Larry Sheldon

said. "If there had been survivors they might have suffered immensely before they finally died."

"I need to share one other thing with you," Billy said. "You may not believe what I'm about to tell you, but I'm going to try and share it as fully as I can communicate it. I had such a feeling of hopelessness and loss for all of the people, and I prayed to God asking Him to receive their souls. When I finished my prayer, the first feeling I experienced was a tremendous rush of hate and terror. I wasn't completely surprised at the feelings, but the next feelings were even more overwhelming. I can't fully describe the incredible euphoria I felt when they entered His kingdom. I know you may not believe me, or believe in God, but I'm telling you it happened."

"I've never shared this with you, but I'm a member of the Logos," Larry Sheldon said. "Not only do I believe you, I believe it was exactly what you thought it was. I believe you know about the Logos and our beliefs."

"Yes, I do, and so does Linda. Our pastor was a member, and he mentored us for several months before we started school. It would seem to be quite a coincidence that several of the most influential people in our lives are members of the Logos. It isn't a coincidence. Is it Larry?"

"Perhaps not, my young friend. But this isn't the right time to pursue the answer."

"Okay, I'll wait. But will you promise me Linda and I can talk about it with you?"

"I promise, when the time is right, I'll tell you everything I know."

A few hours later Billy left them to get ready for their big night. Larry Sheldon had selected Billy's quarters for him. Billy had never taken any real interest in where he stayed, and Larry wanted to make sure his quarters would be suitable.

As he walked in, he took a second to marvel at the accommodations. There was a rock fireplace on the far side of the room, and it automatically ignited into a roaring fire as he entered.

The wall to the right of the entrance was a fish tank. The wall was part of the massive saltwater tanks on the deck above. There were all types of fish in the tank, and they were free to swim down the wall into Billy's quarters.

The living room had an unbelievably comfortable feel to it. Larry used one of the top New York interior design firms to decorate the ship, and he had them take particular care with Billy's quarters.

He was going to explore his new home, but he decided he had better take a shower before their big night. He wandered through his quarters until he found his bedroom and the master bath. It had a large sunken Jacuzzi tub, and a huge walk-in shower. It was made of what looked like rough-hewn granite, and was the nicest shower he had ever seen.

As he showered, he thought back on the amazing and terrifying events of the last few days. Here he was, standing in the fanciest bathroom he had ever seen, in a spaceship that would soon be traveling at half the speed of light, taking a shower.

He thought back to the loss of Klaus Heidelberg, and the billions of people on the Earth they weren't able to save. He remembered John Tyler's bravery helping to save Linda's group, and all of the other people who had worked so tirelessly in order for them to have a chance at life.

He reflected on the tremendous feeling of euphoria he felt after Earth's destruction. Finally, he wondered what sort of life they might end up having. They were destined to spend at least a good portion of their lives on board the ships, and he had no idea if they would ever find another planet they could call home.

When he finished getting ready, he began to think about the coming evening. He and Linda had known almost from birth that they had a special bond, but tonight he intended to ask her to be his wife. He didn't for a minute doubt her answer, but he was nervous for some reason. Like most young men who had ever asked for a young woman's hand in marriage, he had butterflies.

He finished dressing and left to pick up Linda. Her quarters were across the hall from Rob and Beth's. She wanted to be close to them during the first part of their voyage, since her dad was having such a difficult time handling the events. She knew Billy was going to get their dads involved in the operations of the agricultural areas, but she was still worried about him.

It took Billy almost three minutes to reach Linda's quarters. Even by high-speed elevator, it was a lengthy trip across the huge ship.

He was about to knock when she opened the door. "No fair; you were sensing me coming, weren't you?" Billy said.

"Of course I was. I sensed you as soon as you left your room."

"Are you ready to go?"

"I haven't been able to think about anything else all day."

"Are you hungry?"

"I could eat a horse; I haven't had anything since breakfast. I worked straight through so I could have a few hours off tonight."

They took the elevator to the deck where he had spent the day preparing the room for tonight's dinner.

"Where are you taking me?" Linda asked. "The galley is down, not up."

"I have a special evening planned. I don't think we have ever had dinner without someone else present. I've arranged for Richard Patterson to bring our dinner up here, so we can have some privacy."

When they walked in there was a fire burning in a fireplace similar to the one in Billy's quarters. Their favorite music was playing softly for background music. Richard met them at the door and seated them at the dining room table. Neither of them drank alcohol, so he served them their favorite beverage, Coca-Cola.

Most couples, who could have literally any dinner they wanted, would have picked lobster, steak, or some exotic dish. Their special meal was fried chicken, mashed potatoes, and corn on the cob. For dessert, they would have Dutch apple pie and ice cream.

Richard served their dinner, and went to the far end of the room to wait until they were ready for dessert. Billy waved him over. "Thank you so much for all of this. If you don't mind, we'll serve ourselves dessert."

"I understand, and Shirley and I would like to thank you for allowing us to prepare your dinner tonight."

"Thank Shirley for us, and let her know it's very good."

"Good night then. I'll come up tomorrow and get the dishes."

After he left, they continued eating, and enjoying each other's company. When they finished dinner, and were about to eat their dessert, Billy asked, "Would you like a cup of coffee with the pie and ice cream?"

"Is it the good coffee?"

"Yes, it is. Larry made sure we have a couple of lifetimes' supply of our coffee."

They talked for a few more minutes while they finished dessert. He poured them each another cup of coffee. "Come with me, I would like to show you something," Billy said.

They walked into an adjoining room where there was nothing but a single love seat and a coffee table. They put their coffees on the table and sat down.

He put his arm around Linda, and used the remote control to activate the virtual reality system for the room. The ceiling and walls of the room seemed to disappear, and it was as if they were in open space.

Linda gasped. "It's unbelievable. The view takes my breath away. How in the world did you manage this?"

"It isn't that special. It's a real-time virtual simulation of the space outside the ship. Though I do admit, it does seem real. I first used it on the *Imagination* during our test flight to the moon."

"Okay, what are you up to? You've been guarding your thoughts from me all evening. You don't have some sort of bad news for me, do you?"

"Definitely not. In fact I hope you find what I'm going to ask you attractive."

He opened his mind fully to hers, and handed her the ring box. She was about to ask what it was for, when she heard him think to her, *Linda Lou, would you do me the honor of being my wife?*

Just for fun, she didn't let him see her answer right away. After a couple of seconds, she relented and blended her mind with his. *You've always known I would when you asked me. Of course, I want to spend the rest of my life with you. It doesn't matter to me where we are, or how we have to live. I want to spend whatever time we have being your wife.*

We're going to have a fine life together. It's not going to be anything like we expected, but it will be a good life. We have many challenges ahead of us, but we've always known they were coming. I promise you we'll get through them together.

You sound so sure of yourself. I don't know how you can be so positive. The entire planet is gone, and we are on our way to who knows where.

I don't know where we're going exactly, but we'll figure it out. I just know we will find another home someday.

She opened the ring box and squealed. *This is the most exquisite wedding set I've ever seen. I don't think I have even seen pictures of one this nice. How in the world could you afford a ring like this?*

Larry Sheldon helped me out. He has contacts in New York and Amsterdam; well, he had *contacts in New York and Amsterdam. The entire set is a one-of-a-kind custom job. I have no idea what it would have cost, but Larry said it was the least the government could do for us. Besides, as he said, money has absolutely no value anymore.*

Well it's magnificent. Thank you so much, and I can't wait to be your wife. When do you think we can get married?

I think we should be able to schedule our wedding in about two weeks, if it's all right with you?

I guess I can last another two weeks, but what's the significance in waiting two weeks?

I want to put some more distance between us and the asteroid.

We need to tell our parents. They are going to be excited.

Yes, they will, but I don't think it will be a total surprise to them. I'm sure they have believed we would marry someday.

You're right; Mother has even told me she thought so a few times.

She slid over and onto his lap and they kissed for several minutes. She leaned back and said, "We had better stop for now, or we'll need a room."

"I've never heard you talk like that." He connected with her mind again, and said, "Or think like that."

"I've been gone for quite a while, and I am a licensed doctor, after all."

"I do admit it's hard to wait, but we might as well since we have waited this long. Let's go and find our parents, so we can tell them the news."

They knew their parents were probably in the galley having dinner, and if they were finished, they would be playing cards.

When they walked into the dining room, they ran into Richard and Shirley Patterson, who were busy cleaning up the last of the dishes from the evening's diners.

"How was your dinner?"

"Shirley, it was perfect. Thank you and Richard for the special meal. I got a special surprise with my meal," Linda said.

She held her hand out to show them her ring.

"That's the most gorgeous ring I've ever seen," Shirley said.

"I agree; it's huge. What did it set you back?" Richard asked.

"Richard Patterson, you stop that."

"Okay, Shirley, I'm sorry, Billy."

"Nothing to be sorry about, it is an impressive ring."

"Where are you two going in such a hurry?" Richard Patterson asked.

"We're going over to tell our parents."

"You had better get going, and don't tell them you showed us before them."

"You two look like you have a secret," Beth said.

"Not a secret, but we do have some news we would like to share with all of you," Linda said.

"I bet I can guess."

"No need to guess, Billy has asked me to marry him, and I've said yes."

"Oh honey, congratulations," Beth said. "We were talking the first night on board, and we all agreed it wouldn't be too long before the two of you realized you belong together."

For the next several minutes, everyone was busy congratulating them.

"When do you two intend to tie the knot?" Ben asked.

"We thought we would get married in two weeks," Billy said.

"That soon. I thought you might wait until we find another place to live," Beth said.

"It may be a long time before we find another planet to live on," Billy said.

"How long is a long time? It won't be more than a few months, will it?" Rob asked.

"It could be years, I just don't know. Given the distances we have to cover, it's likely to be a long time. Enough of that for tonight, we're both tired so we're going to say good night. We'll talk again tomorrow about what we're going to do for the wedding."

When they arrived at Linda's door she asked, "Would you like to come in for a few minutes?"

"I would love to, but if I do, it probably won't be for a few minutes, will it?"

"No, probably not. I'll see you tomorrow then. I have another busy day planned."

Even though they had almost the entire staff from the Mayo Clinic on board, they were busy all of the time. The ship had two full hospitals, and a clinic on board, and even though the ship was carrying less than half of its capacity of passengers, they had their fair share of health issues.

28

THE NEXT MORNING Billy walked into the galley, and saw his parents sitting at a table with Richard and Shirley Patterson.

"Hi, everyone," Billy said. "What are you doing up this early? It's only five A.M. Why didn't you sleep in?"

"We've been getting up at three-thirty in the morning for as long as I can remember," Richard Patterson said. "We like to have fresh biscuits and cinnamon rolls ready when the first patrons arrive."

"Your father woke up every twenty minutes all night long," Mary said. "He's so excited to get started working in the agricultural area. Rob and Beth just left. Rob wanted to get started and just couldn't wait any longer."

"That's good to hear, I've been worried Rob is depressed."

"He has been," Ben said. "But this has already done wonders for him. I haven't seen him this excited in months."

"Great, I was hoping he would appreciate having something to do," Billy said.

"Speaking of appreciation, we were talking last night, and I hope you know we both love you dearly, but we're also proud of you," Ben said. "The things you have done for us, and the rest of the people in the ships, are truly amazing. We just wanted you to know how we feel."

"I can't begin to tell you how much I appreciate those

kind words. You needn't worry about giving me compliments; I know how much you both love me and you two mean the world to me."

"How excited is Linda?" Mary asked.

"She's almost as excited as I am. We've been looking forward to this moment in our lives for a long time."

"Are you starting to get nervous yet?" Ben asked. "If you are, it's normal. Everybody does."

"No, I'm not. Linda and I are so close that I already know everything there is to know about her."

"Everyone thinks they know everything about their future spouse," Ben said. "But even if you've been sleeping together for years, it's just different."

"We haven't slept together yet. We wanted to wait, and besides, we've been too busy to take time for ourselves. I know people don't know as much as they think they do. But Linda and I can actually blend our minds and converse without talking. Some people think they are close enough to each other to know what the other one is thinking, but we actually can read each other's minds."

"You're serious?" Ben asked.

"I'm serious. We can even do it over long distances if one of us has had some sort of emotional event. We haven't been able to achieve an on-demand connection from a distance, but it's just a matter of time. If we're touching we can do it at will."

"That's so neat," Mary said. "Sometimes your dad and I have the same thoughts, but never like that. I would love to be able to experience it someday."

"You never know, it could happen."

They continued to talk while Billy ate. When he finished, he left to find Linda. When she saw him, she asked, "What do you have planned for today?"

"I don't have any firm plans yet. I need to go to the bridge, and check on our progress. Then I'm going to work on a plan for where we should explore first. What are you going to do?"

"I have a full schedule of patients to see. I got behind yesterday."

"Are you up for dinner again tonight?" Billy asked.

"Sure, are we eating upstairs again?"

"No, I thought we would eat with our parents tonight. Your mom wants to talk about the wedding, and neither of us has spent much time with them in quite a while."

"Sounds good to me. Where do you want to meet?"

"I'll come by and get you, and we'll walk down together. I have scheduled it for seven. Dad can't wait any later for his dinner."

"My dad doesn't like to wait either. All right, I'll see you about six-forty-five."

They parted and Billy went to the bridge. As Billy was reading the logs, he saw they had continued accelerating. They were continuing to accelerate, but it was going to be another twenty-six days before they would reach their top speed of almost 56 percent of the speed of light.

The flagship was capable of speeds greater than 56 percent of light, but the rest of the fleet didn't have the necessary power.

He checked the scanners to see what else had transpired in the Earth's solar system. There was no sign of the Earth. The asteroid had swept the debris from the Earth along with it as it left the solar system.

As he continued to study the scans, he saw the asteroid had destabilized other parts of the solar system. The sun was now several million miles outside its normal position, and Jupiter's orbit around the sun was now roughly the same as Uranus's. The asteroid's magnetic effect had pushed Pluto out of its orbit, and it was now on its way across the solar system.

The asteroid had destabilized much of the galaxy as it

passed through. Since the asteroid would return, he decided their best chance was to leave the galaxy for another one. They were fifteen thousand light years from the nearest edge of the galaxy, and he didn't have a valid frame of reference for what they might find once they were outside of the galaxy.

The ship had all of Earth's accumulated knowledge stored in its computer banks. The problem was the distances were too vast for a detailed study from Earth, so they were of no use to him.

Even though they were going to be traveling faster than humans had ever traveled before, he knew it would take them almost thirty thousand years to reach the edge of the galaxy.

When he designed the flagship, his designs called for the installation of a massive array of magnetic field generators in the front of the flagship. He still hadn't completed his thoughts on how they would use them, but somehow he just knew they would need them to exceed the speed of light.

Shortly before Klaus Heidelberg had become too sick to work, they had several discussions on Einstein and his work on faster-than-light travel. Klaus had not been able to add much more to the ideas he had presented in his paper on the subject, but he had managed to convince Billy it was indeed possible to exceed the speed of light.

He spent several minutes working through how he was going to utilize the field generators. As he was trying to focus, his mind kept wandering to Linda. After struggling to concentrate for several minutes, he decided he would finish his work on the generators another time. He decided to complete his plans for his surprise for Linda.

He was planning to use one of the upper decks for their wedding. He chose one of the purely agricultural areas he designed into the ship. The deck he had in mind was a forest area, and he had a specific meadow in mind for the ceremony.

As he worked on their guest list, he knew Linda wanted to invite all of the staff from the Mayo Clinic.

He wanted to invite Larry Sheldon, Nicholas Stavros, and his crew. When they told their parents, his dad mentioned it would be good if they invited the original population from Clayton.

As he added up the guests, he realized they were already up to at least three thousand people who would want to attend. He also realized the rest of the fleet would at least want to watch on video. When he laid out the seating plans, he realized the forestry area wasn't going to work.

He brought up the layout of the ship to look for a more suitable area. As he scanned through the layout, he decided on one of the lower landing bays.

The ship had two decks designed to be used as landing bays. They only had a few small ships on board, and the original prototype *Imagination*. The other deck was unused, and since it ran the length of the ship, it would provide an immense amount of open area.

He designed the plans detailing the modifications he wanted for the wedding. When he finished, he e-mailed them to Nicholas Stavros so he could put his crews to work on the modifications.

Just as he was finishing, Larry Sheldon came in. "What are you up to?" Larry Sheldon asked.

"I just finished working on the plans for our wedding. I've decided to use landing bay one for the wedding and reception."

"How many people are you inviting?"

"I've set it up so everyone on board can attend if they want to. The landing bay is roughly two miles by four miles, so I'm sure we can fit everyone in. Richard Patterson told me, if they have some help, they can feed everyone in the landing bay. So we'll have the reception there as well."

"You know the rest of the fleet will want to participate in some way, don't you?"

"I know, but there's no way we can bring everyone on board. The plans I just sent to Nicholas's crew included a video system setup which will allow the rest of the fleet to at least watch."

"Good, I know you and Linda don't know most of the people who have been saved, but I do know they all feel grateful. I've already heard from the Russians, and the European Union's ships, and they are all asking if they can send wedding gifts over. I expect everyone else will feel the same way."

"We don't need gifts. Could you tell all of them thank you, but there's no need for gifts?"

"Sure, I can tell them. But I'll tell you they're not going to pay any attention. It will be a matter of pride with them to send gifts."

"I guess I'll just have to deal with it. What are you doing up here at this time of the morning?"

"I've been hunting you. We need to communicate some sort of a plan to the fleet. Everyone is asking questions about where we're going, and how long it's going to take."

"I have been working on it, but the answers I would have to give them right now wouldn't please anyone. The problem is it's going to take thousands of years to reach the edge of the galaxy."

"Can't we just go to a system like Alpha Centauri?"

"We can, and maybe it should be the first one we explore, but it's outside of our range at this time. I'm going to have to figure out how we can travel faster. Traveling the distances we have to go at sublight speed is just not practical."

"What are you babbling about? I've read enough Einstein to know faster-than-light travel is impossible."

"Some of his theories would lead you to believe it is, but some of his and Klaus's work put me on another path. I only got to have a couple of discussions with Klaus about it, but he didn't have the opinion it was totally out of the question."

"I'm not even going to ask you to explain it to me. While I'm considered fairly bright by most people, I've already learned that deep conversations with you or Linda are beyond my ability to understand."

"It's funny you say that, sometimes I don't even understand until it just comes to me. I've never been able to understand how Linda and I come up with the ideas we do. We have discussed it, and it seems like both of us just know the answer when we need to."

"Would you be willing to speak to the fleet to brief them on our current status, and if you're up to it, answer questions?"

"Sure, when would you like to do it?"

"I've already talked to some of the other ships, and if you could do it this afternoon, it would be great. Where would you like to do it from?"

"My first thought was to do it here on the bridge. But I think it might be better if we do it from my quarters. It will give a much softer look and feel to it, and maybe make them feel better about our situation."

"We'll do it in your quarters then. There are cameras in your living room, aren't there?"

"Yes, I believe there are, but let me check to make sure they work."

Billy turned to the console and selected the cameras in his living room. He brought up the four camera views to check the images. "They seem to be working fine. I'll make sure I can control the video feeds from there."

"Okay, we'll do it at one P.M. ship's time. Do you want anyone else with you?"

"If you and John Tyler wouldn't mind, I would like both of you to be present."

"No problem with me, and I'm sure John will do whatever you ask."

"I'll see you at one then."

29

BILLY DIDN'T KNOW why, but he had already come to trust John Tyler, and he intended to entrust him with the fleet's security forces.

While he hadn't actually read any of John's thoughts, he sensed John was someone they would need in the future. Billy and Linda had come to trust their instincts when they had a feeling about someone or something.

Billy called Nicholas Stavros to make sure he had received the plans he sent him.

"Have you had a chance to look at the plans I sent you?" Billy asked.

"I have them, but I haven't had a chance to look them over. What's it all about?"

"I'm getting married in just under two weeks, and I want to hold the wedding in the lower landing bay. I've drawn up the plans, and I would like to retrofit the bay for the wedding. Can I get you and some of your crews to take on the project?"

"We would be more than happy to work on your project. After all, we owe you our lives, and besides we're bored silly. After working almost night and day for over a year, and then having nothing to do, we're ready to get back to work."

"It's a big job, but nothing compared to what you guys

pulled off. I still can't believe how fast you got building ships."

"Thanks for the compliment, but we were just trying to do our part. We'll get started first thing in the morning. Is that soon enough? If you need us to, we can start tonight."

"No need. I don't think it will take you more than ten days."

"You can count on us. We'll do the best job we can for you."

"I never doubted it. Thanks again, and I'll come down and see how you are doing tomorrow afternoon."

Over the next six days, Nicholas's crews worked around the clock. He'd challenged them to finish the work in the shortest amount of time possible.

Billy had posted the landing bay off limits to everyone but the work crews, and Larry Sheldon and himself. When Nicholas Stavros called to tell him they were finished, he had Larry Sheldon meet him in the landing bay for the walk-through.

Nicholas met them at the elevator. "Thank you again for giving us a chance to do this project."

"You finished in record time."

"We decided to work straight through, so you could have some time to check it out, and make any changes you want before the wedding."

Nicholas had his crew leave the landing bay. "They are all gone. Would you like to try out your design? Here's the remote control you asked for."

They spent the next three hours trying out all of the functions he had had them build. He hadn't wanted to do anything to the landing bay that would damage its functionality, so his changes had focused on using virtual reality projectors. They only had a few ships, and they were stored in the other landing bay, but someday they would have many more.

"Wow!" Larry Sheldon said. "I would have never thought any of that was possible. I still can't believe what I just experienced. I completely forgot I was in a landing bay. It was like we were back on Earth."

"That was the idea," Billy said. "I want people to be able to forget for a few moments at least. Please don't talk about this, if you don't mind."

"Don't worry, Nicholas and I know how to keep a secret. The work crews won't be a problem, because they never saw any of it in operation. Without seeing it in action, there's no way they could conceive of what it's capable of."

"Thanks, I want this to be a surprise for everyone, but most of all Linda."

"This is cool, but I need to ask you to do something for me," Larry Sheldon said.

"Sure, what is it?"

"Would you mind trying to brief the fleet again?"

"I can, and it should go off better this time. I didn't realize our thrust fields were going to distort the transmission like they did. I've solved the previous problems, but what do you think I ought to tell them?"

"First, I would like you to announce your upcoming wedding, and let them know they'll be able to watch via video link. A lot of them already know, but I want to make sure everyone is aware. Then we need to name the ship. It isn't right for the flagship of our fleet to not have a name. Once we have covered all of that, I would like for you to take a few questions."

"I think we should allow the entire fleet to help name the ship," Billy said.

"Sure, why not? Can you fix it where everyone can vote?"

"Yes, I can. I'll do it in two phases. First I'll let everyone submit their suggestions, and then I'll let the fleet vote on a name."

"Sounds like a plan; I'll get it set up for tomorrow afternoon at two P.M. Will that work for you?"

"No problem, I'll make sure I'm ready. Where do you want me to do the briefing?"

"Why don't we try to do it in your quarters again?"

"Okay, that will work. I still have the video feeds from my quarters patched into the main system. I would like you to be with me."

"I'll be happy to be there, but it's you the people want to hear from. You're more of a myth to them than real, but they need to get to know you better. People should always know as much about their leader as possible."

"I'm not the leader. That's your job."

"Oh no, my young friend. It might have once been true. But it hasn't been the case for several months now. The last glimmer of that was gone when we left the Earth. You'll be our leader for the foreseeable future, just as it was foretold."

"Foretold, what do you mean? I'm not even twenty-one years old yet. I'm too young to be leading what's left of the human race."

"Leadership is not about age. It's about courage, integrity, vision, and above all a genuine concern for the people you are leading. You embody all of those characteristics and more. You're the brightest person I've ever had the privilege to work with, and that's saying quite a bit. When the time is right, I'll explain the foretold comment. Before Klaus Heidelberg got so sick and had to leave, we discussed you and Linda. He agreed that even including him and Albert Einstein, you two are by far the brightest humans ever born."

"Thanks for the kind words, but aren't you exaggerating?"

"In no way am I exaggerating. You two are the only real hope of all of us. I know it's a huge burden to place on ones so young, but it's the truth. I'm going to help you in any way I can, but in the end, it will be the two of you who determine whether we make it as a race."

"All I can tell you is we'll both try to do what we can. We've always known we had a task to do, but we couldn't quite see what it was. Now we know, and it's a huge task."

"That's all any of us could ever ask, and I believe you two can pull it off. I know in my heart you'll come to know why you think the way you do, and why you seem to sense coming events."

"That's enough of this for now, let me get back to work, and I'll see you this afternoon."

BILLY AND LARRY Sheldon turned on the cameras to begin the broadcast promptly at two. They were in two armchairs facing the cameras. The fireplace was burning in the background, and Billy had just enough lights on for the telecast.

"Ladies and gentlemen, thank you for taking the time to watch this broadcast. I'm Larry Sheldon, and it's my great pleasure to introduce Billy West, the man responsible for the design of the ships we are in."

"Thank you for the introduction. For those of you who don't know who Larry Sheldon is, he's the man responsible for assembling the resources necessary to build most of the fleet. We all owe Larry Sheldon and his teams a debt of gratitude for having the foresight to have a plan which allowed us to assemble the ships we are in. He has asked me to brief you on several things, but I would like to start with a topic dear to me. Linda Bustamante and I are going to be married in three days on board the flagship. I would like to take this opportunity to invite everyone on the flagship to the wedding and the reception. Larry also suggested we telecast the ceremony and the reception to the entire fleet. He has arranged for receptions to be held on board all of the ships of the fleet, so everyone can participate if you wish. Please don't feel you have to attend unless you want to, and please don't send gifts.

"The next topic I would like to address is one I think you'll find more interesting. I'm asking everyone in the fleet to participate in naming the flagship. I've programmed the consoles in the ships to take suggestions for names over the next twenty-four hours. The next day I'll post the list of names so everyone can vote. I'll announce the person or persons who submitted the winning name during the wedding reception. The winner will get his or her choice of quarters on their ship.

"I know you are all wondering where we're going, and how long it's going to take to get there. I'm not prepared to give you a firm estimate of time yet, but I can tell you our first destination is Alpha Centauri. You may have heard of it, but I don't have any specifics on what we'll find. It's simply too far away from the Earth to have been studied properly.

"I've heard there are concerns about whether we have enough supplies for our journey. Let me assure you that we have ample supplies, and we have outfitted the ships to be virtually self-sufficient, and they can actually produce their own oxygen and food supplies.

"Now I would like to open the floor up to questions. I'll take questions for about three hours. If you still have questions after that, I've built a bulletin board where you can post them. I'll attempt to answer your questions as quickly as I can. We'll continue to have at least weekly video meetings until you tell me we don't need them."

"My name is Patricia Collingsworth. How long do you think it will be before we find another place to live?"

"It's hard to say, but it will more than likely be several years at a minimum."

"You mean we're going to have to be cooped up on these ships for years?"

"Yes, I'm afraid so. You'll find we have tried to include as many amenities and reminders of home as possible."

"My name is Salvador Torres, and I don't have a question. I would just like to say thank you from me and my entire family."

"There's no need for thanks, but I do appreciate the sentiment."

The questions continued to flow for over three hours.

"I think that will complete our question-and-answer session for today," Billy said. "Again, we'll do these sessions until we all think they are no longer necessary."

"The session was well done," Larry Sheldon said. "You answered their questions as fully as possible, and you even managed to calm down the ones who were scared and upset. As I told you before, as our leader they are going to look to you more and more. The people want to have hope, and you and Linda give it to them."

"I'm still uncomfortable being the leader. There are senior politicians, generals, and captains of industry on board several of the ships. I would think one of them should be assuming the role of leader."

"The time for their kind of leadership is past. What we need now is someone of your vision and imagination, and most of all faith. The old bureaucracy which ruled the Earth has no place in our new life. Our leader must be capable of innovative thinking and not be afraid of trying something completely new. What else do you have left to do before the big day?"

"I don't think I have anything left to do. I'm going to spend tonight with my parents, and then I'm going to take the night off and get some sleep. I haven't had a whole night's sleep in months."

*   *   *

THE NEXT MORNING Billy didn't get up until 10 A.M. He took his shower, and went down to eat lunch.

Shirley Patterson spotted him at the table, and came over to see what he wanted for lunch. "I'm so happy for you two," she said. "I know you've put this day off so you could focus on helping us all survive. I just want to say thank you from our entire family. I hope you and Linda have as many good times together as you deserve. These are horrible times, but I sense you two are going to be fine."

"Thanks for the kind words, Shirley. None of us know how long we may have, but we intend to savor each moment we're given. You and your family are coming to the wedding, aren't you?"

"We wouldn't miss it for the world. I just hope we can get a seat when we get there. We have to get the food ready for the reception, so we won't be able to get there until the last minute."

"I'll make sure you and your family have seats reserved for you. They'll be right behind where our parents are going to be."

"Thanks, but you don't have to take time out of your special day for us."

"Yes I do, and it's no problem. I expect to see you and your family there."

"We'll all be there, I promise."

When he finished, he spent some time in the lab checking to make sure the ship was all right. Satisfied, he returned to his quarters to get ready. Later he was standing with Earl Williams, their pastor and mentor, as they waited for the wedding to begin.

"I knew the first time I met with you and Linda you would be a couple someday," Pastor Williams said. "I've never been around two people who seemed better suited for each other."

"Linda and I have talked about you and our sessions. Those sessions were a big help to us. Your teachings and counsel helped us immensely. Every time we would feel lost, or left out, we would remember your words, and realize God is always there for us, and in ways we don't always understand, is guiding our way. Even though you may not have always understood us, you helped us more than you know."

"Thank you for the kind words, and thank you for allowing me the honor of performing your wedding."

"We would have never considered anyone else."

The guests had been entering for almost thirty minutes, and the landing bay was starting to fill up. Larry Sheldon had preassigned the seating, and everyone had entered in the correct sequence to facilitate getting everyone seated. Once the guests were seated, their parents and the Pattersons got off the freight elevator beside the pulpit.

The bride's family was normally on one side of the isle, and the groom's on the other. Linda and Billy's family were sitting together. They had never had any friends other than each other, so they chose to sit together. Once they had taken their seats, Larry Sheldon walked over to a control panel and started Billy's program.

The lights dimmed, and a few seconds later the wedding march began to play. Billy turned toward the back of the room and saw the spotlight pick up Linda and Rob as they came off an elevator a hundred feet or so from the front.

They walked to the center, and as they turned to walk up the main aisle, the ship's computers began to generate virtual reality fields around everyone seated in the room.

Even though some of them were more than three-quarters of a mile from the front, they all had the perception they were sitting in the first few rows. Billy wanted everyone to have the same experience, so he had engineered the virtual reality to allow everyone the same view.

As Billy watched Rob and Linda walking toward him arm in arm, he touched Linda's mind. *Are you happy, dear?*

Oh yes. Everything is so beautiful. How in the world did you get the hangar to look like this? It looks just like Westminster Abbey.

You've always said you thought it was beautiful, and I thought you would like it if we were married in it, or at least a replica.

Thank you, and it's impressive. I just wish everyone could see. It's so large, I'm afraid most of them won't even get a glimpse of the ceremony.

Each one of them has a view like they are in the first five rows. Even the people watching from the rest of the fleet have the same kind of view.

Linda and Rob reached the spot where Billy was standing and stopped. "Who gives this woman in marriage?" Earl Williams asked.

"Her mother and I do," Rob said.

Billy stepped closer to them and Rob placed Linda's hand in his, and stepped back. Then he turned and took his place in the front row with Beth. They all smiled at each other, because they had hoped for years that the kids would get married, and now it was happening.

Billy and Linda turned and moved to stand in front of Pastor Williams. As he began the ceremony, Billy touched a button on the remote he was carrying. The church seemed to disappear, and the scene turned into a mountain meadow. There were mountain peaks surrounding them, and you could even smell the pine trees.

The view distracted Pastor Williams so much he stammered and said, "I'm so sorry, I'm somewhat overwhelmed."

He managed to compose himself and he continued with the wedding. About once a minute the scene they were in

hanged. The next view was the plains of Montana, fol-
owed by a pastoral scene of Iowa. All during the twenty
minutes it took Pastor Williams to deliver the marriage cer-
mony, the scenes continued to change.

As Pastor Williams came to the end of the wedding
eremony, the scene changed once more, and they were
tanding in what appeared to be the hills overlooking the
Golden Gate Bridge.

Neither of the kids had ever been to San Francisco, but
when Billy was looking for truly impressive sights, he
hose this one.

Pastor Williams paused, again overcome by the scene.
He caught his breath and said, "I now pronounce you man
nd wife. You may kiss your bride."

As they shared their first kiss as man and wife, they
were talking. *I love you so much. Thank you for being my
wife.*

*I love you even more. I've looked forward to this day
or so long.*

They broke their kiss, and Pastor Williams said, "Let
ne be the first to introduce Billy and Linda West."

They turned to face the people, and everyone stood and
tarted clapping. Billy let the clapping and cheering go
n for a minute or so, and then he called for quiet.

Once the massive room was quiet, he said, "Thank all
f you for coming to share this day with Linda and me. I
hope this marks a new beginning. We have suffered terri-
le losses, but we will overcome our troubles, and make a
ew life for all of us. I want to invite you all to the recep-
on. If you will move to the back of the room, the refresh-
nents are ready."

Most of the guests began moving to the rear of the
oom, but several hundred of them moved toward Billy
nd Linda to congratulate them. It took over an hour be-
ore the crush of well-wishers subsided.

After the last group got the chance to talk to them, they moved to the elevator behind them to make the trip to the back of the hangar.

As they stepped off the elevator, the room's setting morphed once more. This time it changed to one of the beaches in Maui. Even the air had the feel of an ocean breeze, and a faint hint of orchids.

There were all types of hors d'oeuvres, wedding cake, ice cream, and hundreds of bowls of punch. Billy and Linda cut the wedding cake, and fed each other the first piece as tradition dictated.

After they had their first dance together as husband and wife, he told her, "I almost forgot. We need to announce the name of the ship, and the winner of the contest."

"What's the name going to be?" Linda said.

"I haven't even looked to see yet. Let's walk over to a terminal, and I'll check."

He called up the results, and saw the winning name.

"*Genesis* is a good name, and I'm not surprised Larry Sheldon is the one who suggested it," Billy said. "It won by a huge margin, so I guess a lot of people felt the same way."

He walked to the podium, turned on the sound system, and began to speak. "Attention everyone, attention. I would like to take this opportunity to thank everyone for your good wishes, and for taking time to share this day with us. I've just checked to see what the name of our ship is to be. The name you have selected received ninety-two percent of the votes, so I believe it's a good name.

"The name of our flagship and home is to be *Genesis*. Not only is it the first book of the Torah, the Tanakh, and the Old Testament of the Bible, its very definition—birth, origin, or beginning—is appropriate for our situation.

"Even though we had to leave our planet, we've all been given another chance to begin again. The name was

ubmitted by none other than Larry Sheldon. If it hadn't
een for Larry's perseverance and dedication, none of us
vould be standing here today. Larry Sheldon, thank you
or everything you've done and thank you for the name of
ur home, *Genesis*. If you wouldn't mind, step up to the
nike and say a few words."

Larry walked to the podium, shook Billy's hand, and
gave Linda a hug.

"Thanks for the kind words. When I think back to the
first day I realized the danger the Earth was in, I'm amazed
we managed to make it. There were many days where I had
given up all hope, and then I met you and Linda. From that
first moment, I knew you were the ones who would help us
survive. It turns out I was right. Thank all of you for picking the name I submitted, and I believe this ship, and the
fleet we are traveling with, is truly the genesis of the human race."

They spent the next several hours dancing and talking
with their friends and family. Around 10 P.M. they walked
over to the table where their parents were sitting.

Rob saw them approach, and stood to greet them. "Hi
kids. Honey, you made a beautiful bride, and now a lovely
wife. I hope you two have as good a life as your mother
and I have had."

"Let me second that," Ben said. "Mary and I hope you
find as good friends as Rob and Beth have been to us.
Most of all, we all hope you are able to have some sort of
normal life someday."

"Thank you guys so much," Linda said. "Billy and I
can't begin to tell you what all of you have meant to us.
Even though we're both different from what you probably
expected, you've always showed us nothing but love. Ben,
thank you for the words about friends, and I do hope we
can find friends like you have all been to each other."

"On the subject of a normal life, I'm not sure we could

ever be considered normal wherever we go, but I can tell you we're going to have a great life," Billy said. "Now, if you don't mind, I think we're going to call it a night."

"No problem," Rob said. "We were taking bets on how late you would stay, and you've lasted longer than any of us thought. Honey, you and Billy go and enjoy your wedding night, and just this once, think only of yourselves."

They talked for another minute or so, and then they moved to the elevator. Billy punched the button for the top level.

"That's not the floor for your place?" Linda said.

"I didn't tell you? We have a new place. Larry Sheldon said we needed a place that's ours, not mine or yours. I have no idea what it's like. He promised me we would like it, and he wouldn't even let me see it."

"He has great taste, so I imagine we'll like it, but I liked your place just fine."

"Me too, it was the nicest place I've ever stayed in."

They reached the top deck of the ship. "He said the door would be right across from the elevator," Billy said. "The door is already programmed to recognize both of us, so we don't even need a key."

Just as Larry Sheldon had said, the door clicked and swung open ahead of them.

He swept Linda up into his arms, and she squealed. "Billy West, what do you think you are doing? You're going to hurt yourself carrying me."

"Hardly, my dear. One, you're not very heavy, and two, I'm quite strong."

"I know you are. You don't know your own strength most of the time."

He carried her across the threshold, and the door closed behind them. The lights came on automatically, and the sight that greeted them was truly amazing.

The huge fireplace in the center of the room automati-

lly ignited when they entered. There was a large leather
ctional arranged in front of the fireplace. Above the fire-
ace's mantel there was a flat screen TV that was two
undred inches in size. It had a beach scene showing on it,
d their favorite music was playing in the background.

The room had a twenty-five-foot ceiling, with massive
ooden beams running the length of it. Had they still
een on Earth, they could have believed they were in a
ncy mountain lodge.

They walked through the kitchen to the hall leading to
e side of their home. As they walked down the hall,
ey passed a game room and an exercise room. At the
d of the hall was their bedroom. Larry hadn't told them
here to find the room, but like always, they just knew.
hey walked in, the lights came on in a subdued fashion,
d the fireplace in their room ignited.

There was a huge four-poster bed on the far wall, and
the other side of the room was a sitting area.

As they walked around their bedroom, they were over-
helmed by everything they had seen in their new home.
either of them had ever experienced luxury, but Larry
d made sure they had it.

"I have to see the bathroom," Linda said. "There's no
lling what's in there."

They crossed the room to the bathroom. It had his and
rs sinks on either side of the room. The walk-in shower
as fifteen feet long, and had his and hers showerheads.

On the far end, a sunken tub looked like it was big
ough to be a small swimming pool. "I thought we were
ing to ration our water supply," Linda said. "This thing
ust hold a thousand gallons or better."

"We do have to conserve, but everything is cleansed
d reused. The ship's filtration system can clean the wa-
r to a level of purity that's better than the cleanest found
Earth."

They spent a few minutes showering and talking before they went to bed for the first time.

As they climbed into bed, the lights automatically dimmed to a nighttime level. Linda lay her head on Billy's shoulder and as she did, Billy touched a control on the nightstand beside the bed.

The ceiling seemed to disappear, and they were suddenly lying under a starlit sky. It was unlike anything ever seen from Earth. They were now moving at over 330 million miles per hour, so they could actually see various objects in space approaching them.

Billy turned to kiss Linda and begin their first night together.

Not only were they starting their life together as man and wife, they were beginning the adventure of a lifetime as the ship continued its headlong flight into a new life.